SORCERESS AWAKENING

LISA BLACKWOOD

SORCERESS AWAKENING

A GARGOYLE & SORCERESS TALE / BOOK 1

LISA BLACKWOOD

Sorceress Awakening

Gargoyle & Sorceress Book 1

Copyright © 2011 by Lisa Smeaton

http://lisablackwood.com/

(1st edition) Originally titled Stone's Kiss © November 2011

(2nd edition) © June 2016

(3rd edition) © January 2020

COVER DESIGNED BY: Heather Hamilton-Senter

EDITED BY: Laura Kingsley

EDITED BY: Perry Constantine

PROOFREAD BY: Tracy Vandervliet

Special Thanks to Stan H for his eagle eyes.

Print ISBN: 978-1-990608-47-6

EDITION: 10/27/2021

❧ Created with Vellum

BOOKS BY LISA BLACKWOOD

Gargoyle & Sorceress

Dawn of the Sorceress

Sorceress Awakening

Sorceress Rising

Sorceress Hunting

Sorceress at War

Sorceress Enraged

Legacy of the Sorceress

Sorcery & Firedrakes

Scion of the Sorceress

Sorceress Eternal

In Deception's Shadow Series (Epic Fantasy Romance)

Betrayal's Price

Herd Mistress

Maiden's Wolf

Death's Queen

The Prince's Gryphon (forthcoming)

Ishtar's Legacy Series (Epic Fantasy Romance)

Ishtar's Blade

The Blade's Beginning (short story)

Blade's Honor

Blade's Destiny

The Blade's Shadow

First Queen of the Gryphons

The King of the Anunnaki (forthcoming)

The Anunnaki's Blade (forthcoming)

Huntress vs Huntsman (Epic Fantasy Romance)

Master of the Hunt

Night Huntress

Dragon Archer

Soul Mage (forthcoming)

ABOUT THE BOOK

SORCERESS AWAKENING

An untried sorceress teams up with an immortal gargoyle to stop a goddess from enslaving Earth in this epic urban fantasy romance tale.

When Lillian finds herself facing off against demons out of mythology, help comes from an unlikely source—the stone gargoyle who has been sleeping in her garden for the last twelve years.

After the battle, Lillian learns the humans she thought were her family are actually a powerful coven of witches at war with the demonic Riven. Lillian is something more than human, a Sorceress and Avatar to the gods. The gargoyle has been her protector for many lifetimes, but when she was still a child, troubles in their homeland forced him to flee with her to the human world.

But something from her childhood has followed them to this world.

In a heartbeat, her ordinary life becomes far more complicated, and if her overprotective guardian is to be believed, there's an evil demigoddess just waiting for the chance to enslave them both.

SORCERESS AWAKENING is book one of the popular GARGOYLE AND SORCERESS TALES, an epic contemporary fantasy series with a strong romantic subplot. While each book is a complete adventure, the series does have a continuing story arc and should be read in order:

Dawn of the Sorceress (a prequel story)
    Book 1: Sorceress Awakening
    Book 2: Sorceress Rising
    Book 3: Sorceress Hunting
    Book 4: Sorceress at War
    Book 5: Sorceress Enraged
    Book 6: Legacy of the Sorceress
    Book 7: Sorcery and Firedrakes
    Book 8: Scion of the Sorceress
    Book 9: Sorceress Eternal

FREE BOOKS

GET TWO FREE STORIES FROM MY BESTSELLING SERIES WHEN YOU SIGN UP FOR MY NEWSLETTER.

I send regular monthly newsletters with details about new releases,
special offers, freebies, and other bookish news.
If that's something you'd be interested in, just go to the website below.

http://lisablackwood.com/join-the-newsletter-here/

SORCERESS AWAKENING

CHAPTER ONE

*W*hat? Can't I bleed to death in peace? It probably won't even take that long.

At least that was Lillian's guess going by the amount of blood soaking her top and one leg of her jeans. But apparently, the leader of this strange crew was in a hurry and wasn't going to allow her to die peacefully. He and his men had chased her deeper into the spa's gardens for some unwholesome purpose. In desperation, she'd sought shelter in the maze with the hope of losing them within its twisting corridors.

No such luck.

They'd followed her and now had her trapped to finish off at their leisure.

And worse, from what she'd already gathered, fate had decided the normal kind of horrible death people sometimes inflicted upon each other was going to be too mundane for her.

The strangers hunting her wanted something else. Something impossible.

They wanted her magic.

Magic of all things.

Well, that was going to be difficult, wasn't it?

Magic didn't exist.

She'd seen some weird shit since they'd first accosted her in the gardens outside the maze. But the way the small ring of standing stones had flared with blue, crackling light at the first stranger's approach? That could have been some fancy magician's trick.

Lillian peered around the tree's trunk to track her assailants. The leader—Alexander he'd said his name was—now stood a few feet away, studying the shadows under the redwood tree, hunting her exact location among the dense foliage of the lower branches.

Seeking deeper shadows, she shifted her weight and winced as pain stabbed through her side.

Instinctively, she pressed one hand against the worst of her injuries. The pressure only made the wound throb like a bitch.

While some of the other things she'd seen could have been a trick, the shrapnel from the exploding stone ring had certainly been real enough to make her bleed.

And she wasn't the only one bleeding.

She turned her gaze to the rivulets of liquid bleeding down the tree's trunk.

If the exploding ring of standing stones had been a parlor trick, they'd sure as shit one-upped themselves with the freaking bleeding tree stunt.

If the tree was a tree at all.

And what else was more than it seemed?

As a flash of insight bloomed in her mind, she glanced away from Alexander and the bleeding tree to swiftly seek out the familiar statue of the gargoyle where he sat fifteen feet away.

She studied him speculatively.

He still crouched unmoving on his stone perch with his wings mantled around him like a cloak, strength and majesty in his every carefully hewed and sculpted muscle. Could her favorite stone companion with his broad shoulders, burly muzzle, curving fangs, and deadly looking horns be more than a mere statue?

It was only as she narrowed her eyes that she noticed the strange runes glowing on his chest and arms.

Lillian shook her head, trying to clear her vision, but the marks were still there.

Perhaps the gargoyle *was* another kind of protection like the stone circle had been.

Could it be so simple?

Could killing these intruders be as easy as getting to the statue and triggering some protection?

What the hell am I thinking? she scolded herself. *Magic? Are you admitting magic might be real?*

Fuck it. She could worry for her sanity later. She needed to try something. Now. Before it was too late. She was already dead, her vision beginning to go gray at the edges. She was losing too much blood to live, but perhaps she could still protect her family.

The stone ring had done a number on Alexander and his henchmen. If she were lucky, the gargoyle would unleash even greater destruction.

Gathering her will, she straightened. Doggedly, she lurched toward the statue. The ground seemed more uneven than she remembered. Three steps later, she tripped over a piece of broken stone from the ring and fell to her knees.

As she forced herself back up, a sense of something she could only describe as powerful and old flowed through her body, guiding her movements. She surged the rest of the way to her feet and stumbled toward the gargoyle.

With a last, desperate strength, she crawled up the pedestal and over the gargoyle's stone legs. Protected on three sides by his body and wings, she collapsed forward into his lap. She wanted to close her eyes and know no more pain or suffering—to know the peace of cold stone.

Again, those strange instincts stirred within her. All she could think to call it was power: old power, deep and familiar.

Her body tingled.

Was this what dying felt like?

Was this her soul preparing to leave?

Such a strange sensation. It didn't seem right, dying like this. A useless death. Never to know why her world had been turned on its head.

Sleep called, wooing her into darkness. All she wanted was to answer that summons, but that old power within her insisted otherwise. She lifted her head and gazed at the gargoyle.

Her attention drifted to the strange symbols on his chest. She reached out with one blood-covered hand and touched a symbol. A flash of light seared her retinas, and her hand fused to the stone as it turned hot all around her.

She screamed in pain and terror. Both her body and the stone now glowed with a blue light.

Power danced and pulsed between them. A wave grew, about to crest. She screamed again, instinctively knowing she would be consumed if she didn't direct it in some way.

Ancient memories sparked to life and flooded words and thoughts into her mind. With nothing else to do, she screamed the words.

"Dark Watcher, immortal servant of the Light, with my power I summon you to wake. With my will, I do claim you. Hear me and awake. Evil walks the land. Your Sorceress has need."

At her cry, the turbulent power surged into the stone.

Darkness crept across her vision, stealing the sights of the world from her until only the gray-edged image of the brooding stone gargoyle remained.

Under her hands, the statue's surface warmed and softened. The shadow of vast wings moved up and away as his muzzle dipped toward her face. Before fear gripped her, a warm, wet tongue brushed her cheek. A moment later, she collapsed forward against his chest.

This day isn't going anything like I thought it would. Vacuum. Dust the china. Polish Gran's sword collection. Get attacked by mythological creatures. Die in the arms of a gargoyle. Nope, Lillian mused in the last few moments of consciousness before darkness swept in from all sides. *Totally didn't see this coming when I got up this morning.*

CHAPTER TWO

A Few Hours Earlier

"He's just a damned statue," Lillian muttered to the empty kitchen as she smoothed an oiled rag down the length of her grandmother's broadsword one final time. Setting the cloth aside, she frowned at the newly polished blade. "He's stone, nothing more."

The microwave's clock glowed pale green in the dim light. Not really wanting to know the exact time, she avoided focusing on the digits and returned to sweeping the rag across the blade in a rhythmic motion. "I don't..."

Need him?

That was a lie, though, wasn't it?

Tension built behind her eyes and little flashes sparked in her vision, promising one hell of a headache in the making.

She pinched the bridge of her nose and closed her eyes. It didn't help.

The scent of rich, warm coffee reached her a few seconds before the sound of gurgling announced the coffeemaker was finished.

Lillian welcomed the distraction. After a few more swipes of the rag, she set the sword aside.

Polishing her grandmother's entire sword collection had seemed like a suitable task when she'd jerked awake from a nightmare at some ungodly hour before dawn and couldn't get back to sleep. Usually, nightmares and insomnia didn't plague her, but there was something new—a restlessness that reared its head every night just as the stars faded and the first pink tinted the sky with a hint of dawn.

Only one thing calmed the restlessness—sitting with *him*, her stone gargoyle.

All the signs pointed to the same problem. The inability to sleep, polishing her grandmother's sword collection in the middle of the night, wanting to spend hour after hour with a stone statue under the shadow of her favorite tree, a growing dependence on coffee...

Yep, she'd lost her mind.

The solitude registered heavier now that her hands weren't busy. Mechanically, she wandered over to the coffee pot and filled the largest mug she could find.

She was putting the cream back when she noticed one of her grandmother's dog-eared romances sitting on top of the fridge, half-hidden under a pile of junk mail.

Taking a sip of her coffee, she eyed the romance. It was one of those hormones-take-notice, blush-inducing covers, complete with drops of water cascading down the hero's picture-perfect chest. Gran always claimed a little escapism never hurt anyone. With a grin, Lillian tucked the paperback under her arm. As an afterthought, she scooped up her cell phone on her way to the back door.

Outside, air crisp with a hint of last night's fog greeted her nose. Gravel crunched under her shoes as she walked the twisting garden path. A cedar maze with twelve-foot-tall walls stretched out before her.

A few feet ahead, a tan-and-brown blur streaked across the gravel path. As she followed the resident chipmunk deeper into the living corridors, her earlier worries fell away.

Reaching the maze's middle, she came to a small clearing ringed by upright, waist-high stones. At its center, a juvenile Dawn Redwood grew strong and proud, dwarfing its surroundings. Ten feet from the tree's trunk, a stone statue lurked, partially concealed by dense shadows.

He crouched over his stone perch with a knee resting on the pedestal and wings mantled around him like a cloak. While his one hand rested on his raised knee, his other arm gripped his side in a rather odd position for a sculpture.

It saddened her a little, for there was a narrowness about his squinted eyes and a crease in his brow that hinted at pain.

Interestingly, he didn't look beaten.

His shoulders were broad, head proud, legs corded with muscle, strength and majesty in his every line.

"Hello, old friend." She looked up into his face with its burly muzzle and curving fangs. His muzzle merged flawlessly into wide cheekbones. Large eyes were hooded by a broad forehead. Crowning his head were two massive horns that curved back and up like an African waterbuck's. A thick mane flowed in a stony river midway down his back.

The gargoyle was one of her first childhood memories. At the age of eight, after a near-drowning accident stole her memories, she'd been drawn to the stone statue as if he was pivotal to her survival. Lillian had always assumed her strange need to be near him was a result of her childhood trauma.

She brushed a few spider webs and tree needles from his pedestal. Then, as she'd done since childhood, she climbed up the stand to settle upon the gargoyle's knee. While he was a little cold and hard, he still made a good chair.

Lillian opened the book and leaned back against his arm.

She jerked awake to the sound of her book crunching against the gravel. Her heel slipped off the edge of the pedestal, and with a desperate grab at a stone arm, she avoided joining her book on the ground.

"Insomnia. Going to break my neck... my own damn fault."

She grumbled while she climbed down and hunched over to pick up her book.

Straightening, she realized she'd slept half the morning away.

"I suppose I should get back to work. Gran will be home soon," she told the stone gargoyle and patted his knee. "Goodbye, my old friend."

She'd only just exited the maze when she skidded to a halt. A pale-skinned stranger dressed in a gray business suit strolled along the garden path to her left. With his hands clasped behind his back, he studied the perennials on either side of him.

Occasionally patrons from her family's spa would wander over into the private gardens, but the resort was closed, undergoing renovations. Besides, this man looked out of place. The longer she studied him, the more out-of-place he seemed.

Unfamiliar instincts blazed to life so suddenly she found herself coming to attention as alarm hummed through her veins and sweat began trickling down her spine.

Lillian eased back toward the walls of the maze just as the lone man raised a hand in greeting. The gesture was normal enough. She berated herself for being foolish, and then relaxed a bit and waited for him.

He'd almost reached her side when she heard the crunch of many feet on gravel coming from the path to her right.

She whirled around as more strangers emerged from around a big, ground-sweeping magnolia. There were nine of them: five men and four women. She didn't know them, but they stalked forward with the smooth grace of predators and arranged themselves in a semi-circle in front of her.

Her earlier sense of alarm returned tenfold.

Lillian backed up, but there was nowhere to run except into the green, leafy corridors behind her.

The maze, which had always sheltered her from childhood fears, wouldn't keep her safe from real danger.

CHAPTER THREE

*T*he shortest among the group, the man who had first waved at Lillian, stepped toward her. Dressed as he was in a well-tailored business suit, the man's appearance spoke of money. Yet his shaggy, gray-peppered brown hair was at odds with his otherwise tidy appearance. Other than that, he would have been an unmemorable fellow—from a distance.

Up close, she could detect the lie.

Hostility radiated off him in waves.

"You may call me Alexander." The short man smiled, but the cold glint in his eyes canceled out any friendliness that might have been there. "My associates will not harm you if you come with us willingly. I have a few questions for you." He gestured for his people to give her room. All but two of them moved.

The remaining two, a woman with a short, stocky build, and a ginger-haired man with a six o'clock shadow, turned their unblinking gazes to the shorter man. Alexander narrowed his eyes and said something too low for Lillian to hear.

The man in need of a shave backed off, but the woman showed her reluctance by the way she changed her stance without giving ground to Alexander's command. She turned her feral eyes upon Lillian and tilted her head to sniff at the air.

Too frigging weird. Time to leave.

"I don't know who you are, but I think there's been a misunderstanding. Perhaps I can help you find your way back to the road." Lillian rushed the words together in her hurry. "The gardens can be confusing."

"There has been no mistake. I can smell your power," Alexander said.

Lillian's one eyebrow arched at his words. *I can smell your power? Seriously?*

With luck, she could ditch the crazies in the maze.

A breeze picked up and whipped her hair into her face. In the brief moments it took to tame her hair, she realized she'd missed something. The others now looked past her, deeper into the maze, in the direction from which the breeze had come. The woman with the feral eyes backed away with a hiss.

First singly, and then in twos and threes, the others retreated from the green cedar walls. Lillian didn't know what was hiding in the maze, but it couldn't be much worse than this group of menacing strangers. Even if they hadn't blocked her path back to the house, instinct demanded she run into the concealing greenery.

She bolted into the maze's entrance and ran as if monsters out of her darkest nightmares were giving chase. The first branch of the maze loomed in front of her. She darted to the right. Two more sharp turns and she was well into the intricate maze.

The others hunted her, crashing through the narrow rows not far behind her. By the sounds of snapping branches and swearing, someone was trying to go through the walls instead of around them.

She was nearly halfway to the center before the noises of pursuit started to fade. If fate was kind, her pursuers were now hopelessly lost. Her slight advantage would only last until she emerged on the other side, but it might be enough to escape into the forest. And the lengthening shadows of dusk would give her an advantage in her home forest if she got that far.

When she emerged in the center of the maze, she ran past the first ring of stones. She was under the shadow of her redwood by the time a figure raced from another opening. She froze behind the tree. The man didn't see her and continued across the small glade, heading toward the path leading out of the maze.

Damn, he'd be ahead of her now. She hugged the tree trunk while she caught her breath. This wasn't going well. *Think, think, think.*

A flash of movement at the east entrance betrayed another man a moment before he walked into the clearing. He sniffed at the air as he jogged up to the first ring of stones. His eyes locked on her tree. A smile slowly spread across his face.

Fuck! She wished she had one of her hunting bows. It was swiftly escalating into a 'shoot first, deal with the police later' kind of situation.

The man reached the first stone and rested his hand on it. With a yowl, he jerked back. Smoke rose from the stone, like grease dripping onto the coals of a barbecue. While *that* was an unusual sight, she didn't have time to dwell on it.

Survival first. Weird shit later.

More strangers appeared, spat out by the maze. No one else tried to enter the perimeter of the waist-high ring of stones, even though there was plenty of room between each stone to cross without so much as brushing against them.

A tense silence engulfed the clearing.

Alexander entered last, his steps unhurried. With his head tilted to one side, he looked from her to the redwood and back again.

"I'd thought the ones with strength like yours had gone extinct centuries ago." He said it as if his words explained everything. After another half-dozen steps, he stopped outside the ring of stones. He frowned at them a moment. "Not that it matters. It's your magic I want. You have two choices: surrender your magic or swear allegiance to serve our cause."

"I have no idea what you're talking about, but that handy circle of stones seems to be keeping you at bay. Unless you plan on camping out here for the next few days, I think you'd better move on." She didn't believe for a minute they'd do what she advised and doubted telling them to screw off would have much of an effect either, but maybe if she kept them talking, she'd eventually wake up from this nightmare.

He smiled, a charming curve of lips, then he tilted his head in the direction of the house. His merriment vanished. "That's a grand house. And these gardens, they're rather large for just you to take care of. If I wait, I imagine your family will come home soon. Your husband and children, perhaps?" His expression took on a faraway look as if he were thinking about something else. "Or am I wrong? You have the ageless look of all dryads, but perhaps you're actually very young, newly come to your powers. Is that why I've never sensed you before? No matter. I'm sure you have loved ones, and they'll be along shortly."

Lillian couldn't hide in the shadow of the tree forever. As he'd said, her family would return home and be captured. Clearly Alexander wanted something from her. Her magic, he'd said. She didn't know what he was smoking, but it had to be some bad shit.

Even seeing the stone smoke when the other man touched it could have been a trick. However, that didn't mean they weren't dangerous.

"I am patient up to a point," Alexander said. "If you make me go through these stones to get you, my patience will run out before I reach you. Your choice."

She shook her head.

He frowned and his eyebrows scrunched together, annoyance pinching his features. Without another word, he focused on the stone standing nearest to him and began a chant low in his throat. Placing one hand upon its surface, he grimaced as power arced, its blue light lancing out from one stone to the next in line. Unseen until now, a dome of energy encircled her and her tree.

"This can't be happening," she muttered.

But it was.

Whatever he was doing weakened the dome. Where at first the dome had appeared a solid blue, its coloration was now patchy and frayed. A fissure formed along the base of the stone he touched, the finest of cracks. She didn't want to know what would happen when it gave way.

Behind Alexander, a disturbance in the ranks as they drew back from the stone ring distracted her, and she missed the exact moment the stone shattered. Shards flew in all directions, damaging the other stones and cutting down meadow grasses and prairie flowers like a scythe.

Agony bloomed to life along her right hip — more along her waist.

She should have been safe hiding behind the tree's trunk, yet some of the stone shrapnel must have hit her. Blood—hot and sticky—dampened her t-shirt and one leg of her jeans. Seconds later, the burning sensation turned numb. A deep cold started to throb in her side as if her life was being sucked away by the wound.

She stumbled over a root and slammed her shoulder on one of the redwood's ground-sweeping branches. Teetering against it, she gathered herself, then ducked under the branch to see what was going on. Instinct guided her eyes up the tree. Two thin, blade-like fragments of stone were embedded in the side of the tree's trunk.

Pink liquid dripped off the fragments and dropped onto the ground below. More ran down the trunk. Astonished, she touched the liquid. It was slick like sap but smelled coppery.

Tree sap mixed with blood?

Another rivulet flowed down the trunk and coated her fingers.

Her legs grew rubbery. Numbness crept up from the wounds, seeping through her blood and across her thoughts.

"Your lifeblood is watering the dirt and leaf litter. Such a waste of magic," Alexander mused.

What? Can't I bleed to death in peace? It probably won't even take that long.

At least that was Lillian's guess going by the amount of blood soaking her top and one leg of her jeans. But Alexander was in a hurry and wasn't going to allow her to die peacefully.

She also doubted she was going to die the normal kind of horrible death people sometimes inflicted upon each other.

No, Alexander wanted her magic.

Magic of all things.

Well, that was going to be difficult, wasn't it?

Magic didn't exist.

The way the small ring of standing stones had flared with blue, crackling light had to have been a trick.

Lillian peered around the redwood's trunk at Alexander only to wince as pain stabbed through her side.

Fuck. She pressed one hand against her side. The pressure only made the wound throb like a bitch. *Fuck everything.*

Alexander stood a few feet away, admiring the tree she was sheltering under, his head tilted to look up at its top, thirty-five feet above them. He walked around the redwood's circumference, studying it from different angles, seeking her exact location among the dense foliage of the lower branches.

While he was distracted, she eased one hand above her head.

Sliding her fingers along the bark, she sought the rivulets of liquid bleeding down the tree's trunk and used the dampness to guide her to the first stone fragment. Her fingers closed on a cold, sharp object. She clawed at it with her nails, dragging it from the wood.

Agony burned in her hip. She embraced the pain. It was

better than the cold, sucking sensation of having her life drawn out of her injury.

Yeah. That was the other situation her mind couldn't rationalize away, no matter how hard she tried. As impossible as it seemed, her own injuries were somehow linked to the tree's. But that was an impossibility she could mull over later...if she survived.

Not for the first time, she wished she had one of her hunting bows.

But she didn't.

Moaning about it wasn't going to change that fact.

Her fingers worked at the second piece of stone as Alexander finished skirting the tree and came to face her.

With a grunt, she freed the second shard and flung it with all her strength. Sap-blood flew in a splattering arc.

Her aim was true, and the stone coated in a tree's blood collided with Alexander.

He roared in agony, a tone of near glass-shattering quality.

Take that, you bastard.

Hopefully, such an unholy sound signaled a mortal injury.

The fragment had embedded itself in his neck where an artery should have been.

And...was the stone smoking and hissing?

Yes...yes, it was.

Alrighty then. Shit's getting weird again.

Other drops of the tree's blood had eaten away at Alexander's skin like she'd tossed acid upon him. A human would have hit the ground, dead by now. She didn't know what he was, but he wasn't human.

Silent now, the creature collapsed to his knees but continued to smile at her. Oh, he was in pain. She could see it in his pinched expression: the white skin drawn tight across his face, the slight grayish hue of his complexion. But it was the sharp fangs when he hissed at her that gave him away.

A vampire?

"You've got to be kidding me," she whispered to no one in particular.

Impossible. There was no such thing as a vampire.

Yet what else could he be?

And what else was more than it seemed?

Her gaze landed on the gargoyle statue and studied him speculatively.

It was only then that she noticed the strange runes glowing on his chest and arms.

Lillian shook her head and blinked, trying to clear her vision, but the marks were still there.

Could it be so simple?

Could killing these creatures be as easy as getting to the statue and triggering some other form of protection?

She needed to try. She was already dead. She was losing too much blood to live, but perhaps she could still protect her family.

Gathering her will, she straightened and held the second stone fragment like a knife. Doggedly, she lurched toward the statue. The ground seemed more uneven than she remembered. Three steps later, she tripped over a piece of broken stone from the ring and fell to her knees.

As she forced herself back up, she saw someone in her path: a blurry blob with a cloud of dark hair around it. The strange, feral woman she'd first noticed outside the maze stood between Lillian and her goal. Anger stirred to life.

A sense of something powerful and old flowed through her body, guiding her movements.

She surged to her feet; the stone fragment held low against her good thigh. Lillian darted forward, the land around her a blur. Her opponent was moving far too slowly. One more step, and then she snapped her arm up and forward, burying the stone shard in the woman's stomach. Her opponent's mouth fell open as she gasped in shock.

Growling, the woman clawed at the stone fragment. Lillian sidestepped her enemy and continued toward the gargoyle. Three strides from her destination, a heavy weight slammed into her and claws ripped into her back.

Kicking desperately, Lillian dragged herself out from under the crazed woman.

With a last, desperate strength, she crawled up the pedestal and over one of the gargoyle's stone legs. Protected on three sides by his body and wings, she collapsed forward onto his lap. She wanted to close her eyes and know no more pain or suffering—to know the peace of cold stone.

Again, those strange instincts stirred within her. All she could think to call it was power: old power, deep and familiar. Her body tingled.

Was this what dying felt like? Was this her soul preparing to leave? Such a strange sensation. It didn't seem right, dying like this. A useless death. Never to know why her world had been turned on its head.

Sleep called, wooing her into darkness. All she wanted was to answer that summons, but that old power within her insisted otherwise. She lifted her head and gazed at the gargoyle.

Her attention drifted to the strange symbols on his chest.

She reached out with one blood-covered hand and touched the nearest symbol. A flash of light seared her retinas, and her hand fused to the stone as it turned hot all around her.

She screamed in pain and terror. Both her body and the stone now glowed with a blue light.

Power danced and pulsed between them. A wave grew, about to crest. She screamed again, instinctively knowing she would be consumed if she didn't direct it in some way.

Ancient memories sparked to life and flooded foreign thoughts and verses into her mind. With nothing else to do, she screamed those words.

"I trust the Father's choice. Dark Watcher, immortal servant of the Light, with my power I summon you to wake. With my will, I do claim you. Hear me and awake. Evil walks the land. Your Sorceress has need."

Darkness crept across her vision, stealing the sights of the world from her until only the gray-edged image of the brooding stone gargoyle remained.

At her cry, the power surged into the stone. It softened under her hands. The shadow of his wings moved up and away as his muzzle dipped down.

A warm, wet tongue brushed her cheek as she collapsed forward against his warmth.

This day isn't going anything like I thought it would. Vacuum. Dust the china. Polish Gran's sword collection. Get attacked by mythological creatures. Die in the arms of a gargoyle. Nope, she mused in the last few moments of consciousness before darkness swept in from all sides. *Totally didn't see this coming when I got up this morning.*

CHAPTER FOUR

Stone no longer, he answered his lady's call. The dark world came alive around him as his senses awoke, one by one. The thump of many hearts hummed in his ears. One fluttered rapid and weaker than the rest, on the edge of death. He inhaled a deep breath, and three things became apparent:

Air tainted with blood and death-scent filled his lungs.

A warm weight slumped across his lap.

Blood covered him in a sticky coating.

He opened his eyes for the first time in many years as his mind slowly sorted order from the chaos of his senses. A woman sprawled across his lap. Surprise melted away, replaced by cold dread as his soul recognized her.

She was still. Too still, her pale skin gray-tinted. A sheen of sweat covered her face. The only color was the bright splash of her blood.

His lady's blood. Horror clamped his stomach and unleashed a churning void in his middle.

Why had he not known she was in danger?

He dragged in another great lungful of air, the lingering scent of her desperation and fear strong on the back of his tongue. Blood and burning fury rushed through his veins with each beat of his heart. Pointing his muzzle at the nearest enemy, he roared. But it didn't expel all the hate and helpless rage trapped within him. Again and again, he howled out his agony until it echoed across the width of the glade in a deafening wave.

Rage destroyed reason. Muscles tensed for battle as talons sprang from his fingertips. He gathered his lady into his arms and fed her power while he straightened from his crouch to face his enemies. At the sight of them cowering away, another low rumble built within him. His lips curled back from his fangs, the need to rend and destroy overwhelming.

The invaders fell back as they retreated to a safer distance. By the scents permeating the meadow, his enemies were a mix of fae-bloods. A breeze picked up and blew the weakening essence of evil to his nostrils.

Silent now, he curved his wings around his shoulders and cupped the escaping scent closer to him. He'd nearly missed it —the corruption of a demon-touched corpse. A Riven. An ancient weapon used by blood witches.

One of his lady's attackers knew what he was, and the Riven had run to save itself.

He lowered his lady to the ground with gentle care, then standing over her, he began whispering spells to slow the flow of blood. While he unfurled his wings, he gathered more power. Using his soul-link to the Spirit Realm, he tapped into the torrent of creative magic.

The cold power from the Spirit Realm mixed with the

warm air of the Mortal Realm, creating lift. Magic whirled around him like gale winds before a thunderstorm.

A fae-blood shapeshifter with a gaping hole in her stomach growled and started to back away from him while three of her comrades advanced. By her unmistakable wolf-musk scent, she was a dire wolf. With the flick of his tail, he decapitated the female. Before her body toppled to the ground, he was moving.

He swept out a talon-tipped hand, ripping out the throat of one of the males and then gutted a third with a kick from his hind legs. He pushed the body over backward and lunged at the next creature within reach: a silver-skinned female with pointed ears. A snapped neck freed her soul from the anchor of her body.

He was winning, but there were too many to fight his way free quickly, and half his attention was trained on his lady. She was losing her battle to live. Why was her magic not healing her as it should?

Then a memory floated up from the depths of his mind. She couldn't touch her magic because he'd caged it. But why? Nothing made sense.

Another dire wolf female darted at him. His tail snaked up and speared her in the throat. A prolonged battle was too dangerous with his lady so vulnerable. This needed to end, now. He directed his magic at the encircling horde. Threads of power condensed in the air and the shadowy wisps latched onto any warm-blooded creature near enough to touch. The scent of burning flesh filled the air, and the screams of his enemies echoed in his ears.

Seeing he had devastated half their companions, the other

creatures vanished into the shadows of a surrounding maze. He curled his lips and caught their individual scents on his tongue, committing each to memory. When he had them all, he sent deadly little shards of his shadow magic to hunt them.

Turning his full attention back to his Sorceress, he gathered her in his arms and studied her. She was far paler than she should have been. Even without her magic, her wounds shouldn't have been fatal.

Detaching a portion of his consciousness from his body, he sent it into the woman in his arms. Her power still drained away.

He checked the weavings he'd placed over her wounds, but they were holding. No magic or blood hemorrhaged from those points. Elsewhere then, but where? His consciousness stretched beyond his body, following the scent trail of magic back to its source. A tree. Two long gashes. Heartwood deep.

By the Light! His lady was a dryad. How had he missed that fact? His memory was full of unexplainable holes. But his proximity to the dryad's tree explained why he hadn't at first felt his Sorceress's distress. The hamadryad tree was much stronger in magic and overshadowed her dryad. The tree had tried to wake him instinctively, but she wasn't the Sorceress. Though, that still didn't explain why he hadn't felt danger.

Nothing was as it should be, but he'd have to solve that mystery later. He had greater concerns.

Looking up at the tree, he admitted he had *much* greater concerns than a few foggy memories.

Blood leaked down the tree's majestic trunk and saturated the ground at its roots. Instincts jerked him into motion, and he summoned wards to shield the wounds. The prickle of power danced along his skin a moment before he directed the spell. An insubstantial webbing spun out between his outstretched hands, like a delicate, blue lattice. It adhered to the bark and sealed the wounds, preventing further loss of the hamadryad's blood.

The Sorceress never chose to be reborn as a dryad. It would be too great a temptation for their vows. Yet she was obviously a dryad and must have had a small cutting of her hamadryad with her when he'd rescued her from the Battle Goddess's kingdom and brought her here.

At the time, his dulled senses and the stench of blood magic had disguised her scent, and he'd mistaken her for a sidhe.

Her soft moan brought him back to the present. It didn't matter how her spirit tree came to be here. Here it grew, and here it bled its lifeblood upon the ground. He dropped to all fours and circled the tree. He sniffed at the ground until he pinpointed the area where the greatest concentration of magic saturated the loam. The scent of sap and blood trig-gered instincts and dragged him back to memories of his infancy.

Many times, in many lives he'd come to awareness hearing his mother's deep, slow heartbeat and the sounds of wind and lashing rain in her branches as he grew within the heart of her tree.

There was something here in this memory he needed.

Safe in his watery cocoon, deep inside his mother's wooden heart, he'd grown strong.

Ah, yes.

Along with the food and water of the earth, he had absorbed his dryad mother's memories.

There it was—the knowledge to heal his mistress.

More of his memories returned, both recent and ancient. Heal her hamadryad and the dryad should live.

Tonight, the second time his lady had called to him in this life, had been as chaotic as the first. Worse. Now she lay dying along with her tree. If her hamadryad had been older, he could have put her in the tree to rest and heal, but such an attempt in this magicless place might kill the tree. He scrounged his mother's memories for other healing methods and found what he needed.

He had to act quickly. The power was dissipating, sucked up by the earth like water on drought-cursed land. He dropped into a trance and summoned his power for the delicate work of separating his mistress's magic from the magic-starved land.

The highest concentration of magic pooled just below the grass, in the layer where small, fibrous roots sought food and water. With one hand pressed against the hamadryad's trunk and the other on the ground, he flexed his talons. After he absorbed the magic from the soil, he drew it up into his body, purified it, and returned it to the spirit tree. He drained the small pool and reached deeper. His mind rushed down into the earth, probing for the smallest tendrils of power. He continued until the smallest scrap—every little fragment, no matter how tiny—was returned to the hamadryad.

After he reinforced the wards on the hamadryad's larger wounds, he healed the small punctures his talons had made. Those larger wounds would need intensive healing but must wait for now. Mending the tree would be useless if...

No, he would not permit failure.

Returning to the prone dryad, he sat on his haunches and lifted her into his lap. He licked at her face. Feeling her skin's clamminess and noting her gray-hued pallor, he knew he didn't have long to prepare for healing.

Before he began the arduous task of healing her, he'd need to find a shelter more defendable than this maze. He repositioned the small dryad in his arms and broke into a ground-eating stride. He navigated his way free of the leafy corridors and emerged into a lush garden. The cool shadows beckoned to him, offering a way to hide from the sun's revealing rays.

Summoning the shadows to him, he swiftly wove a cloak of invisibility.

He exited the gardens and encountered a stone home, large and spacious but surprisingly empty of people. He wondered where the servants were, and the guards. There should have been some defenses guarding this house, yet he detected nothing.

After one more probe of the house and surrounding lawn, he tightened his hold on his lady and entered the stone cottage by a back entrance. As a precaution, he placed a ward around the entire structure and keyed it so only he could pass. Then as an added measure, he mentally scanned the area immediately around the building.

Still no one.

With the outside of the building as safe as he could make it, he turned his attention to the inside of the dwelling. A stone-tiled floor stretched out under his talons. He made soft clicking sounds with each step.

A large table of polished wood sat at the room's center, and a counter stretched around two sides of the room in an *L* shape. The table held a loaf of freshly baked bread and a basket of sweet-smelling fruit. The room lacked a hearth, but he guessed it to be a kitchen of some sort.

He laid his precious burden upon the table. The rapid beat of her pulse worried him, and her breathing was too shallow. Dropping into a deeper trance, he summoned his magic. At his silent command, the magic flowed out from his body. It was less than he'd hoped, lacking the wild turbulence he was accustomed to, but it would be enough to heal the Sorceress. It had to be. He bowed his head until his muzzle touched her breastbone and he breathed more power upon her.

Nothing happened. His magic didn't even penetrate her skin. What had the Battle Goddess done to her when she was a helpless child that his power could not now meld with hers?

Panicked, he leaped upon the table and hunched closer, attempting to will power into her. Then he remembered he'd caged her magic for reasons that still remained elusive to him. With no other choice, he reached with his power and unraveled the spell preventing her from calling upon her own magic.

She jerked awake, her chest heaving as if a nightmare suddenly gripped her. Her eyes focused on him and her expression softened in recognition.

A shaky hand caressed his muzzle, before reaching back into his mane, circling his neck. Still, she didn't take what he offered, power she desperately needed. He bumped her face with his muzzle and licked at her skin but was careful not to sip even the smallest drop of her dryad blood for fear of losing his concentration.

She moved again. Her arms tightened around him as she nuzzled the underside of his jaw. Then her fingers shifted, grasping his shoulders and clinging there a moment before sliding down his arms. One of her hands grazed the slashes where a dire wolf had gotten in a lucky swipe.

Gentle fingertips paused in their downward descent and reversed, gliding back over the broken skin. Light caresses turned to a savage prod. He grunted more in surprise than pain, but her hand dropped away in the next moment.

Slowed by his shock, his reflexes didn't spur him into action until her bloody fingers were halfway to her lips. She no longer looked at him. Instead, her gaze riveted on the bright smear on her fingers. Before they reached her lips, he snatched her wrist.

She hissed in frustration, struggling weakly before falling back against the table, her energy spent.

He reared away from her, dropped to all fours, and began to pace with his wings mantled, tail whipping with agitation. He froze at what his mind tried to tell him. She craved his blood, hungered for its power like a mate would. Yet they were not mates.

They could never be mates.

Sacrilege.

A soft sound, followed by a watery gasp, dragged his attention back to the table. She was paler than before, gray, and her breath came in a death's rattle. Unable to watch her struggle alone, he returned to her side and caressed her cheek.

He knew what he had to do.

After gathering her into his arms, he carried her over to a corner and sat with his back braced against a wall, her slight form resting in his lap.

She was so light, so fragile. He didn't yet know what changes the Battle Goddess had forced upon her, but what if he could share blood without shattering his oath and forging mating ties? No matter how slim the chance, he had to try. He slid her hand closer to the warm dampness he could feel making its sluggish way down his arm, but her fingers didn't tighten upon the wound as they had before. She was too weak even for that.

His talons rested cool against his breastbone for a moment. Then, uncaring of the consequences or that he was breaking one of the sacred laws binding them, he dragged the point of one talon down his chest a finger's length. With his other hand, he lifted her head to the wound.

He could live as an oath breaker. He didn't think his sanity would survive her death so early into this new lifetime together.

Eyes still closed, she shivered in his arms and inhaled a deep breath. Then, following the coppery scent to the wound, she sealed her lips over his blood-dampened flesh. At the first lap of her tongue, his concentration shattered like mist before a strong wind. Magic surged and flowed into her. She drank his magic along with his blood, growing stronger with each heartbeat.

Soon his Sorceress pressed against him, becoming more demanding in her feeding. Ecstasy threatened to destroy his discipline. The soft caress of her fingers feathered along his abdomen as she stirred in his arms. Her gentle touch shocked him to his core, rousing instincts better left to slumber. Fire settled in his groin.

He groaned, then cursed his response.

His horns grated against the wall behind him, sending white dust and bits of debris raining down upon them both. He tightened his arms around her, wanting her closer while at the same time trying not to crush the life from her. His tail coiled around her uninjured leg as if it had a life of its own.

It seemed endless, the pleasure-pain of her feeding on his power, yet it was over too quickly. With one last lick along the length of the wound, she tilted her head back and looked at him. A half-smile graced her lips, and then she tucked her head against his shoulder. A few moments later, her breathing evened out as she drifted to sleep.

Rest was far from his thoughts with his lungs working like a forge's bellows and his pulse thundering in his ears. He called on what remained of his discipline and fell into another trance to order his body's rhythms to calm—it would last moments, at best.

Once he was calmer, he opened his eyes and checked her wounds. They were healed. Only faint, pink scars remained. She may have been healed, but her dryad blood still called to him, its coppery, sap-sweet scent enticing him down a dark and forbidden path. He shook himself, fighting deeply rooted instincts. Only after he'd won that internal battle was he able to deposit her back on the table.

Leaving her side was difficult, but he needed to get clean of her blood, her intoxicating scent. Now.

Sniffing the air, he scented water but couldn't pinpoint the source at first. He paced around the room and continued scenting. Then he heard the faint plop of water dripping onto an unyielding surface somewhere above his present location.

With a huff, he sought out the source of that sound, tossing his arm and wristbands on the ground as he walked. His knee-length loincloth landed on the carpet. Its ornate beads rattled against each other for a moment before falling silent.

Following the sound of water to its source, he went up a broad set of stairs and down a short hall, at last entering a large room. Beyond that room was another, smaller one. A silver spigot of some sort dripped water into a white basin.

On one wall, a glass alcove took up a quarter of the room. It smelled of soap and dampness.

Blessed relief.

CHAPTER FIVE

A coppery taste coated Lillian's tongue. Her mouth was dry, gummy with old blood. She must have bitten her tongue, and unless her mattress had suddenly turned to stone, she'd managed to knock herself out and was lying flat on the floor. Of all the stupid things to do, bashing her head hard enough to lose consciousness had to be one of the clumsiest. She ran her hands out to her sides. Cool, polished woodgrain took shape under her searching fingers. Interesting. None of the floors felt like that. She blinked open her eyes and peered to one side: the honey color of oak met her vision. Kitchen table?

Yep. Kitchen table.

She'd somehow managed to knock herself out and then landed on the table?

Not bloody likely.

She scoured her memory. A void blocked her way. She panicked, fearing she'd lost her memories for the second time in her life... but she remembered that, so her memory still functioned. Something else, then. Something so frightening her mind didn't want to remember.

She could deal with frightening. Fear was better than the nothingness of vanished memories. She scanned her surroundings. The kitchen looked normal. She wasn't sure what she sought, but nothing in this room jogged her memory. Sitting up, a wave of dizziness swamped her, and she curled her fingers around the table edge in a death grip. The rush of blood and the crackle of white noise hummed in her ears.

After blinking several times, Lillian's vision cleared enough for the room to come into focus.

Okay, that's better. I can do this, she reassured herself.

Seeing no point in postponing the inevitable, she jumped down from the table and wobbled around until her legs remembered they had bones in them. God, it felt like she'd donated half her blood to a blood bank. The thought of blood summoned an image of her grove, her favorite tree dripping gore onto the ground. Her mind shied away from the vision.

She took in the room again and noticed something she'd missed before.

A thick, gold bracelet sat abandoned on the floor. Bracelet? Hell, that word didn't even begin to describe the hefty chunk of gold and jewels sitting on the tiles. She was reaching for it, her fingers poised to curl around it, when she saw the blood smeared on the floor next to it.

More blood marred the bracelet, staining some of the intricate knot-work along its one side. Her eyes swung back to the smudges on the floor. There were others, farther apart, and they headed toward the living room. Those smudges, they couldn't be tracks, not unless a velociraptor walked the earth again and it happened to come into her kitchen, following the scent of good baking.

Yet there they were, tracks the size of a small dinosaur, blood smeared and marching off into the depths of her house.

Out.

She had to get out. Maybe then the nightmare would end. She eased her way across the kitchen floor, careful of squeaky floorboards and the groans of an old house. She didn't want to face what had made those tracks. Now that she had a goal, reaching the back door as quietly as possible, she could control the panic lurking at the edges of her mind.

The doorknob turned under her hand. As she pulled open the door, it loosed a groan fit for a haunted house on All Hallows' Eve. She threw herself through the doorway and slammed square into... nothing?

"What the hell?" she cursed, her breath escaping in a grunt.

Stunned, she stumbled back and rubbed her sore shoulder.

Luckily, the abused shoulder, and not her face, had taken the brunt of the impact. She ran her hands across the entrance and saw a nebulous, multihued blue light swirling around her fingertips where they made contact with the barrier. It was not unlike the oily surface of a soap bubble with its cascade of colors.

Words solidified in her mind.

Ward. A spell for protection.

Where the hell did that bit of information come from?

Her newly acquired knowledge was scarier than the blue ward thingy.

On a hunch, she checked the windows and found them

blocked by more of the strange substance. She braced her hands against it and pushed.

Nothing.

She might as well have tried pushing through concrete.

Looking out beyond the pale barrier blocking the window, she could see her maze in the distance. Scattered lumps dotted the lawn, some in plain view while others remained partially hidden by the garden's tall, ornamental grasses.

Bodies.

She swallowed hard and looked again to be sure. No. Body parts.

The barrier her mind had erected to protect itself from the traumatic memories vanished, and everything from that afternoon flooded back.

She'd been attacked by monstrous wolfmen, feral cat-like women, and sallow-skinned creatures with hunger in their eyes. She remembered a power flooding her, and then joy at the feel of the stone warming and softening under her hands. The fog of mixed-up memories ended there.

Fear fluttered in her stomach, and her breath hitched.

Nothing she remembered clarified how she had come to find herself on the kitchen table with a strange blue light preventing escape. With another glance at the bodies in the garden, her idea of possible escape in that direction lost some of its luster, especially since there might be more than just bodies out there.

Backtracking, she returned to the kitchen table and paced around it twice, and then came back to the tracks.

None of the attacking monsters could have made tracks like those. But there was one particular stone fellow she'd sat with every day since childhood, and his feet were large and ended in talons. If her gargoyle had come alive, he might have made tracks such as these.

Her heart lurched at that thought, but it wasn't in fear. After a brief moment of euphoria, her rational mind told her she probably didn't want to come face-to-face with whatever creature was still standing after the battle.

Occupied by thoughts of escape and what those prints could mean, she jerked at the soft rumble of the water heater as it started up in the laundry room just off the kitchen. She hadn't at first heard someone taking a shower upstairs, but now that she listened, she could hear the faint sound of water in the pipes.

As if it wasn't bad enough that she was locked in her own home with a bunch of dead bodies out back, the gardens reduced to a warzone, her grove violated, and blood and God-knows-what tracked all over her grandmother's antique carpets, the last monster standing had apparently come in and made himself at home.

Lillian frowned and squared her shoulders. She could hide somewhere, whimpering in fear until whatever was in the house found her and dragged her from her hiding place, or she could arm herself and face the threat head-on.

CHAPTER SIX

While she would have preferred her crossbow, her fencing sword was better than nothing, its weight a solid reassurance in her hand. She retraced her steps until she came to the living room and the curving stairway that led up to the second floor. Discarded pieces of jewelry and the occasional smudge of blood marked the path the creature had taken. She cleared the stairs and turned down one dark hall. The first bathroom on the second floor was silent and empty. That left one other. She entered her bedroom, intent on her master bathroom.

The door was ajar. A curl of steam drifted out across the floor. Inside, the bathroom was dark and so full of steam she couldn't see anything. The monster didn't know how to turn on a light switch but could figure out a shower? She pondered that a moment. Perhaps it didn't need light. Just her luck. The damned monster probably had night vision.

She eased into a defensive stance as she reached in and flicked the switch. Her breath caught as the room was flooded with yellow light. Her sword's tip clanked against the tiled floor in her shock. She jerked it back up into position until the point hovered at shoulder level.

Her rational mind had expected to find a monster, and there was one. He filled her walk-in shower, and the massive shower still wasn't big enough for the entire gargoyle. His wings arched across the length and width of the large bathroom, and his tail sent water droplets spraying across the room as it lashed back and forth, its blade-tipped end twitching like an agitated cat's.

One wing arched back and gave her a view of the rest of the gargoyle. His head brushed the ceiling, and his horns clinked against the small tiles when he moved. With eyes partially squeezed shut against the sudden intrusion of bright light, he turned his muzzle in her direction and flared his nostrils, drawing in a deep breath. She had the distinct impression he tasted the air, and by the way he snorted like a horse and shook his head, she didn't think he liked the smell.

His muzzle dipped down, and his eyes locked on the sword she held. He turned fully toward her. At least with him eyeing the sword so intently, he might not notice the vivid shade of scarlet she'd just turned. Had there been any doubt in her mind about his gender, it vanished in a heartbeat. Male. Lacking in modesty.

He had muscles most men would envy. Then she reminded herself he also had a tail, wings, horns, and talons. Still, even in all his otherness, he was majestic. Scary as hell but lovely as a predator.

Fear was absent, and she should have worried about her sanity, but somehow it all seemed right. The gargoyle was a prominent part of her childhood. He had always been home to her.

And 'home' was presently extracting himself from the shower. When he stepped out, he straightened.

The bathroom shrunk.

Mercy, he was still hunched over.

He was massive. Over eight feet of gargoyle crowded her master bath. She couldn't beat *that* in a fight. Her sword's point dipped again, but she didn't lift it back into a defensive position. One solid hit and he'd put her through a wall. Heck, he could probably snap her blade in two with a thought. At least the sword's weight stopped her hands from shaking.

"Hello," she said. Her voice came out faint, hollow-sounding. She cleared her throat, unable to stop the nervous reaction. "I'm Lillian."

How intelligent, she muttered in her own mind. At least her voice sounded stronger.

He cocked his head, his jackal-like ears sweeping forward from the depths of his wiry mane. She hadn't noticed his ears earlier. They'd blended into his ebony mane and the crown of bone that formed the base of his two large horns.

He expelled the breath he'd been holding and took another. His nostrils pinched shut.

Good lord, she must smell worse than she thought.

His talons clinked against the tiles as he took another step forward. She backed away until she slammed into the doorframe. A squeak escaped past her lips. He snatched a clean bath towel off the rack and snapped it open with a flick before she could think to run at his sudden move. No matter which way he tugged, tucked, or arranged it, the towel wouldn't reach around his muscular girth.

With a deep rumble, he grabbed a second. Tied together, the two towels proved large enough to fit around his waist and haunches. But he still didn't seem happy with the arrangement. Constricted by the material, his tail flicked and jumped like a downed power line, offering a new threat to modesty. It occurred to her shock-slowed brain that all the poor creature wanted was some privacy. A blush burned across her cheeks a second time.

She was backing out of the room when a flowing language issued from his mouth. Deep, beautiful, smooth like the wind in a forest. It reminded her of night's shadows and the lull of beckoning sleep. He repeated himself, or she thought he might have. She couldn't be sure because she didn't know what he'd said the first time, and it became no clearer on the second try.

He was gesturing at her now. She nodded and pointed to herself. "Lillian."

"Lillian," he repeated in a clear, deep voice. He pointed behind him.

She followed where he pointed.

Did he mean the shower? Shrugging, she pointed at it and said, "Shower."

He nodded his head, pleased. "Lillian, shower." Then he ducked under the doorframe and marched away, leaving her in the steam-filled room with the shower still running.

Too shocked to follow, she stood gawking like an idiot. Her first conversation with her gargoyle, something she'd dreamed about as a child. It had finally happened. Two words. He'd told her she reeked in two words.

CHAPTER SEVEN

Freshly showered and now dressed in a clean T-shirt and jeans, Lillian stood over the pile of her discarded clothes and frowned at the evidence that proved she hadn't imagined the last few hours. She poked the bloodied and shredded clothes with a bare toe. *No hope of ever getting them clean enough to warrant mending.* The mess of ruined fabric landed in the garbage with a wet sound. She rewashed her hands.

Hopefully, she now smelled better to a gargoyle's delicate nose.

During her shower, she'd washed away the remainder of her fear. How could she fear anyone who looked as ridiculous as he had, jammed into the shower with wings and tail jutting out, horns scraping the ceiling? Besides, she was still alive. If he'd wanted her dead, he'd had plenty of opportunities. Instead, he'd told her she reeked and fled the room as fast as he could.

"Well, fine," she mumbled to herself. "No more procrastinating."

As she exited the bathroom, the sword caught her eye. It sat propped where she'd left it next to the door. Since she wasn't going to attack him, the sword was pointless. Besides, the mere thought of doing him harm sickened her. She needed answers. Something to explain away the strange link of kinship she felt with the gargoyle—if that was really what he was.

As she left the room, the bedroom door creaked loudly enough to shatter glass. She winced at the noise but continued her march down the length of the hall until she reached the stairs, which she stomped down with a heavy tread. She couldn't say how she knew where he was, but like a bird aligning its migration flight to the Earth's magnetic field, she set her mind seeking his and followed where that tug led.

She found him in the kitchen. He paced around the island table, his bath towels slapping at his thighs as he walked. Seeing her, he stopped.

Once again, she was reminded of stone; he held himself so still. The spell broke a minute later as his jackal-like ears swiveled toward her. When she stayed rooted in place, he took measured steps in her direction. Slow and cautious, like he was wooing a bird or closing in on a skittish horse, he reached out a clawed hand. She didn't spook that easily and held her ground.

He approached with a gentle caution, but all his muscles were tensed like he was ready for a fight. Her throat tightened, and her heart felt like a weight in her chest. With his hand outstretched before him, he inched nearer until only a few feet separated them. She took a half step toward him and another.

He leaped forward, tackling her. His wings enveloped her a moment before his strong arms crushed her to his chest. She squeezed her eyes shut, and she couldn't even scream since fear and surprise held her jaws locked. Her heart pulsed strangely, fluttering like it didn't know how to beat. Then it remembered and took off with a vengeance.

Slowly, the dark world behind her closed eyes expanded. The sweet fragrance of soap registered on her senses. The feel of warm skin over hard muscle. The echo of his heart. The pulse of his blood. Forest scent and male.

Her gargoyle was real.

Without reason or logic, joy engulfed her soul and the remnants of panic melted away. She locked her arms around as much of his waist as she could reach.

He nuzzled her hair, blowing into it with great puffs of breath. His muzzle dipped lower, his tongue laving at her face in broad damp swipes. Stilling, he inhaled deeply before resting his muzzle on top of her head, just holding her to him as if he feared she would vanish.

Apparently, he considered her natural smell to be an improvement over dried blood and gore.

"You're certainly friendly," she mumbled into his chest.

Mumbling was all she was able to do with his arms locked around her; his chest may as well have been made of stone. She should have been screaming and fighting, driven by panic, but she wasn't. She trusted him without question, which likely should have worried her more.

He shifted her in his arms as he folded his wings against

his back. Then he unbalanced her more, reaching for something on the table behind her.

"You could let me go. I can stand on my own. I won't even run away. Promise." Her words went unanswered.

A loaf of bread appeared an inch in front of her face.

"Okay. A little room, please." She shoved at his chest. After the third time, he seemed to get the point and allowed her to put a little space between them. She was still locked in the circle of his arms, but at least now she could take a deep breath without cracking a rib. He gestured with the bread again.

"Persistent fella, aren't you?" She could stand there with a loaf of bread bombarding her face, or she could take the food.

With a sigh, she accepted the loaf and tore a chunk off, cavewoman style. When she dutifully started to chew, he gestured for her to eat more. She swallowed and took another bite. He nodded his head and released her. Somehow it didn't surprise her he'd be pleased by her compliance.

When she finished her chunk, he tried to get her to eat more.

"Sorry, no." She shook her head and hoped he would understand.

He gestured again.

"Not unless you plan to force-feed me." She crossed her arms and glared at him. "I have questions. To start, what's your name?"

She pointed to him and he grasped her hand. His head tilted to one side as his ears flicked forward and then back.

Lillian sighed. *This is going to be a long day.*

She tugged on her hand until he released her. While pretending to brush at crumbs, she stepped out of his personal space. He didn't follow her, so she walked over to the sink and filled the teakettle with water—all the while fighting the urge to turn around. After she placed the kettle on the stove, she glanced out the window. Her breath caught. Bodies slumped near the maze. How had she forgotten about them? Seeing them again, the horror rushed back. But unlike the first time, her mind was sharper, and now a greater concern wormed its way into her consciousness. Her family would be home from the airport soon, and there could be more of those monsters outside somewhere. A spike of dread lanced her insides.

Her back muscles clenched into knots, winding tighter by the minute, and her jaw ached with the need to do something. If she called her family and told them to stay away, they would only rush home faster.

"Lillian."

That voice again, lulling as the night breeze. His arms enclosed her from behind and her moment of panic dissipated. Of course he would have killed all the monsters. Her gargoyle would never let them hurt her family.

Interesting. She narrowed her eyes in thought. If she was in physical contact with him, calmness engulfed her. But when he was away, something rose within her. Fear or panic, she wasn't sure which, but either reaction was concerning.

Was he controlling her thoughts, her emotions?

Doubts grew. She again stepped away from him to think.

He remained a calm, solid presence behind her until the kettle's sudden, shrill whistle spurred the gargoyle into action. He swept her up into his arms and spun in a circle, seeking the source of the noise, his talons poised to rend his enemies.

"Easy," she soothed. "Whoa. It's okay." She placed her

hands flat against his muzzle and eased them up to his temple.

The room swam, blurring with motion. When her vision cleared, the ground was a greater distance away, the room smaller, claustrophobic.

Impossible as it was, she was somehow seeing and feeling the world around them from his point of view—and, yes, she was presently feeling her horns rasp against the ceiling unpleasantly.

Her tail lashing in agitation at the shrill sound hurting her ears, she looked to the small object causing the noise and backhanded it. It sailed across the room and landed with a clatter, but at least the horrid sound bouncing around the room died off.

"What on earth!" Lillian jerked her hand away from where it rested against his temple. "What the hell was that?"

She twisted in his arms and pushed at his chest, attempting to slip free. When that failed, she slumped against him. He still didn't release her, but at least the strange parade of foreign sensations stopped.

"Okay," she said, more to calm herself than him. "We need ground rules. No more of the mind-merging crap. I don't want to ever know what it feels like for my horns to scrape the ceiling ever again, nor do I want to discover anything else deeply personal about you either by accident or intention on your part. Hands off until you can keep that under wraps."

A soft whine issued from his throat as he bumped his muzzle under her hand a second time. Warmth and contentment, like a deep radiating sense of peace she'd never known before, surrounded her. Then it was shattered. Accompanying the new sensation was the image of the whistling teakettle. Foolishness. Embarrassment. Regret.

After a moment, she understood he was using touch to communicate, trying to apologize for his rash behavior. He'd been caught off-guard by the shrill teakettle. He'd thought it was an attack. She might have found it funny if it hadn't unfolded in her kitchen.

By way of apology, the gargoyle retrieved the teakettle, refilled it with water, and placed it back over the element. Then he returned to her side and watched in his silent way.

His ears flicked forward, and back—like a horse listening for reassurance in his rider's voice. *A gargoyle with insecurity issues?*

"I'm sorry," she said in a calmer voice. "I get pissy when I'm scared. And I've been more scared today than any time in my life." She took one of his larger hands with its deadly talons into both of hers, hoping he could pick up on her emotions like she had his, and concentrated on projecting her feelings of gratitude and the lessening of her fear. "You saved my life, healed me. I can't even begin to figure out how or why, but I'm alive, and you seem genuinely interested in keeping me that way. The least I can do is hear you out."

Now her day would improve if she could find a way to communicate in complex sentences. His touchy-feely voodoo gave her an idea, and she intertwined her fingers with his. She felt like a child. His one hand could engulf both of hers without difficulty and his claws... the term 'huge' didn't do them justice. But for all his massive strength and formidable weaponry, he hadn't harmed her. She patted his hand and tugged him in the direction of the cupboard over the kitchen sink. Pulling out a package of English Breakfast tea, she held it out to him. He blinked at her, but dutifully sniffed at the packaging.

"Tea," she said, giving it a little shake. She took a teabag and dropped it in the teapot, then poured the boiling water in after. Next, she showed him how the stove worked.

He absorbed knowledge with an unreasonable quickness, and she wondered if his magic was aiding him in some way, or if he was able to pick the meaning of her words from her mind directly. Whatever the case, in less than a half-hour he was pointing at random objects in the kitchen, saying the words, and demonstrating how they worked. From the kitchen, they moved to the living room and then to the other parts of the house. The TV and stereo he didn't understand, but at least he didn't try to 'kill' the television like he had the teakettle.

After an hour, the gargoyle could recite a couple hundred words. She was mildly envious of his ability to learn so quickly. Sentences were still beyond him, but that was probably her lack of skill as a teacher. She didn't know how to teach him something she couldn't show or demonstrate.

Since she had grown tired of merely thinking of him as 'the gargoyle,' she tried to persuade him into revealing his name, but he merely blinked at her, his gaze giving no hint to his thoughts.

Frustrated, she tried again, slapping her hand against her chest.

"Lillian," she muttered, and then pointed at him.

He blinked at her and then nodded, giving her a flash of teeth.

He found it funny. He was laughing at her. Great.

The tip of his tail flicked like a cat's, and he suddenly leaned down and licked her across the cheek.

She sputtered and swore.

His grin stretched even wider, showing white, curving fangs. His tongue darted out again, catching her across the ear. "Lillian," he rumbled.

"I know my name, Sherlock." She pointed at him again. "Do you have one?"

"Yours," he said, his expression turning serious. He bowed until his horns touched the ground and his wings pooled around him like a silk cloak. "I am yours. I have always been yours."

CHAPTER EIGHT

A deep laugh rumbled in his chest at his lady's expression. When he placed a finger under her chin and closed her mouth, her teeth came together with a soft click. The sound must have galvanized her, for she snapped out of her stupor.

"Yours? As in mine—like you belong to me? I... I don't... Wait one minute! You can speak perfect English." She folded her arms under her breasts and stood there, attempting to stare him down. "You've been holding out on me. After that info bomb, you can't stand there all silent and stoic."

The word games weren't necessary, but they gave him a chance to study her, and since she thought she needed to touch him so he could pick up her thoughts, she'd held his hand most of the time. He found he craved contact after years locked in stone.

He was also stalling. His own memories were still spotty. He'd taken her memories for some reason; though, frustratingly, he couldn't remember why. Something to do with the trauma she'd suffered while in the Battle Goddess's kingdom, perhaps? He wouldn't have taken such a drastic measure without reason.

And he'd already restored her ability to reach her magic so she could heal. Best he not restore her memories until he knew why he'd taken them.

Even telling her their names from their last life might be enough to trigger her memories.

As for his own, there seemed to be a few unnatural holes. He suspected that during his escape from the Battle Goddess's kingdom one of the blood witch's spells might have infiltrated his defenses. Then once he had surrendered to the healing sleep, the spell broke dormancy and ravaged his mind until his own defenses rid him of the spell while he was still stone.

Caution was in order until he'd filled in the gaps in his own memories. For now, he'd only share with her what she absolutely needed to know. If they couldn't use their old names, it was time for new ones.

"I am your protector. It's your right to give me my name. What would you have of me, my Mistress?" he asked.

"Mistress?" She sucked in a breath, held it a moment, and then expelled it through her teeth, her expression thoughtful. "Okay, you're really going to have to explain the mistress thing to me and answer some questions."

Remaining silent, he tried and failed to come up with a way to answer whatever questions she might ask without triggering memories he wasn't ready for her to recall just yet.

She cleared her throat. "First question—you saved me.

Why? Who am I, and what am I to you? Those creatures, why did they attack me? What do you...?" She let the sentence die as her eyes widened. "You know something about my childhood! Please, if you have knowledge... I need to know. It's all a blank void to me. Please." Her voice cracked on the last 'please.'

Maintaining his silence while she looked at him like that was undoubtedly one of the hardest things he'd ever endured. In fact, he wasn't sure how long he could keep his secret. They were not designed to lie or withhold information from each other.

Lillian's expression of desperate yearning changed to a frown when she realized he wasn't going to say anything more. "Oh, don't think you can play 'mute beast' now. I heard full sentences come out of that muzzle of yours."

He recalled she'd said she got 'pissy' when she was scared. He was unfamiliar with the term, but it was a good word for the way she stood with her hands fisted at her sides and her narrowed eyes tracking him like an enraged bear's.

Now was not a good time to explain. She was already under enough stress.

"Talk." She hissed something else under her breath that sounded like *no more handholding* and paced away from him.

She was adapting too quickly, her agile mind thinking up too many questions. It would make hiding the truth harder, and he didn't actually want there to be falsehoods between them, but he needed more time to understand what had been done to her as a child. There were too many unknowns. And for every uncertainty, new dangers could arise.

She exhaled a deep sigh. "Okay. Trust goes two ways, and I

gather you're not comfortable talking about everything yet."
He heard her heart rate slow as she calmed. "Fine, we'll take it
slow. No pressure. What would you like to talk about?"

"My name?" he replied.

"Wasn't that what I was doing before *you* blurted the 'mistress' thing?" She sighed out another long, frustrated sound.

He couldn't prevent the corners of his lips from curling
away from his teeth in a gargoyle smile, so he dipped his head
down in a bow, hiding his expression.

"The Sorceress has always named her Gargoyle Protector."
And just like that, he revealed a critical piece of information.

He winced, admitting he should be the last person in the
universe to be trusted to keep a secret from his other half.
Besides, he reasoned, she deserved to know something about
their relationship, didn't she?

"Right, so what?" Lillian drawled. "Was she negligent?"

He tilted his head to the side, puzzling over her words.
Once he gathered the meaning from her thoughts, he grinned
and tapped her gently on one shoulder. "Yes, my lady is very
forgetful in this lifetime."

Again, her expression reflected an unpleasant surprise, but
she recovered faster this time and snapped her teeth together
a moment later. "Well, you must have been smoking that
same stuff as the other guy blathering about my magic. I'm
neither a sorceress nor your mistress."

Her words were spoken in a firm tone, but there was an
underlying doubt coloring them as well.

"I'm very certain. You are my Sorceress, and I am your
gargoyle, your protector. It's your right to name me."

"You've got to be freaking kidding me," she hissed more to

herself than him. But she merely sighed and closed her eyes. After a moment, the wrinkles on her forehead smoothed out, and her expression turned deceptively peaceful. "Fine. You win."

"You will name me?"

"Yep." She flashed him a mischievous grin.

He waited with ears poised forward, tail flicking gently.

"Gregory."

"Gregory?" he said, trying the foreign name on his tongue. It was short, like the name Lillian, and he wondered if all the names of this world were as short and clipped and lacking in beauty. Although, he didn't completely dislike it. She'd gifted him with this name, after all.

"Gregory Livingstone." She started to laugh.

He supposed it could have been worse, and he did see the humor in being named living stone.

A distant rumble caught his attention. He spun away from Lillian and loped to the back door. There were many strange sounds in this realm, and he didn't know what this was, but it sounded large and dangerous. Whatever it was came closer, roaring up the stone-covered lane.

An open window allowed the breeze access. Upon the wind, he detected an oily odor and the tang of fumes like the deep vents in the earth gave forth. A moment later, one of the metal-and-glass-enclosed carriages that the people of this world used for travel sped up to the stone cottage. He'd learned of these things from Lillian's thoughts, but the noise and smell were much muted in her memories. Or she was merely nose-dead.

Now that the vehicle rolled to a halt, the noise was less, but a quiet hum still set Gregory's teeth on edge. He eased into a crouch and flexed his talons on the tiles as he limbered up stiff muscles. From Lillian's memories, he knew these people were her family.

However, there was no guarantee that they had not been infected by the Riven. If they intended Lillian harm, he would send them on their way to the Spirit Realm regardless of her affections for them. The tip of his tail twitched as he waited for the ones within the carriage to show themselves. After a moment, the vehicle rumbled to silence. His ears swiveled forward as he advanced another step.

From behind, Lillian wrapped her hands around his arm. Her fingers bit in, nails scratching at his bicep while she tried to tug him away from the door. He didn't know what she thought she'd accomplish. He weighed four times as much as her. She jerked on his arm with greater panic. Her nails bit into his arm hard enough to break the skin.

Surprised, he glanced down at the few scarlet drops beading up along the length of the scratches. Strange. Dryads didn't have claws. Before he could study her nails, she dropped her hands to her sides.

Her nostrils flared as she locked eyes on his small wound. An unfathomable expression crossed her face. After a moment, she shook her head and mumbled an apology. She continued in a clearer voice. "Don't hurt them. Get away from the door." She renewed her tugging on his arm. "Please let me talk to them."

He swung back to face the newcomers.

"Wait, you said I am your mistress—I order you to stay here. I need to go talk to them first. It's bad enough the gardens look like a war zone. They certainly won't be expecting an eight-foot-tall gargoyle in the kitchen! Let. Me. Talk. To. Them."

In all other situations, he would respect her wishes, but not when her safety was at risk. While she might know and trust these people, he did not.

A series of soft creaks and metal groans came from the direction of the vehicle. He spun back to the humans. The doors on either side of the carriage stood open, and with a slow caution, the occupants eased out. A male of average human height and short, windblown brown hair emerged first, a crossbow gripped in one hand and a quarterstaff in the other.

Behind the first man, another male emerged, his white hair a startling contrast with his youthful features. He was empty-handed as far as Gregory could tell. Last, an old mother with many years of wisdom upon her exited the vehicle.

The elder also carried a quarterstaff in her hands. Each staff was carved and painted with runes that glowed to Gregory's magic-enhanced sight. He eyed her quarterstaff more intently. Perhaps it was more than a weapon. A vague recollection of the woman walking between two trees on a wintery night surfaced. He'd met her before.

The breeze carried their scents to him. And while there was no stink of evil, he wasn't done studying them yet. They had power, and all power could be dangerous. He called the shadows for concealment.

After he faded out of sight, he paced forward until he stood in the threshold of the cottage. Lillian crowded him from behind, trying to squeeze past him to rush out the door. Winding his tail around her waist, he held her secure against his side for a moment, just enjoying having her close. When he looked down at her, she had her eyes closed.

An intense look of concentration spread across her face. A moment more and her thoughts flooded his mind. Like a waking dream, images formed before his eyes. The first showed him releasing her so she could go join her family and explain. A second image formed—in this one he was waiting patiently for her to finish explaining the situation to her family.

He called his own magic to dispel her visions, then he lowered his muzzle and swiped his tongue across her face from chin to hairline. Her eyes popped open, and she flailed her arms, hollering and trying to push his muzzle away. Punishment complete, he shoved her behind him and stalked forward. Lillian grabbed at his tail, her fingers locking around it in a pinching grip. With a powerful flick, he slipped free of her grasp and darted through the ward blocking the door. She, however, smacked into the solid blue shielding magic.

An irate sound, part-huff, part-growl escaped her.

"No. Dammit!" she shouted. "Stop, you great brute!"

Her actions caught the attention of those waiting below. Three sets of eyes gazed up with looks of suspicion and worry. Unable to see him, they stared through him to where Lillian stood. By their baffled expressions, they wondered why Lillian was pounding her fists against empty air.

He added a layer of sound-deadening magic to his ward, then inhaled another deep breath and began sorting the different scents. Only the old woman from the night he'd first come to this realm was familiar. In the chaos, he'd not had time to learn the grandmother's name, but this was her—a few years older certainly, but still the same woman who'd stood before him without fear, the one he'd trusted enough to raise the Sorceress while he slept and healed.

"Sis, are you okay?" The brown-haired man asked as he advanced one slow step at a time.

"Jason, stay back!" Lillian yelled from inside the house, proving just how fast she could annihilate a sound-deadening spell guided by only her instincts.

Gregory grunted in annoyance but didn't bother setting a new ward.

"It's okay, Lil. Tell us what happened," the one named Jason said as he continued forward. Gregory moved to intercept.

"No! Leave him alone. Don't hurt him." Lillian's voice mirrored the panic he felt growing in her mind. She'd seen too much today, and now he was forced to threaten her family.

"Jason, do as your sister says."

Gregory swung his muzzle in the direction of the new speaker—the older woman he'd met before.

Growling low in his throat, Gregory warned off Jason again. The grandmother tensed at the sound, alert and ready for battle. Her bravery earned her a mote of respect.

Still, they were too close to his Sorceress. He rumbled a second time, and Jason tightened his grip on his weapon until his knuckles stood out white against the dark wood of the staff.

"Easy, don't panic." The older woman's voice exuded calm. She held her quarterstaff horizontal before her, her arms relaxed.

"Gran, what the hell is going on?" Lillian sounded bewildered. "Why are you carrying a staff?" Her gaze riveted on the woman's quarterstaff.

The old woman cleared her throat. "Lillian, it will be all right. I'll explain everything." While the old woman spoke in reassuring tones to Lillian, her sharp eyes searched the shadows where Gregory stood.

He scented her summoning magic. Like wood smoke, it tickled his nose with its pleasant, warm odor. The runes on the staff faded for a moment as her eyes took on an unfocused look. After a moment, her gaze sharpened and she scanned the area to either side of him, then above his head. She smiled.

His ears slanted forward with interest. She'd found him by seeking the void her magic couldn't penetrate. Clever woman. His estimate of her crept up another notch.

"Lillian, I know this is very strange. You must have a lot of questions," the old woman didn't look away from Gregory's direction while she calmed Lillian, "but I need you to focus for me now." She put force behind her words. "I need you to tell me what happened. Are you aware there is another creature here?"

Lillian suddenly stopped worrying at his ward. He could practically feel her expression transforming from annoyance to uncertainty as she realized he might have tricked her in some way. The scent of her rising fear thickened in the air.

"I was cornered by strangers. They weren't human. They hunted me." She paused, likely trapped in her recent memories. "I ran, hoping to lose them in the maze, but they found me by scent. Something there stopped them, a power in the stones. But a man named Alexander did something to the ring of stones and they erupted. Shrapnel flew in all directions. I was hit... I'd lost so much blood. I was dying." The flood of words issuing from Lillian choked off. She drew a shaking breath.

Gregory's wings unfurled with the urge to comfort. Lillian's need almost swayed him from his mission. Instead, he used the distraction to stalk the group.

"Lillian, it's all right. Tell us the rest." The old woman's voice soothed like the night breeze—calming, reassuring. It nearly swayed Gregory into answering the woman himself. With a shake, he broke away from the older woman's subtle spell.

Lillian continued in a daze. "I was dying. All I could think was I must reach the gargoyle. And I did. He... he came alive. I felt the stone warm under my hands. I thought my soul was leaving my body." Her voice shook. "I blacked out the moment I touched him. Later, I awoke on the kitchen table."

Following the long shadows cast by the tree trunks, Gregory circled the small group and came up behind the grandmother. When he stood on two legs again, he exhaled across the back of her neck. She stiffened, but no other sign betrayed her fear. He grinned, his lips curling back from his muzzle with humor, pleased she'd not seen him move. The woman's scent was clean, free of evil's taint like the last time they'd met.

"I know it's unnerving that only Lillian can see the gargoyle, but let him get your scent," the woman said, her words a blunt order. "Do nothing he will perceive as a threat to Lillian."

Jason shifted his quarterstaff from one hand to the other in a nervous fashion. "Shit. Are we going to stand here all afternoon until he decides to eat us?"

"Jason, hold your tongue," the grandmother said.

"This sucks shi—"

"Jason, quiet!" Lillian shouted from her position on the porch. "And listen to Gran for once!"

The male held his position next to the vehicle, but his sour expression said he wasn't happy about it.

"I swear, if the invisible beastie sniffs my crotch, I'm—" The male bit off his sentence as Gregory exhaled a lungful of air across the human's forehead, blowing his fine, brown hair straight back. The human jumped away with a yelp. There was no darkness upon this one either, so Gregory left him to dance in place. The human whirled one way and then the other, flapping his arms like a startled goose.

Gregory dropped to all fours and started toward the last human, who had backed some distance away from the vehicle. When pale blue eyes followed the motion of his strides, Gregory realized this man could see him.

He mantled his wings and allowed the wind to catch at them until they unfurled. Destructive magic bled between the membranes in a blue-white sheet in obvious threat. Still, the blond-haired human showed no fear. Instead, his features were frozen in a look of awed disbelief. Slowly, his look altered as it changed to belief, and then subtle hope.

The breeze shifted, carrying the stranger's scent. Clean, like spring's return after a long winter, and a hint of loam and wild forests. This was no human.

He paced closer and studied this new creature while he circled. Ah, he recognized what the man was now. Another surprise in an unusual day, but he had greater concerns, like when the Riven would return to threaten his lady again.

Dismissing the other immortal, Gregory turned back

toward the old woman. The scent of crushed grass and the sounds of footfalls coming up behind him served as his only warning. Had the blond-haired male cared to tread more quietly, he might have succeeded in disguising his approach. Gregory turned to confront his opponent, and the smaller immortal collided with his chest.

Driven by his crazed need, he smashed a fist into the scratch marks on Gregory's upper arm. The smaller male grunted and cradled his fist against his chest, but whatever pain the injury caused was quickly forgotten when he spotted the dark smudge coating his damaged hand—gargoyle blood. The blond-haired male's expression changed to one of rapture.

Gregory growled, more in annoyance than pain. He licked at his wound before any other magic-starved beast decided attacking a gargoyle was a good idea. A minor wave of weakness shivered down his wings as the other male began siphoning magic through the link of Gregory's blood.

"I'm sorry," the male said. "So many years surrounded by death. Death coming closer with each turning of the seasons. I couldn't continue like this."

"You might have asked."

"And you might have said no."

The gargoyle couldn't fault him for his reasoning. In this magic-starved land, he might not have wished to waste magic on someone he didn't know when Lillian might require it at any moment. But now he couldn't stop the other male from feeding without killing him.

"How long have you been trapped in this form?"

"Centuries."

Gregory, about to award the other with a suitable punishment for the theft of his blood and magic, decided anything he thought up would pale in comparison to what the other immortal had just done to himself. Besides, it might prove useful to have another immortal to help guard the Sorceress. There couldn't be many others he could trust in this strange land. *"It will hurt to shed your human form. Your body won't remember its true shape after all this time."*

"I don't care," the smaller male whispered between clenched teeth. "If I live, I shall never again allow a woman to bewitch me into another form."

The gargoyle snorted. That promise wasn't likely to live long, knowing what he did about this one's kind. *"This is going to hurt. Perhaps more than you realize. Many lives ago, when my lady was born into a dragon body, I spent much of that life as a dragon since shapeshifting wasn't one of her gifts. As I recall, when I periodically returned to my true form, it was exceedingly painful."*

"Thanks," the stranger hissed. "Might I learn the name of the gargoyle who is returning me to my true form?"

Remembering Lillian's wicked smile, he hesitated a moment before answering the stranger. "My Mistress named me Gregory Livingstone."

"Gregory... Livingstone? Seriously? That's not a name; that's a walking pun. Poor bastard, what did you do to piss her off?" The male's laugh was cut short by a gasp as a wave of pain rolled across his features.

If the stranger would have said more, Gregory never knew. The body of the smaller male began to glow. A pale light hovered like a thick mist above his skin. Then his bones began to grow and shift under his too-tight skin. It split and his moans turned to screams. In an act of mercy the fool probably didn't deserve, Gregory placed his talons on the male's forehead and commanded him to sleep. The smaller male lost consciousness a moment later. Quiet returned to the yard, and he turned to seek his lady.

Lillian watched him with an expression of horror like he'd expect to see if he'd eaten her beloved brother. He didn't know what he'd done to earn such a look. He glanced over his shoulder to the body quivering a few feet from where he stood. It continued its change and was quite hideous to behold. Surely not. She must realize this wasn't his fault. The fool had stolen his blood. It was out of his hands.

Her look of horror changed to one of rage. Oh, perhaps she did believe him responsible. Stupid, magic-starved unicorns. Unfortunately, killing this one would be a waste of magic, so he let the equine continue to drink from the well of his power.

"Jason, no!"

The grandmother's warning wasn't necessary. Jason's progress was reminiscent of a wounded deer crashing through thick undergrowth. Gregory whirled around, realizing as he did the human could see him and was heading directly toward him.

Gregory was weaker than he thought if the unicorn had already consumed enough of his magic that he couldn't hide in shadow. Seconds later, the human was upon him, swinging a quarterstaff, and he didn't have time to worry.

Jason swept the quarterstaff at Gregory's legs, forcing him to leap out of the way. While still in the air, he snapped his tail around the human's weapon. With an abrupt heave, he tugged Jason off balance. In a quick move, the human twisted in midair and landed a kick to Gregory's ribs. A moment later, the youngling released his hold on the quarterstaff and lunged away with a curse.

"There was no evil within him!" Jason yelled. "He was my friend." Drawing his knife, he continued to circle.

Gregory rubbed at his abused ribs and tracked the human with narrowed eyes. So far, he'd been gentle on this human because the Sorceress would be angry if he damaged her brother, but he was starting to care less about niceties as his annoyance of this strange land and its people grew. First, he'd been attacked by the creatures of darkness, then by a crazed unicorn, and now a cocky human child challenged him.

Jason came at him again.

"Enough!" Gregory snarled. He grabbed the human by the shoulders and lifted him into the air. He jerked the dagger from Jason's hand and flung it away. Then, uncaring if he clawed the fool of a human to shreds, Gregory roughly turned him until he was suspended upside down above where the unicorn rested, exhausted from the change, but whole.

"*Not—my—doing.*" Gregory punctuated each word by shaking the human. "He stole my magic. To stop him would have killed him. He did this to himself. But if you continue, I will damage you. Mortal, do you understand me?"

"Yes," Jason moaned.

"Are you sure?"

"Yes." He sounded weaker. "I think I'm going to be sick."

Gregory deposited the human on the ground next to his unicorn friend. They were both crazy. It might be contagious. Turning, he ran into Lillian. She glanced beyond him to the unicorn, concern drawing her eyebrows together.

"What did you do to him, and why?"

"I did nothing. He stole my blood so he could return to

his true form. Did you not know your brother's friend was a unicorn?"

She mouthed his words, and then shook her head, looking lost. Her skin was paler than before, and he worried shock was setting in. His suspicions were confirmed when she started to shiver. He pulled her closer until her smaller frame was a solid line against his side, and then he wrapped a wing around her shoulders. She leaned into his warmth and didn't look up at her grandmother's approach.

"Forgive my grandson and his friend, ancient one," Lillian's grandmother said. An elegant bow accompanied her formal greeting. "You may call me Vivian, and as you can guess by the evil you've already discovered, these have been trying years for everyone. But let there be peace between us and let us share food and histories. There are dangers which must be explained."

He didn't miss how she glanced worriedly at Lillian, but he didn't question her further. There would be time for inquiries later. For now, he was more concerned about Lillian. She was so small—fragile, even—and she'd been so close to death when he'd first woke, no wonder she was now on the edge of shock. She'd suffered much trauma in the last day. There was also her hamadryad tree to think of, but the tree was safe for now. He'd see to the hamadryad's healing tomorrow.

"Lillian needs rest," he said.

"Of course." Vivian made a sweeping gesture with her arm. "This way."

He inclined his head to Vivian in thanks before urging his lady back in the direction of the house. Lillian allowed herself to be herded.

Inside, Gregory followed Lillian as she made her way

through the kitchen and on into the living room. There, she collapsed into a chair and held a pillow in her lap, her eyes glazing with recent memories. Her grandmother stood next to her and whispered words of comfort. Right now, Vivian was the one Lillian would find safe and familiar, while his presence would only lead to more questions and worry. So, he faded, blending into the room around him until he was once again part of the shadows.

CHAPTER NINE

*D*istracted by her grandmother, Lillian missed when the gargoyle vanished. She leaned forward in her chair, her fingers biting into the armrests. He'd been standing right in front of her a moment ago, and now he was gone. Nothing moved that fast. His magic must cloak him in some way she didn't understand. A laugh bubbled up. She suppressed it with difficulty.

What *did* she understand? Magic. Gargoyles. Unicorns. Her entire life was a lie.

When her mind threatened rebellion, she took several deep breaths. Calmer, she approached the problem with a rational mind. What was she to do? A gargoyle followed her around like a lost dog. He must have a reason. She needed to find out his motives. But how? Question after question whirled through her mind, but no reasonable explanations presented themselves.

"You've had enough shocks for one day," Gran whispered in her ear. "Come with me. The gargoyle is right. You need to rest. Everything will seem better after a good night's sleep. Then I'll explain everything I know in the morning."

She should be demanding answers now, tonight... but she was so damned tired. Her body felt heavy, her limbs nearly numb.

"Come," Gran whispered.

Lillian was sure her grandmother was weaving some kind of spell to make her sleep, but she decided she was too tired to care.

Gran ushered her up the stairs, pushing on her shoulders to steer her in the right direction. After a few turns, Lillian found herself in a room. Her grandmother handed her a bit of satin. Lillian blinked. Her favorite indigo nightgown. And yes, that was her oversized bed. It had never looked so good.

When the door's click announced her grandmother's departure, Lillian started shedding clothing as she crossed the floor.

Then, the satin nightgown still a cold presence against her skin, she crawled across the bed and scrambled under the covers. Her eyes were already closed by the time her head hit the pillow. Before sleep claimed her, a worried thought flashed through her mind.

Where had her gargoyle gone?

A soft, slow whooshing teased the edge of her hearing, rhythmic like the ocean, almost a purr. The soothing noise had a steady thump as its counter beat. Delicious warmth radiated throughout her body, and she instinctively burrowed closer to that warmth.

While a part of her mind wanted to embrace sleep, other senses were sharpening. She inhaled a deep breath. Air perfumed with the scents of home baking filled her lungs— her grandmother's pancakes and sausages, if she was not mistaken. Her stomach growled, waking her further. Still, she didn't open her eyes—something was dancing at the edge of her consciousness, something she didn't want to acknowledge or remember.

She squeezed her eyes tight and wiggled even closer to the heat, determined to recapture the mindless oblivion of sleep. Another scent crawled across her senses and seeped into her mind like a drug, one reminiscent of wild places and the pleasant, musky warmth of a purely male being—the scent of a gargoyle.

She froze. Memories of the last day wouldn't be denied and came crashing down upon her peaceful world. Muscles tense, she cautiously opened her eyes—to an expanse of ebony skin stretched over a defined, muscular chest. A heavy weight was slung across her shoulders, preventing her from sitting up, and something else with the grace of a two-by-four held her lower legs imprisoned. Five minutes' worth of wiggling and the gargoyle's arm was down almost to her waist. Being careful not to shake the bed, she sat up.

The two-by-four turned out to be his tail.

There was an eight-foot gargoyle occupying her bed.

Tramping down rising panic, she did a quick survey of the bedroom. Her robe was on the other side of the room, tossed over the back of her reading chair next to the antique oak dresser. With a new goal firmly in her sights, she held the panic at bay a little longer.

After several more minutes of slow, cautious wiggling, she

was out from under the gargoyle's wings. A few deep, calming breaths and she inched off the bed in slow motion. Her bare feet touched the floor. A glance over her shoulder confirmed her new bedmate hadn't so much as stirred a talon. Fear made her breath shallow and rapid. She bolted for the robe in a mad dash. In under ten seconds flat, she had the robe clutched in one hand and had reversed direction for the door.

She reached the old walnut door—a gate to sanctuary, the way to freedom. But she did not turn the knob. Poised, frozen between moments, she was unable to decide which way to go.

Whatever was on the other side of the door was just as much the unknown as the big beastie sleeping in her bed. Worse, perhaps. The gargoyle had never lied to her, which was more than she could say about her family. For years they had hidden all this from her. Magic. Of all things, magic existed.

She needed answers. Perhaps then the chaos of the last day would order itself into something resembling a normal life.

Ten feet away, sleeping soundly in her bed, was someone fully capable of answering her questions. All she had to do was confront him.

Determination flowing in her blood, she spun away from the door and faced the bed.

How long had she slept next to the big, eight-foot-tall monster, with his massive talons that could have torn her apart? Even as she thought it, that older foreign part of her spirit knew he would never harm her—not even in his sleep.

Indecision held her rooted in place for several more seconds. Then curiosity and that strange, fierce need to be near him reared its head and overruled wisdom. Instead of running away, she slid one foot ahead of the other until she stood at the end of the bed.

The opportunity was too tempting to resist. After a moment's consideration about the foolhardiness of what she was about to do, she reached out with shaking fingers.

Keeping her touch light so he wouldn't wake, she slid her fingertips along warm skin. The deep rise and fall of his chest confirmed he still slept deeply. He was curled in a fetal position, his tail tucked around him like a cat—the biggest damned cat she'd ever encountered. It was nice studying him while he slept. He seemed less scary that way.

Even curled on his side, his eight-foot frame dwarfed the king-sized bed. One massive wing stretched out behind him while the other blanketed him like a cloak of shadows. His head rested pillowed on his bicep, and one arm still reached out to where she'd been tucked against him. His large fingers, with their three-inch claws, were uncurled, relaxed in sleep. If he'd had a nightmare, he could have gutted her. Her eyes traveled the length of him again. While he wasn't human, he was undeniably male. Overprotective guardian non-withstanding, he'd be finding himself different sleeping arrangements very soon.

Without conscious thought, her fingers found his hand and touched the black, curving claws. She really should be running away, she reminded herself. Instead, she sat on the edge of the bed and explored the gargoyle.

Oddly, she could deal with the strangeness of the gargoyle better than seeing her family in their new roles. Or seeing a man she'd known all her life turn into a unicorn. It was like something out of a fevered dream. Abnormal. Surreal and completely creepy.

That the gargoyle seemed the most normal part of her life didn't bode well at all.

She stroked his mane for several minutes. Calm returned, followed by clearer thoughts. With confidence she didn't know she possessed, she sat on the bed and investigated the spiky ridge of hair between his horns. If Lillian thought she could get away with it, she would have tried to brush his mane for him, but the motion might wake him, and she rather liked watching the gargoyle sleep. She wasn't sure why or how, but he was a natural part of her existence. Like air and food and water, her gargoyle had transformed into a component she needed to live.

From downstairs, the distant beep of the kitchen timer reached her ears. At the noise, the gargoyle made a huffing sound as he wiggled his muzzle under the edge of her robe until his entire head vanished beneath a fold of the dark-green fabric. Only his horns and ears stuck out and she started to laugh.

"No, I stand corrected. You're not cat-like. You're more dog-like." His ears twitched at the sound of her voice, but he still didn't wake up. Instead, he burrowed farther under her until he threatened to push her right off the side of the bed. "Definitely dog. I don't suppose I can teach you to fetch breakfast? Oh, well. At least—"

Her next words froze on her tongue as the gargoyle exhaled a grunted exclamation. In one beat of her pounding heart, he was fully awake. His powerful tail snaked out and reached around her shoulders. That heavy, unstoppable weight forced her forward and down until she was sprawled flat on the bed, the gargoyle poised over her. Then he leaped from the bed and landed on all fours, his tail lashing. But before she could ask what was wrong, a disturbance outside in the hall reached her ears. It came a second time. Closer now, she could make out the sounds—dishes rattling on a tray.

"Jeez, you need to calm the fuck down. It's probably just Gran with breakfast. She's nice like that."

Gregory advanced on the door with grim interest just as it creaked open. Gran strolled in and shoved the door shut with her hip. Gran eyed the disheveled bed with an arched eyebrow, and then looked the gargoyle up and down as she detoured around him. On her way by, she waved the two trays close to his muzzle, and then continued forward with a knowing smile. The gargoyle padded after her, sniffing at the dishes as he came.

"Did you sleep well?" Gran asked. Again, that same eyebrow rose in question.

"Yes, very well...considering a rather large *gargoyle* was sharing the bed. Know anything about that?"

Gran graced Lillian with a most innocent look. "Yours is the biggest bed in the house."

"Ha! I knew it. You said you ordered the wrong size for the resort and didn't want to pay to ship it back."

"I couldn't very well tell you it was for your gargoyle, now could I?"

Lillian huffed, turned to the gargoyle, and speared him with a look. "You're not a dog—you don't get to sleep in my bed."

Gregory seemed more interested in what Gran was carrying than in the conversation.

Gran cleared her throat. "Anyway, I imagine you both

must be hungry, so I brought a little something to hold you over until lunch. Eat, and then we'll talk."

Lillian was about to tell her to talk now, but the mingled scent of maple syrup, pancakes, and sausages reached her nose. She tracked the trays as avidly as did the gargoyle. Deciding she could multitask, Lillian uncovered the first tray and snatched up one of the sausages. She was taking the first bite when the gargoyle leaned in close and sniffed at her food.

"It's not poisoned." Too hungry to worry about manners, she ate with her fingers. "Relax for five minutes." She waved at the bounty. "Eat."

He didn't obey immediately, so she lifted a second finger-length sausage off the tray and held it out to him. One moment he was sniffing at it, then she blinked, and it was gone. The only clue he hadn't used magic to make it vanish was a slight movement as he swallowed.

Gran handed him his own plate and motioned for him to eat. The gargoyle didn't need more prompting and folded a pancake in half and shoved it in his mouth. A second vanished as fast as the first one. Gran smiled and turned back to Lillian.

"I know you have questions. I'll tell you all I know, and then we'll see if we can get our new friend to tell us what he knows." Gran graced the gargoyle with a calculating smile. He stopped eating long enough to bob his head in assent. She turned back to Lillian. "Good. First, no matter what you learn here, I want you to know you *are* my granddaughter in all ways that matter."

Gran paused, closing her eyes like she sought a long-ago memory. "You came to me on a January night twelve years ago carried in the arms of a hulking shadow, a creature of immense girth and height—your gargoyle."

Shock descended on Lillian like a blow.

"Six months earlier, we had lost my granddaughter, Lily, in a drowning accident. It was just before we bought the spa and moved here. My Lily was such a good girl." Gran continued, "She wouldn't have minded you taking her name. You even reminded me of my little Lily. When the gargoyle asked me to guide and protect you like one of my own, giving my word was no hardship."

Lillian swallowed hard. God, she'd stepped into the life of a dead girl and made it her own. Horror cramped in her belly. Everything she knew was a lie.

A numb, seeping cold held Lillian in its grasp. Her world was built on a hundred thousand lies. *Who am I?* She remembered the blood running down her tree, and the sensation of her life force weakening as blood oozed from the wounds. *What am I?*

"But why name me after her? Surely it triggered painful memories for you."

"Painful, yes. But sweet, too. It was my way of honoring her memory and my promise to the gargoyle." Gran looked at Gregory where he crouched next to the bed. His empty plate sat on the floor next to him, his full attention upon Gran as she told her tale. "We were new to this place. No one knew Lily. They wouldn't know you were not the same girl. So, you became Lillian." Gran sighed. "I have kept my promise to the gargoyle as best I could, but now there is an enemy beyond my ability to defeat. Yesterday they came here to destroy my coven and found you here alone. I am sorry. We had no idea they were ready to move on our territory."

"Who are they?" Lillian asked. "And why don't I know any of this? Why keep the truth from me?"

"Forgive me for the lie, but the gargoyle told me to say nothing of magic. So, I thought it best if you believed you were Lily. I then came up with the idea about you losing your memories in a near-drowning—a half-truth is easier to accept than an outright lie. And brain damage explained why you would need to learn our language and details about our world." Gran paused again and looked down at her hands. When she looked up, she gave the gargoyle an intense look. "I'm interested in hearing the reasons why the gargoyle wanted you to know nothing about magic. That was a curious stipulation."

Lillian followed her grandmother's gaze. Gregory balanced on his haunches, one hand braced against his bent knee, muzzle bowed until it touched his chest, eyes focused unseeingly on the ground. He looked about as talkative as a rock.

"Right. Better luck next time." A cold sweat broke out along Lillian's back. She wasn't sure she wanted to hear the gargoyle's reasoning—her gut told her there was more amiss than just bad guys trying to kill her. She returned her attention to Gran. "What do you know about the creatures who attacked me?"

"Not enough. They call themselves the Riven. We don't know their agenda, but they are a gathering of evil-tainted magic wielders. Before, we speculated they were led by creatures that legends call vampires. Now after your attack, we know that to be true."

"Why attack me? Why now?"

"I don't know." Gran broke eye contact and glanced out the window. "But this isn't the first time they've made a move against us," she said, her voice strained. She took two deep breaths. When she spoke again, her voice had smoothed out. "Six years ago, we were caught unawares. There had been rumors of a dark underground movement, one that could unbalance our community and expose us to the humans, but no evidence was found to back up our theories. Then the disappearances started. At first, we thought a blood feud had broken out between the Clan and the Coven."

"Wait," Lillian interrupted. "I gather the Coven is made up of your people—the witches. But this Clan, who are they?"

"Yes, you are correct about the Coven. We are the descendants of the few ancient human bloodlines gifted with magic. The Clan is a mix of the other magical races, many of which were once enemies. But our diverse peoples banded together for one simple reason: survival. The Clan's numbers were always less than ours, but now they are many, many fewer. While they may not age, dwindling magic has killed many of them. If they don't find a way back to the Magic Realm, all the Clan will perish in time."

Lillian rubbed at her temples. "So, the unicorn is Clan, and my brother is Coven. And the Clan and Coven are allies?"

"Now we are, but that wasn't always the case. At the thought of another blood feud, members of both Clan and Coven became paranoid and defensive. The council gathered to put a stop to this, for a blood feud would expose us to the humans. The last time such a thing happened was long ago and ended with members on both sides burning at the stake. The council ordered an investigation. The order was barely three hours old when we were attacked. The Riven showed us how woeful our defenses were against them. We lost eighty percent of the council in one night."

Grief and anger glinted in Gran's eyes, the two emotions melding into a steel-hard resolve. "Nothing like that attack had ever happened before. Individually, we didn't know what to do against such a powerful new enemy. For the first time in recorded history, the entire membership of the Clan and the Coven came together, like a herd seeking safety in greater numbers. When we did, we saw how many were missing. At first, we thought those absent were dead, hunted down by the Riven. But later we learned the truth. Better had they been dead." Gran sighed bitterly.

"Some old and trusted friends we never thought had a speck of darkness within them were serving these Riven. It soon became clear the Riven plan to consume all the magic of this realm and rule over what is left. I fear some of the Clan and Coven traitors may not have had a choice. We caught one of the traitors, a dire wolf. He seemed relieved when we put him to death, as if he was at last freed from intolerable servitude." Gran shook her head. "I don't know what was done to that poor creature but granting him death was the kindest gift he'd received in many years."

"What is a dire wolf?" Lillian found herself asking with genuine curiosity.

"Ah." Gran cleared her throat. "You've heard the legends of werewolves, no doubt."

"You're saying a dire wolf is a werewolf?"

"Nope. And don't ever call a dire wolf that in one's hearing." Gran started to chuckle. "That'll make them cranky. Like many of the fae-bloods, dire wolves are shapeshifters, but their natural shape is that of a large wolf. Instead of a human changing into a wolf, it's the other way around. The fae-blood wolf learned to shapeshift into a human."

"Oh." There was so much Lillian didn't know, and by the set of her grandmother's shoulders, there was more to come. "Tell me the rest. My parents... I mean Lily's parents." She frowned. "They didn't die in a car accident, did they?

Gran spun her wedding band around her finger in slow, measured turns. "My son and daughter-in-law were on the council, members representing the Northern branch of the Coven. They were present when the council was attacked."

Lillian glanced down, assimilating her grandmother's story. The glossy hardwood floor reflected the morning light. Her gaze tracked the stream of sunlight back to the window and beyond to the beauty of the world outside.

The sight of her favorite tree surrounded by the large maze usually brought a sense of peace, but today it couldn't fill the hollow ache in her heart. So much of her life was a lie, and much of what was real felt like a fantasy.

She glanced at the gargoyle. At least he hadn't vanished into the shadows. "Why bring me here? Where am I really from?"

He remained silent.

"Even fed, you're still not much of a talker." Lillian crossed her arms over her chest and glowered.

Gran patted her shoulder. "I think he wants me to tell you the rest."

"There's more?"

"Lillian, by now you must realize you're not what you thought. You're Clan, not Coven. You're not human."

Lillian wanted to deny her grandmother's words, but after all that had happened, she knew there was something different about her. She inclined her head to her grandmother and asked as calmly as she could, "If not human, what am I?"

"I, too, wondered that at first. Your gargoyle was injured, as were you. I think he used a lot of his power to heal you and didn't have enough left over for healing his own injuries. His time was limited. He was already turning to stone, and he couldn't tell me much about you beyond the fact he didn't want you familiar with magic. I didn't even know what species you were at first."

Lillian held herself perfectly still, her muscles tensing as if for battle. "Go on. I can handle this."

"I found my first clue clenched in your hand—a small cutting from a tree, its leaves still fresh like it was newly picked. I put it in water. Within a day, it had sprouted roots. That it rooted at all would have been enough to signal that this was no ordinary cutting, but there was also a trace of magic in its leaves. You are a dryad. The cutting was from your hamadryad, your spirit tree. You are a guardian of the forests. I didn't know enough about dryads to know how to look after one, but I knew a sick child when I saw one. There was an unhealthy look about your skin I didn't like. Your little tree sickened until just a few needles remained. Fearing I'd lose you, I contacted the Sisterhood of the Dryads and told them about you, your tree, and your gargoyle. They were here in less than a day. You're alive because of them. I don't think I would have thought about giving your tree gargoyle blood."

Lillian absorbed what her grandmother said. She couldn't accept everything now. It was too much. Later, when she was alone, she'd replay this conversation in her head and maybe then it would make sense.

Trapped in her own memories, Gran continued like she was unaware Lillian was there with her. "The first night he arrived, he'd been injured, and his blood was splattered across the snow. That magic-laced substance shimmered under the moonlight—I remember seeing it, and in my state of shock I'd thought it beautiful like the stars in a cold, winter sky. The next morning, my senses returned, and knowing the power locked in an immortal's blood, I gathered up all I could find and kept it frozen."

The gargoyle stood, his sudden movement interrupting Gran's story. He made a short, coughing bark as he glanced out the window. His tail lashed and his ears snapped forward. Someone was coming, judging by his body language.

Lillian eased off her bed and came up behind the gargoyle. Her viewpoint was all wings, mane, and flicking tail. A small thrill of gratitude flowed through her veins when he shifted a wing out of the way and made room for her to stand next to him.

Through the open window, she heard a vehicle coming up the lane. The boulevard trees blocked her line of sight and obscured the vehicle until it turned up the main driveway. Her brother's truck came into view.

The gargoyle's lips pulled back from his muzzle. Jaws parted slightly and nostrils quivering, he sniffed at the air. She touched his arm—and his thoughts came to her. No, not smelling the air—tasting it to search for magic.

"Ah, the Sisterhood's representatives have arrived," Gran said. "I sent Jason to pick them up from the airport."

"Other dryads?"

"Yes. They're the closest biological family you have in this world, but don't be fooled for a moment. They are a dying race and have an agenda of their own. They saved your life, but I think they did it more to curry favor with the gargoyle than out of actual concern for you."

"You think they're dangerous." Lillian meant it as a statement, but Gran answered anyway.

"No," Gran said, then paused as if selecting her next words with care. "I don't mean to poison you against them. They serve the Light, not the Shadow, but they are not human. They don't think like us. And as much as you're biologically like them, you were raised as a human, with a human's view of the world and our moral concepts ingrained in you from a young age. You may not like what they have come seeking."

"I'll deal. Our biggest problem is with the Riven."

"Indeed."

Lillian glanced at the gargoyle. He was now silent, unmoving. Only his eyes showed any life in them. They glittered like black ice, a predator's stare directed down at the women exiting the truck.

Both strangers had the tall, lean grace of swans. They looked like they belonged on a Paris runway. "I thought you said these women were the same species as me. I fail to see the resemblance." Apparently, nature had given her the curvy and slightly plump gene.

"Oh, they're just half-starved. Their trees didn't have the nutrition of nice gargoyle blood to make them big and strong." Gran chuckled. "Don't worry, dear. They'd blow over in a storm. Do you still regret you're not like them?"

"Nope. Not when you put it like that."

"Well, we can't hide up here all afternoon. Shall we introduce you and your gargoyle to the dryads?"

"Sure." Lillian couldn't muster much enthusiasm. She didn't want to meet them, not when she was feeling like the poor, uneducated cousin.

Gregory remained silent as he padded to the door. He held it open for them.

Not seeing any other choice, Lillian followed Gran out.

The gargoyle vanished into the shadows, but he trailed along behind, his heat and magic a reassuring presence. Up until the moment he'd awakened and saved her, she'd always felt alone and hadn't known why. Now she knew the reason. Her gargoyle belonged at her back. She smiled and reached out behind her as she descended the stairs. The warmth of a muzzle bumped under her fingers. A moment later, a tongue licked at her palm. She smiled as contentment warmed her heart.

CHAPTER TEN

*L*illian took the curving stairs in a slow, measured step to allow herself time to study the two strangers. Their backs were to her, but her brother was below, attentive as a servant, which told her enough about these women. Her poor, beguiled brother. While she wasn't familiar with dryads, these two looked capable of eating her brother alive.

Ahead, her grandmother sailed down the steps, showing no signs of weakness or age, her floral-print summer dress billowing out behind her. She moved as a queen or matriarch would, quietly assured of her right to rule her domain.

Gran tilted her head in Jason's direction. "Be a dear and finish cleansing the gardens."

A smile tugged at Lillian's lips as she took in her brother's look of disgruntlement. But Jason only grumbled something as he left.

At Gran's approach, the paler of the two dryads stood. The newcomer made the simple motion one of slow grace.

"Vivian, we thank you for contacting us." A long-fingered hand swept sable-colored hair off her shoulder as she spoke. The sleek locks looked like they had never seen the abuse of a blow dryer or flat iron. But otherwise she looked normal, human in appearance.

Lillian wondered if the dryad used magic to disguise her fae heritage in some way.

Sable-hair's lady-in-waiting, as Lillian decided to call the other woman, bowed to Vivian and then stepped back.

Like two queens meeting to negotiate a treaty, Gran and Sable-hair regarded each other with hard gazes.

"The gargoyle is awake and remains in this realm? He hasn't returned to his own yet?" Sable-hair's voice tightened with worry on the second question.

Her jaw tightening at the dryad's words, Lillian glanced over her shoulder to confirm the gargoyle was still invisible.

He was.

She could still feel him but not so much as a ripple of shadows betrayed his presence to the naked eye.

Handy trick that.

With a frown, she returned her attention to the two newcomers.

What did these dryads want with her gargoyle? What was so important they couldn't take the time to exchange names first? She didn't like the implications already.

Gran nodded at the dryad's words. "He is here, and he will remain here as long as my granddaughter does. He shadows her every step. Whatever his purpose, if you wish to speak with him about your problem, you'll need to communicate through Lillian. The gargoyle is shy, reclusive, and disinclined to speak to us folk of lesser magic."

Lillian's jaw tightened. Gregory wasn't like that. Sure, he didn't have much to say, but he'd never done anything to make her think he regarded the rest of them as lesser beings. Gran caught her eye and shook her head the slightest bit. That one motion told Lillian all she needed to know.

If her grandmother wanted to keep these strangers guessing, she would play along. The gargoyle remained silent, hidden in the shadows. Apparently, he agreed with Gran's plan.

The second dryad, the brown-haired lady-in-waiting as Lillian had decided to call her, turned her attention fully upon Lillian. "This gargoyle is your servant?" Her sculpted brows rose in question. "Does he await your command?"

Lillian's stomach soured. Her grandmother's plan suddenly didn't look so appealing. This new sense of authority, where others looked to her for answers, was not something she wanted. Reluctantly, but seeing no other choice, she answered.

"If anyone is in the other's debt, I am in his. He saved my life twice. First from the monsters who attacked me, and then later when he used his own strength to heal me. I was dying." Her words drifted to silence as she remembered those moments of horror.

"But he *does* remain at your side?" Sable-hair interrupted.

"I'm not his master." True. But he had said, 'I am yours,' and called her 'mistress' whatever that might mean. She didn't think she'd share that piece of information.

Sable-hair gritted her teeth, a noticeable change compared to her earlier serene expression. "Tell me how you came to be in this realm in the company of a gargoyle."

Gran cleared her throat. "Perhaps introductions are in

order." She glanced in Lillian's direction. "The dryads, like many of the fae races, don't give their true names freely. This is a dryad Elder of the North American Sisterhood. You may call her Sable."

How creative, Lillian thought to herself as she smiled at the dryad in an attempt to seem friendly. When she held her hand out to the Elder, Sable hesitated.

Gran gave the dryad a frosty smile. "Elder Sable, this is my granddaughter. As you have said, she is in the good graces of a gargoyle."

After a brief pause, Sable returned the handshake, the dryad's soft, unblemished skin completely different than Lillian's own garden-roughened hands.

Lillian grinned at Gran's implied "play nice or else."

While the Elder returned Gran's frosty smile, Lillian peered at the other dryad.

The lady-in-waiting took a step forward and made eye contact. "May I ask what is your relationship with this gargoyle? Is he blood relative or future mate?"

"What the hell?" Lillian's jaw dropped. *Blood relative or future mate?* She hadn't known what to expect, but that wasn't it.

"But surely you know that much?"

"I've no idea what you're talking about. I don't see how..." Heck, she saw zero family resemblance between dryads and gargoyles. There were a few genetic differences, for starters.

"How long has he been awake? A day? Two? Even if you honestly don't remember your past, that's still long enough to experience the draw between our races."

Lillian didn't even know how to formulate an answer to that odd line of questioning. Shaking her head, she denied the woman's words. But as she took a step back, she remembered that just an hour ago, she'd been running her hands over the gargoyle while he'd slept. Was magic why she kept wanting to touch him? That complicated things.

Gran sent Lillian a look of sympathy. Then, her expression darkening, she transferred her gaze to Sable. "Did you read any of the reports I sent you? Lillian knows nothing—absolutely nothing—about her history. She only found out this morning she wasn't human."

"Her lack of education is hardly my fault."

With a snort of disgust, Gran flung her hands up and muttered to herself.

Sable cleared her throat. "Perhaps we should return to the reason we came."

"Yes," Gran smiled coldly. "Tell Lillian what you seek."

"We seek the same as you. To learn why and how the gargoyle came here."

Suspicion started growing in Lillian's mind. "And once you have your answers, what will you do with that knowledge?"

Sable tilted her head to the side to study Lillian in turn. "Leave this world. We're a dying race and can't remain here. There isn't enough magic to beget healthy children. We must flee back to the realm of magic if we can."

Lillian was trying to listen and make sense of everything they'd said, but her mind kept going back to when the dryad asked what relation the gargoyle was to her. Damn it all to hell! She had to know. "Explain what you said earlier about gargoyles and dryads... being related." She locked gazes with Sable.

The dryad folded her hands and composed herself as if

preparing for a long tale. "You are aware there are no male dryads?"

"No, but Gran did call you the 'Sisterhood.' Go on."

"Long ago, when we wanted a child or companionship, we'd seek out males from the other magic races. Sometimes even a human male would do. But over time, we grew weaker. The oldest of our bloodlines were failing to produce viable, strong girl-children to continue our race." Sable's eyes unfocused, her thoughts turning inward.

A ghost of a smile hovered on her lips. "Long and long ago, when we still lived within the Magic Realm, a dryad queen grieved over her barren state. Her tree had taken to blight, and she was dying without an heir. She feared for all her people. On the border between life and death, she first saw the gargoyle. All of the magic races have their legends about those demon killers, Light's Assassins, but she'd never met one in all her years." Sable paused a moment, as if gathering her thoughts before continuing.

"He had frequented her forest for many centuries and found the peaceful glade where she took root soothed his soul. He'd watched her from the shadows for a very long time without revealing himself. It wasn't until he found her dying, as she prayed for another to take her mantle of power before she passed on, that he realized he loved her noble spirit and the kindness of her heart. He showed himself and told her he knew what would help her tree, save her life, and make her fertile, but he had a request of his own. He sought a mate."

Sable paused and met Lillian's gaze. "Now, this wasn't the usual type of bargain. He told the dryad he'd heal her regardless of her decision. He was lonely and wished to experience the joy of raising a child—which for every other creature upon the earth, in the seas, and flying through the air is a normal occurrence. But gargoyles are different. The first gargoyles were created to serve and protect the Lord of the Underworld's kingdom, and like him, they dwelled alone. There are no female gargoyles."

Lillian frowned thoughtfully. Gregory hadn't said much about their relationship, but she didn't think he was looking for a mate. He'd called himself her protector.

Was he a blood relative?

Lillian found that thought strangely disturbing and decided she wasn't ready to poke at the reason just yet.

"For eons, they served the Lord of the Underworld and destroyed evil in his name. Though it wasn't forbidden, no gargoyle had sought a mate or tried to sire a child, content to continue their silent battle with evil among the shadows," Sable said, lost in her tale. "But this gargoyle had found and lost his heart in the peaceful forest glade. Placing his talons upon his flesh, he slashed open his own hide. Then he mixed his blood with water and poured it upon the ground under the dryad's tree. Her tree drank, healing and growing stronger as the queen watched. When the gargoyle came up behind her and placed one of his talon-tipped hands on her shoulder, she shied away, unable to hide her fear at his touch. It was only after she saw what he held that she calmed: grasped in one clawed hand was a stone bowl, filled to brimming with his potent blood. He instructed her to mix a few drops in water and feed her tree each day. She took the bowl, and while she was distracted, the gargoyle vanished back into the shadows of the forest."

Interesting and disturbing. Hadn't Gran used Gregory's

blood to save the hamadryad cutting? Just what did her gargoyle think of that?

Unaware of Lillian's thoughts, Sable continued her tale. "With the dawn, the gargoyle still hadn't returned. Days sped by as the queen waited, both dreading and hoping he would come back. The seasons changed and years matured and died. Then on one early spring day, while the mist still shrouded the land, a shadow darker than the surrounding forest crashed into her quiet glade and collapsed under her tree. The dryad woke and left her tree to find the gargoyle wounded. Uncertain what else to do, she took the strength she gained from his blood and used it to heal his many wounds. Under her care, the gargoyle recovered from the demon-inflicted injuries, which would have killed most other creatures."

Again Lillian frowned, thinking she knew where this story was going.

"When he was strong once more, he made to leave, but she persuaded him to stay and make his home in her glade. He gave her many dryad daughters, and she gave him his gargoyle son. And that was the beginning of dryad and gargoyle life pairings."

Lillian started laughing at the absurdity of the story. She couldn't help it. "That story sounds a little like a Greek legend, like the bull from the sea and how the Minotaur was sired. Kinky sex, anyone? Have you ever *actually* seen a gargoyle? I've seen smaller horses."

"Your thoughts are polluted by a human's outlook. We are not human." Sable's response dripped with disdain.

"But you're human-sized and human-shaped! And he's not. I don't see how..." She let the sentence die while she still had a wee bit of dignity left.

"If you have no interest in him as a mate..."

"You're welcome to him," Lillian blurted. A moment after she'd uttered the words, she already regretted them. Gregory deserved better from her. He was his own thinking, intelligent being, worthy of respect.

Gran cleared her throat. "Maybe this gargoyle doesn't want to be bartered away. I think you'll find he left as soon as you started talking about him as if he were a pair of hand-me-down jeans."

"Sorry," Lillian muttered, and then directed her next question at the dryads. "But have either of you actually seen a gargoyle up close?"

The second dryad cleared her throat and quietly introduced herself as Russet and then continued in a soft-spoken way. "I have. Once, long ago. While they are fierce in their true forms, they are also capable of great compassion and gentleness."

"True forms?"

"Lillian," Gran cut off Russet. "We'll talk more about dryad and gargoyle history later, but now Sable and I need to discuss business. Why don't you make some tea?"

Lillian winced at the dismissal but got up from her chair and went to the kitchen. She couldn't sense her gargoyle anywhere near. Like Gran said, he must have disappeared at some point during the conversation about kinky sex. Smart fellow.

Alone in the kitchen, she put the kettle on to boil while she thought over the last conversation. It was for the best the gargoyle wasn't around. It would be beyond awkward to ask him outright if he expected fringe benefits for saving her. And the stress of the last day had obliterated the filter between her brain and her mouth. No telling what would come out if she talked to him now.

She gathered her grandmother's fancy cups and saucers from the cupboard by the back window. While placing them on a tray next to the teapot, she glanced out. Her brother was cleaning the gardens, which involved lugging an oversized jerrycan.

It hadn't occurred to her what "cleaning up" would entail. Now she witnessed the gruesome details as he poured a generous amount of fuel on one dark spot. And of course, they'd need to burn away the blood and remains. If a gargoyle's blood could heal, there was no telling what evil-tainted blood might do.

A match ignited the spot.

Mesmerized by the flames, she watched until the kettle's shrill whistle broke her concentration. She shook herself and made the tea. Earl Grey, her grandmother's favorite. Maybe it would put Gran in a talkative mood. With each new piece of knowledge Lillian gained, more questions surfaced. Topmost was *'Why am I here?'* but *'What did the gargoyle want?'* was a close second now. That a gargoyle, one of the Light's Assassins, was glued to her side couldn't bode well for a peaceful future.

Well, the kitchen tiles weren't going to give her any information.

She scooped up the tray of cups in one hand and the teapot in the other. Armed with tea and cookies, she went to find more answers.

Back in the living room, Gran and the dryads had turned the coffee table into a combat command center. Maps with topographical overlays showed rivers and land elevations.

One looked like a modern road map, except instead of the familiar towns and cities, there were a strange lot of squiggles and foreign names around boundaries she didn't understand like some alien civilization had taken over the world she knew.

"They violated Clan territory to get here." Gran frowned down at the map. "I want to know how they escaped the dire wolves' notice."

"What if they *didn't* escape their notice?" Sable asked.

"No. I don't believe it. They wouldn't sell us out."

"Not normally," Sable agreed. "But it might not even have been maliciously done. A dire wolf is loyal to its pack first."

"They suffered as much as we did in the attacks six years ago."

"Yes, and they might be desperate to protect their remaining members. What would you be willing to do to protect a loved one?"

"You're guessing."

"No more than you," Sable countered.

Gran grunted. "Fine, we'll be on guard. The alphas are coming here tomorrow after the Hunt. I will question them then. And if they are deceitful, the gargoyle may beat me to them."

"Why not bring Lillian and the gargoyle to tonight's Hunt? If the wolves are hiding anything, the gargoyle will smell their deception."

"Yes, I plan to talk to the gargoyle about that." Gran looked up and motioned for Lillian to serve the tea. "Ah, lovely."

Lillian let her mind go blank as she filled teacups, politely asking what everyone wanted in theirs. She was pouring her grandmother a cup when movement on the stairs caught Lillian's attention.

A tall man glided down the stairs with an athlete's grace— a nearly naked man, she amended. A rather handsome, nearly naked man with a vast expanse of warm brown skin on display. His knee-length beaded loincloth, gold torc, and gem-encrusted armbands were suspiciously like her gargoyle's. A silky black mane reached mid-way down his back and was tied with a piece of hide. His bare, human feet made no noise as he descended.

"I think that's enough tea, Lillian," Gran said.

Lillian glanced down. She'd overfilled the teacup and flooded its saucer. A pool of steaming tea spread across the walnut table. Cursing, she snatched some napkins to sop up the mess.

She tightened her grip on the teapot.

While Gran and Sable, trailed by Russet, went forward to greet the gargoyle, Lillian hung back by the coffee table.

"Darling," Gran said, disrupting Lillian's thoughts, "now that we've told you all we can about your kind, I think Gregory wants to tell you a little about your history."

Gran's shit-eating grin told Lillian her grandmother was aware how much the gargoyle's changed appearance had her flustered.

The gargoyle didn't give her long to worry, though, and gestured for them to take a seat.

Lillian sat and noted a problem. There weren't enough chairs. Before she could go retrieve one, the human-form gargoyle walked to her side and stood at her right shoulder. His one hand rested on the arm of the wingback chair. Up close, it was hard to miss a few anomalies. His nails were a proper human length, but it looked like they'd been painted with black nail polish, and their shape was off—too pointed, both at the tips and the nail base. He flexed his fingers and the nails lengthened a half-inch. When he relaxed his grip, the nails returned to their original length.

Oh boy.

His little demonstration let her know he was aware of being studied. Since she'd been found out, she studied him frankly, following the hand up the wrist to the smooth, hairless arm.

Ah! That was what caused the slight hint of foreignness that had nagged at the back of her mind when she had first looked upon him. Like his gargoyle form, the only hair was on his head. Wide, dark eyes fringed with a generous amount of lashes studied her in return. They were his only soft feature.

A strong jaw and nose combined with a broad forehead gave him a rugged look. Certainly not pretty-boy handsome, but still striking—if a woman could tear her eyes away from his perfectly proportioned body long enough to take note of the face.

Damn, but he was built like a master sculptor had personally had a hand in his shaping.

Brushing back a few strands of his hair, she tucked them behind his pointed ears. He smiled, his lips stretching back from white teeth. He had two large canines on both his upper and lower jaw that would put a vampire to shame.

She looked away, only to realize everyone else in the room had watched her while she'd ogled the gargoyle's altered form.

Great.

A wave of heat spread all the way down her neck, but she raised her head and pretended she was a queen, and these were her subjects. It lasted until her brother entered the living room from the kitchen. He glanced at the gargoyle and then at Lillian's face.

Jason tried to say something, but he started laughing too hard and couldn't get it out.

She glared at him. It wasn't her fault the damn gargoyle had suddenly decided he wanted to look more appealing for the two pretty dryads sitting across from her. He'd had plenty of time to wander around looking sinfully handsome, and he hadn't bothered for her. Not knowing what else to do, she pretended she hadn't just spent the last five minutes admiring Gregory. She gave her grandmother a baffled look for good measure.

Gran didn't bother to hide her smirk. "Jason, see if any of your clothes will fit the gargoyle. The nights still get cold."

Gregory reached for Lillian's hand where it rested against the armrest. Caught by surprise, she let him intertwine their fingers. Baffled, she studied his features to discern his mood. His expression remained blank a moment, and then with a sudden smile, he turned and dropped to sit cross-legged on the floor at her feet.

He leaned back against her legs, and placed her captured hand on his right shoulder, then laid his own over top.

She would have jerked free of his grasp, but she didn't want to draw any more attention to herself. Fixing her gaze on the back of his head, she willed a calm mask to cover her rioting emotions.

CHAPTER ELEVEN

*N*ot for the first time in his many lives, Gregory wished he was just a gargoyle and Lillian was simply the woman he loved. But no amount of wanting on his part could make them anything other than the Avatars. Lillian was the Mother's Sorceress. He was the Father's Gargoyle Protector. Nothing could ever change that fact—stone was more flexible. Yet he still played this stupid and dangerous game with the Sorceress. He couldn't help himself. Anger had stirred in his gut when the dryads talked of him as if he were a stud to win over with words of seduction and coy looks. Then Lillian had said she didn't want him, that the other dryads could have him. He narrowed his eyes, but didn't speak of it, the ache in his heart still too fresh.

While the Divine Ones forbade their Avatars from mating with each other, his lady had always loved him without regret throughout their many lifetimes. Even if they never fulfilled their deepest longing for fear of birthing a monster with godlike power upon the three Realms, they had their millennia-enduring love to rely upon when sadness became bitter.

Until now, when the Sorceress had said she didn't want her gargoyle.

Her careless words had hurt more than he would ever let her know, but then he'd come and sat with her and her nearness soothed some of the rejection.

When he inhaled a deep lungful of air, it was impossible not to taste Lillian's essence, they sat so close. It was sap-sweet but thankfully lacked the heady tang of her blood. He'd already broken one oath to save her life. How many others would she tempt him to break in this life? He glanced down at his hybrid form. Unwise as it might be, perhaps he was the one doing the tempting now.

It was the nagging worry she saw him as more beast than man that had prompted him to first change his shape. His judgment was compromised when he was in the same room with his lady. It was the only explanation. For why else would he complicate the situation more than needed?

He grimaced as the truth came to him. Had he been thinking rationally instead of acting like a hormone-drunk fool, he would have let her believe him a beast, some kind of loyal pet. Instead, his anger had swayed him into taking this form to show Lillian what she was throwing away, what she did not want.

All this would be so much easier if Lillian remembered who she was, but he dared not restore the Sorceress's memories until he had time to investigate what the Lady of Battles had done to her. There was no telling what traps the dark goddess had cast upon Lillian's soul.

He'd stalled long enough. While he couldn't tell the full truth, there *was* information Lillian needed now.

"I don't know your world or its troubles," he began, "but I have sensed an unbalance growing in this Realm while I slept in stone. It grows stronger with each season. The Riven, these creatures are known to me, an ancient enemy I'd thought eradicated." He glanced at Vivian. "I listened as you told Lillian about your troubles with these Riven, but when did these problems start?"

"A few years ago. Why?"

"Lillian and I first came to this Realm twelve years ago. Is twelve years a reasonable time estimate for when the dark ones began their conquest?"

"Are you saying you and Lillian are responsible for the creatures of darkness coming here?"

"Yes, I believe so. I will start from the beginning so you can understand what has happened." He stared at Lillian while he talked, focusing on her until the others in the room became distant to him, unimportant. "First, you must know we share a link of magic and spirit, one that has endured many lifetimes together." Lillian stiffened behind him at the word *lifetimes*, but she remained silent.

He watched as she reached out to caress his hair. Her lips shaped his name. He intertwined his fingers with hers and brought her hand to rest over his heart. At the contact, her thoughts flowed to him from where her hand rested on his chest: an overwhelming sense of peace whenever they were together. Wonder and curiosity. Excitement mixed with a hint of fear at her new awareness of him. But eclipsing all else was her unconditional trust in him.

Basking in that warmth, he continued, "When I was still gestating in my mother's tree, I reached for you and found you among our enemies, a prisoner. Newly born, the fluids of my mother's tree damp and sticky upon my flesh, I went to you. I was still learning how to coordinate my limbs when all the memories of our past lives came to me, awakening with my power. Not yet a day old and I already knew my purpose—to protect you."

Her gaze flicked from his face to their interlaced fingers, then back again.

She didn't pull away, so he resumed his story. "Had my father not been near at the time of my birth, I would have run off in pursuit of you without any weapons but for what I was born with. He couldn't stop me from seeking you out, but he gave me his warded jewelry as added protection until my magic awoke fully. I went on the hunt, following the direction of your spirit. That led me to the Battle Goddess's domain. I rescued you, but the escape cost me much of my magical strength. Without magic, we would never have avoided recapture. There was only one path left to us. Passing through the Veil between the Realms is something only a limited number of immortals can survive. Injured as we were, the Veil came close to killing us. But we survived the trip here where I found this family to raise you. Then I surrendered to the healing sleep of stone until you woke me."

He paused and glanced up at Gran with an unhappy look. "But before I rescued Lillian and made my escape, I battled a blood witch. I believe a spell that later grew into a Riven may have made the trip with one of us."

"Newly birthed. Sleep of stone," his lady mumbled half to herself. She jerked her head up and met his gaze. Her eyes widened and a surprised breath hissed past her lips.

Baffled, he waited.

She brushed her hand along his mane, and her expression softened. "God. You're just a child. You were born, found and rescued me in less than a day, and then came here and turned to stone only to wake and rescue me again. You're not even three days old."

"You're looking at it like a human again," Sable corrected her.

"No, I'm thinking like a non-perv. There's a difference." Lillian came to her feet and faced off against the other dryad. Gregory stood as well in case he needed to intervene, but he was ignored by the two women.

"No matter what you think, he *is* a gargoyle. If you don't believe me, ask him. Dryads normally gestate their girl-children within their trees for three years. But a 'gargoyle child' is more prolonged, closer to ten years. When they are finally born, they are mature, fully developed."

Lillian glanced in his direction for confirmation. He nodded. "I was only two years away from maturity. I finished maturing while in stone."

"I don't care. That's not the same as life experience." Lillian transferred her scowl to him. "You're still a child."

"No more than you. We departed the Spirit Realm together and were conceived within moments of each other."

Lillian's teeth clicked together, and she exhaled another hissing breath.

"Fine," she said and patted his hand, her voice calm. "But you still slept through childhood because you needed to heal. You took injuries protecting me, and you lack the experiences you would have during childhood and adolescence."

He grinned at her dogged determination to protect him. "We have lived many lifetimes. I have all those memories."

"We'll talk about this more later." Lillian stood between him and the other dryads with her hands fisted at her sides, her spine rigid. "I'm dead serious."

The scent in the room changed to one of challenge. His little dryad was so very protective of him. It was... endearing. Gregory hastily swallowed a rumble of laughter.

"Well," Vivian said into the silence. "Glad we've aired that laundry. Now, where were we, Gregory? You were saying about how you came to rescue Lillian."

"Indeed." His humor vanished with the reminder that creatures of darkness were still abroad in this realm, creating havoc and killing innocents. "As I said, I think I carried more than just Lillian to this realm when we fled the Lady of Battles."

Lillian tapped him on the arm to get his attention. "Who or what is the Lady of Battles? Same goes for a blood witch." To judge by Lillian's somber tone, her earlier anger at the dryads was forgotten.

"The Lady of Battles is a creature of extreme darkness. She wanted your power. I put a stop to her plans." Gregory winced at his evasion. *I hope*, he added silently.

"Go on," Lillian prompted.

"She was not always evil. She once served the Light as a..." Gregory paused, and then sorted through Lillian's mind for the proper word. "A warden-like demigoddess granted powers by the Divine Ones to hunt out evil and keep it in check. As their daughter, the Lady of Battles had great power. For millennia, she served the Divine Ones. She had a twin, the Lord of the Underworld. The Lady also had a consort, the Shieldbearer. Although her consort was a demigod in his own right, he lacked the power of the twins. Jealous of the power the Lord of the Underworld commanded, the Shieldbearer attacked the Lady's twin, intent on taking that power for himself. The Lord of the Underworld saw the evil growing in the Shieldbearer's heart and deemed him incurable. And as his nature dictated, Lord Death destroyed that evil the only way he knew how. He killed the Shieldbearer and sent his soul back to the Divine Ones to heal.

"If he had realized what that one act would bring about, the Lord of the Underworld would not have killed his twin's mate. The Lady of Battles went insane. She blamed her brother for her pain. And so, the war began. The Battle Goddess tapped into the power stored in the Veil between the Realms, turning it into a weapon to use against her twin. Lord Death responded by severing her connection to the Veil. She then turned to other methods."

Gregory paused and made a wide, all-encompassing gesture. "The Twins would have destroyed entire worlds had the Divine Ones not intervened. They punished both Twins by ordering them banished from the Spirit Realm and chained to their respective temples within the Magic Realm." He did not mention that he and his Sorceress were the ones ordered to carry out that punishment.

He continued his censored tale. "But during the war, many who lived in the once-peaceful Magic Realm fled for their lives. Some sought shelter with the Lord of the Underworld, but a great many more fled to the Mortal Realm while the Veil between the Realms was still weak enough to allow travel."

"That is how our ancestors arrived in this world," Sable added in a soft voice.

Gregory nodded. "But the Divine Ones' punishment didn't stop the Lady of Battles. Even imprisoned, she drew a great army to serve her, the very creatures of darkness she was supposed to keep imprisoned. The Lord of the Underworld gathered his own army. I, like all gargoyles, serve him. For centuries, the Lady has been growing her army and not all her warriors served willingly. By capturing Lillian, she planned to make me serve her as well. As for a blood witch, they use blood, life energy, and souls from innocent creatures to fuel their dark spells."

Lillian closed her eyes, her lashes a dark line along her cheeks. She spoke without looking at him. "So... I was captured by this Battle Goddess?"

"Yes. And I think the blood witch infected one of us—me most likely—with a spell that would infect another, turning that poor person into a Riven." He turned to Vivian. "In the first days after I arrived, did others come to examine me?"

Vivian grunted. "Only every powerful fae on this side of the pond."

"One of my visitors must have been infected before my body rid itself of the spell. That fae then infected others. Forgive me."

"You didn't create the spell," Lillian offered. "If I hadn't gotten captured, none of this would have happened. That makes this mess my fault. It's up to me to make it right. You said the Lady of Battles wanted my power. If I have power, it must be good for something. What can I do to force the Riven back to their prison?"

"You claim responsibility that is not yours to take. You

were a child, innocent of any wrongdoing. Before you challenge the Riven, you must first be trained in your magic."

Mild panic churned in Gregory's stomach. If she started to probe for her magic, there was no telling what would happen.

Until he had time to discover what had happened to her in the Battle Goddess's kingdom, he couldn't trust her, no matter how much his heart wanted to.

"Then tell me what I need to know. Teach me. Tell me about the Realms and our enemy."

"You make it sound so easy. There is so much you must learn. I scarcely know enough of your words to explain it in a way you'll understand." He sighed, his brows drawing together in thought. What was safe to tell her? He rubbed at his forehead, mildly surprised when he didn't encounter horns. Already this hybrid body was beginning to feel ordinary. Natural—like the tenderness he felt for his lady. And that was the danger.

There was so much *he* didn't know.

For now, a half-truth would have to do. "Think of the Realms as layers making up the universe. The layer we reside in now is the Mortal Realm. Surrounding this one, is the Magic Realm, where the Twins were banished. The last and greatest, the Spirit Realm, surrounds the others. All the Realms are protected and separated by the Veil—a great weaving of magic composed of all the elements. Most creatures can't cross the Veil. The Riven can't, so they are trapped here in this magic-starved land. That lack of magic likely slowed their spread."

"How do we stop them?" Lillian asked.

He hesitated while he chose the next fragments of truth he hoped would satisfy Lillian's curiosity. "I must hunt all of them down and destroy them with purifying magic. Depending on how many of these Riven are here and how strong they have grown, I might require help to kill this infection."

"Why do you remember all this when I don't? What happened to my memories if it wasn't a drowning accident?"

His stomach contracted into a tight knot. "You were not strong enough to travel through the Veil. You were damaged." His words sounded rushed to his own ears. *Merciful Divine Ones, please don't let her guess the truth, not yet.*

"Will I heal in time? Remember all these past lives you mentioned?" she said, her eyes thoughtful.

"Yes. Though I don't know how long it will be before you remember."

"Please," he whispered in his mind, *"don't let that be another lie."*

Lillian frowned, as if sensing his lie, but her expression smoothed out after a moment and she asked, "In the meantime, how do we go about hunting these Riven?"

"I will be able to hunt and track them once I find a trail. However, there is a more immediate concern that needs our attention," Gregory explained. "Your hamadryad tree was wounded during the attack, and I didn't have the strength to heal both the tree and you. I placed a weaving over the injuries to protect against further damage, but the wounds need tending. I would appreciate it if one of the dryads would guide you in learning a dryad's magic."

He pointedly focused on Sable. "I can supply strength and my blood as needed, but the actual act of healing isn't one of my greater skills."

"I would be honored." Sable bowed, and then after

straightening, she glided up next to Lillian. "Come, Sister. I will direct you in the use of a dryad's power."

Lillian glanced back at him questioningly, but Sable tugged on her arm and dragged her in the direction of the back door. He tracked the pleasant sway of his lady's hips as she descended the stairs outside.

Alone now, shadows curled around his body, hiding him as he summoned his gargoyle form. When he had his familiar shape back, he dropped to all fours and followed the lingering scent of dryad.

CHAPTER TWELVE

*H*ot, humid air hinted at the chance of an evening thundershower. Gregory hoped for one. Perhaps it would wash away some of the stink. He wrinkled his muzzle in distaste. The mixed odors of slaughter, old death, and burnt flesh hung over the grove. If they managed to awaken Lillian's dryad magic, it might help purify the grove. Her natural dryad magic wouldn't be linked to her powers as the Sorceress, so it should be safe for Lillian to summon it without triggering any trap left by the Lady of Battles. He hoped.

Shadows cast by the maze's west wall stretched across the glade as the sun eased closer to the horizon. A slash of white glowed among the darkness. As it came closer, the pale shape glided between the slender trunks of the trees, weaving and bucking in his joyous frenzy.

Had the unicorn kept up his antics all day?

Probably.

Gregory had eaten rabbits with more intelligence.

The stallion bolted straight toward Gregory. He wished the unicorn's natural power wasn't to see through deception; in this case, a gargoyle's shadow magic. Dirt and bits of grass bombarded him as the unicorn skidded to a halt within arm's reach. Gregory's displeasure increased when the unicorn pranced over to Lillian with his neck arched and tail sailing like a banner in the wind.

The unicorn bobbed his head and rubbed his muzzle against the dryad. Lillian laughed and stroked the unicorn's nose, then moved up to scratch the base of his spiraled horn.

Gregory directed his thoughts at the stallion. *"Have you forgotten it was a woman who tempted you into taking human form and caused your... predicament?"*

"I have not forgotten." The unicorn rolled an eye in Gregory's direction. *"But she's stunning and she smells delicious."*

"And you look and smell like food, too," Gregory warned.

"Predators are all the same, but you're worse than most. Do you even know what a sense of humor is?"

"No."

The unicorn inched away from Lillian.

Content, Gregory returned his attention to Lillian, where she stood between Sable and Russet. The three women were standing at the base of the hamadryad. Sable had begun the first lesson, unaware of what went on between gargoyle and unicorn.

"Feel your tree," Sable was saying, "her life force humming under your hands. She is the source of your power and your strength. From her, you draw life. Without her, there is only death."

Lillian glanced back at him and then beyond the arch of one of his wings to the remains of the shattered stone circle.

She paled. But a moment later, she straightened her shoulders and placed her hands on her tree in a decisive move.

Pride swelled in his heart. His lady was strong. The Sorceress always had been—but this lifetime, he had worried she would not be strong enough. For once he was happy to be proven wrong.

Lillian leaned forward until her forehead rested on the rough bark of the tree, scant inches beneath the lower of the two long slashes. The blue lattice of his weaving still glowed in the shade cast by the upper canopy.

"Do you feel it?" Sable asked her student.

Lillian nodded her head. "Yes, it's... it's so much—such strength. Why did I not know of this before?"

"I'd ask your gargoyle that question, were I you. Perhaps because you didn't know your true nature, you had no idea this was even possible, so didn't try." Sable gestured at the hamadryad. "Now direct some of the power you feel into the redwood. Visualize the wounds. Imagine all signs of dirt and disease pushed from those wounds. Good. Now envision the wound knitting together, the edges closing, the bark intact once again." Sable patted Lillian on the shoulder. "Excellent, young one. It comes so naturally to you. It will not be long until you are truly a dryad in all ways—wait! What are you doing?"

The startled edge to Sable's tone jolted Gregory into action. Power raised the hair at the back of his neck and tingled in his lungs as he drew another quick breath. This was not a dryad's weaving. This was energy drawn from the Magic Realm—an act of power as the Sorceress, not just a dryad. He rushed to Lillian's side and placed a hand on her shoulder. When she turned to him with power bright in her eyes, he knew how dangerous the situation had grown. Energy bled from Lillian. It bubbled from the Magic Realm, flowing across the land like a spring-fed brook, Lillian its headwater. The current caught at his wings, tugging at them.

"My lady, you have healed your hamadryad and using more magic now might be too taxing." He spun another web of half-truths, not caring if she figured out later she had been lied to. The Magic Realm was bad enough, but if he didn't stop this now, she might switch and draw power directly from the Spirit Realm.

"I don't feel tired at all. This is wonderful... I can feel the evil shriveling and dying all around the meadow. It's magnificent. Look," she said as she pointed toward where the stone circle lay shattered. Magic shimmered along her arms, barely visible, like heat waves in the desert. "I can fix it and make it stronger, watch."

Sable took one look at Lillian's arms and took several steps back. With shock replacing her usually serene expression, the older dryad's gaze followed where Lillian pointed. Gregory held his breath.

Fragments of stone rose up from the grass as Lillian returned the shattered stones back to their proper places. Stone pillars formed out of the rubble. Not a stone or piece of gravel was out of place or showed even a hint of damage. Power continued building. She'd said she could make it stronger. No doubt she could, but not with the supplies she had at her call here. She needed additional materials and better-quality stone if she wanted to create a more powerful ward.

Small tremors under his feet warned him he needed to stop this now. He wrapped his arms around her shoulders, subtly absorbing the power she'd summoned before it could cause an unbalance in the natural world. "Enough. Listen to me. You're not yet ready for this. You don't have what you need to make the circle stronger—if you try to force extra power into those stones, the circle will erupt like it did when the Riven attacked you."

"I can control this. I know I can." She sounded drunk.

He shook her. "Do you want to be responsible for the deaths of Sable and Russet?"

His meaning must have penetrated her power-drugged mind. She froze and then paled. "I wouldn't harm you or the others. I'd stop before the stones became stressed."

"How would you know when they reached that point?"

"I..." Her shoulders hunched and the vast flow of magic dwindled. "You're right. What am I doing?"

He held her until the last trickle of power died away. Magic strained under his skin, filling him to the point of pain. A neigh from behind him had never been so welcome. A moment later, the unicorn started siphoning power. When the magic was a more manageable presence, Gregory looked over his shoulder and inclined his head in thanks. The unicorn echoed the motion, and then with a spray of grass and clumps of mud, the stallion bounded off into the shadows of the grove.

"I'm sorry." Lillian's voice broke. She swallowed and tried again. "That was stupid. But it felt natural, so right. Forgive me. I'll always listen in the future."

Gregory snorted with humor. "You're forgiven. Though I doubt you'll obey that last oath. You've never been very good at listening."

She didn't rise to his baiting. Her thoughts were too guilt-ridden, and he worried for her. If he released the block he'd put on her memories, all the knowledge and skills she'd learned in her past lives would return, and she could wield her magic safely. But the memory of what the Lady of Battles had done would return as well.

Gregory couldn't risk it. He wanted his Sorceress restored in a way that ate at his resolve, but it would have to wait for now. The healing of her hamadryad hadn't confirmed anything.

While he hadn't detected any evil tainting her magic, she'd acted dangerously and that was something the Sorceress would never do. Instead, she'd reacted as thoughtlessly as a child with a new toy. Her loss of control could have been an accident due to inexperience. Or it could have been the Battle Goddess's influence.

There was only one way to know for sure here in this Realm. Once Lillian trusted him absolutely, he would risk the deep merging that would allow him to learn what had been done to her. By the grace of the Divine Ones, he would be able to reverse the damage, and then they could go home.

Lillian tugged on his hand. "If we're done here, I'd like to go help Gran with dinner."

"Go. I'll be along after I've had a word with the unicorn. I'm appointing him guardian of the maze. I'll only be a few moments."

"Sure," Lillian agreed like she barely heeded his words, already retreating into her own thoughts.

After she had gone, he sat alone, troubled by his own dark worries.

CHAPTER THIRTEEN

*A*fter an awkward dinner, where Gregory was the only participant with an appetite, Lillian hung back to question her grandmother.

"So?" Lillian asked as she deposited another pile of plates on the counter.

Gran looked up from loading the dishwasher and gave her a questioning look.

"No one has told me where we're going tonight. By the way everyone bolted after supper to go get ready, I assume this isn't the usual trip to the neighbors for coffee and cards."

"No, not exactly," Gran said. A smile crossed her lips and faded a moment later. "The magical community has many different celebrations. While most are private and solitary, once each month we must come together to raise magic, reaffirm the bonds of kinship, and to strike fear into the hearts of our enemies. Tonight is the Wild Hunt. Even the threat of attack will not stop the Hunt, for without the Hunt all magic spells would wither and die."

"I've heard the legends about the Wild Hunt." Lillian tucked a few strands of hair behind her ear, then smoothed it in place. It was a telltale nervous gesture she'd been trying to ditch for years. Oh, well. She didn't care if Gran knew she was edgy tonight. "The Hunt, isn't it supposed to be dangerous? And by that I mean evil. I thought people were the chosen prey."

Gran released a long-drawn-out sigh. "In this age, the Hunt is no more evil than one of those swords hanging over the mantle. It's a tool. One we use to raise and gather magic so we may survive. A tool can be used for good or evil. That depends on the heart of the wielder." Gran resumed loading the dishwasher. "And yes, in centuries past, the Hunt was dangerous. It was used to hunt down sacrifices or to kill oath breakers. Some of our rulers had an unnatural streak of cruelty. During those earlier times, most humans with the misfortune to run into the Wild Hunt didn't survive to report the encounter. Later, when we were ruled by more just rulers, we would take the human's memories but leave them alive. Upon occasion, a fae would find a mortal interesting and return with the human."

"You mean they abducted the poor person, right?"

Gran cleared her throat. "Yes."

"And you want me to go with you on this Wild Hunt?"

"Lillian, I don't want to put you in unnecessary danger, but the Hunt is needed for everyone's survival. I won't leave you behind after what happened yesterday. Just stay close to me this evening, and all will be well. I'm more concerned about how your gargoyle will react to the rest of the Clan and the Coven. Now, you should go get ready. The dryads have constructed something for you to wear." Gran patted Lillian's shoulder and then walked away.

CHAPTER FOURTEEN

*W*ith her wet hair wrapped in a towel, Lillian sat on the bed and fiddled with the belt of her terry robe, which covered the new forest-green bra and panties. One eyebrow had wedged itself in her hairline a while ago. There wasn't much else she could say or do except wait for the other two women to finish with the gown.

She had never before seen a garment made from moss, fluffy Maidenhair ferns, and the broad sweeping fans of Bracken ferns. The gown's individual parts were held together by a fine webbing of magic. There was a first time for everything. Of late, she was witnessing new "firsts" every other hour.

The headboard creaked as the bed shifted under her. Her brows scrunched together. Unless there had been a minor earthquake, the room held one occupant too many.

"Out," Lillian ordered.

The two dryads paused in their work and looked up at her

like she'd sprouted horns. Well, horns *were* part of the prob-lem. Twisting to look behind her, she scanned the empty bed and frowned. "Nice try, but I'm not indulging you in a free peepshow. Out now, or I'll braid some pretty flowers into your mane."

A snort and more shaking of the bed marked Gregory's position. Unfortunately, it came too late. A warm, damp tongue washed across her face. A moment later, the invisible gargoyle jumped down, landing with a thump. He material-ized next to where the dryads worked. Butting his nose into the pile of greenery, he pushed their hands away from their work and sniffed every petal and leaf. Presumably happy with his findings, he padded from the room, the tip of his tail flicking gently.

The dryads watched him go.

Lillian was still wiping gargoyle kisses off her cheek when the others brought the dress over to her. The skirt—woven of moss so soft and refined it looked like lace—fell to the floor in graceful folds. Over the green lace was a second sheer skirt of interwoven ferns. When they gestured for her to try it on, she eyed it with suspicion. Magic gave the greenery a lushness the natural plants lacked, and the entire gown gleamed with a faint shimmer as if silver dusted the woven-plant fabric. With a sigh, Lillian shimmied into the hip-hugging skirt but soon marveled at the silky comfort. Slits ran up both sides for ease of movement.

A form-fitting green top made from the tiny leaves of meadow rue and the flowing Bracken fern blended with the moss lace, creating the prettiest gown she'd ever seen. It might be beautiful, but it didn't seem practical.

"If I remember correctly, this didn't work out so well for Cinderella."

The dryads blinked at her.

Lillian sighed again. "Magic made this. If I'm left with only my undies at midnight, I'm *not* going to be happy."

"But Gregory might," Sable said with a smirk.

Lillian flashed the other woman a twist of her lips, more fang than smile. But she let the dryads fix her hair with cream ribbons and white flowers. Around Lillian's neck, Sable fastened a necklace of silver and what looked like tiny drops of dew. Matching earrings completed the look.

"You are a striking creature," Sable said, circling Lillian to better view her work. "No wonder the gargoyle hovers near you like a hopeful suitor."

Lillian decided to let the silence speak for her. It was better than trying to come up with a reply to that loaded comment.

Sable smoothed her fingers along Lillian's hair and tucked the last stubborn strands in place. "Thank you for allowing us to attire you in our way. There are so few of us left, we must preserve as many rituals as we can."

"Sure," Lillian mumbled, her thoughts elsewhere. At first, the gargoyle hadn't done anything to make her think his emotions went beyond the relationship of long-standing ward and protector. She silently laughed at her own reasoning—a day and a half was hardly long enough to become acquainted with another person's dreams and longings. But what would she do if there was truth to Sable's comment and Gregory *did* see her as more than his ward?

After a moment's thought, she decided that was a problem for another time.

First, she had to survive this Wild Hunt and try not to make of fool of herself or expose the depth of her ignorance to the rest of the Clan and the Coven.

CHAPTER FIFTEEN

*T*he road divided two worlds. On one side of the winding gravel road, a deep, wooded ravine waited, calm and mysterious, and on the other, the metal ribs of a derelict sawmill jutted up into the star-speckled night sky. The moon illuminated the land around the mill. The area had gone wild again, forest creeping back in, ready to reclaim the land. The contrast was eerie, like the surreal footage of a post-apocalyptic world. She shivered, cold down to her core. Instinctively, Lillian looked in the rear-view mirror, hoping to catch a glimpse of the gargoyle riding in the truck bed.

Her eyes found no sign of him, but she could feel him in her mind, his legs braced to hold him in place, and his wings cupped to catch the wind. He loved the speed and the cold air. Lillian's lips turned up at the gargoyle's joy.

Lillian heard the heavy pulse of drumming before Gran turned into an overgrown driveway. The chain-link gate was thrown wide, tilting off to one side, partially unhinged where rust had eaten its way through the metal. Other cars were already parked, and more arrived from different directions as she took in the scene.

"All this is ours." Gran swept her arms up and out, the gesture encompassing the mill and the surrounding forest. "The Coven and the Clan pooled resources and bought it from a logging company back in the seventies. It was one of our first joint acquisitions. It didn't look like much then, but it came cheaply. As far as anyone knows, we're an environmentally minded company specializing in rehabilitation, restoration, and sustainable forestry." She smiled. "While it's not the whole truth, it isn't a lie, either."

Lillian grunted. That sounded like her life. There certainly hadn't been a lot of truth-telling there, either. If anything, the gargoyle was the most honest with his long silences.

Smoothing her skirt over her legs, she wiggled as she tried to get out of the truck without flashing everyone. Lillian silently damned all trucks to hell, and double-damned skirts with slits up the sides. And then triple-damned clothing made from ferns, moss, and ivy. At least by the look of things, they were meeting in the old sawmill, so she hoped that meant she wasn't going to be tromping around in the forest at night in a damned dress.

Before Lillian could blink, Gregory was next to her, shapeshifted to look human once again. He gripped her around the waist and lifted. With a squeak, she slapped her hands down on his shoulders for balance. Even after he'd set her on her feet, his hands lingered a moment. She stood there staring, unable to think of something to say even when he captured one of her hands and ran his thumb over the back.

"Come," Gran said. "The others are waiting."

Lillian returned to herself with a blush. A large group of

newly arrived strangers had gathered to watch. The gargoyle's invisibility magic was an interesting power and one she would have put to use about now.

She ducked her head, and when Gregory trailed after Gran, Lillian followed. She didn't have much choice. Gregory hadn't released her hand. She was so focused on not stepping in puddles or doing something else to embarrass herself, she missed when the crowd of strangers broke up into smaller groups. They all headed toward the vast crouched shadow of the abandoned sawmill.

"Is it safe?" Lillian asked. That wasn't the real question she wanted to ask, but she didn't know how to put into words the sensation of cold fear hovering just below her heart.

"The mill? Yes, of course." Gran gestured at the building. "We've done some work to the inside, but nothing that would show on the outside. We don't want questions."

Lillian nodded absently. The drumming she'd heard as they neared was stronger now. Heavy and primal, it called to her. Gregory released her hand and fell a step behind.

Doors on giant tracks slid open at their approach. Two men waited on either side of the entrance. Calling them doormen seemed wrong. Each had the intensity of a bouncer mixed with the lean muscle of a ballet dancer or a martial artist. Whatever they were, they gave off a sense of strength, training, and menace.

Lillian glanced behind to ask Gregory if he felt whatever hovered in the air around the two men, but her gargoyle had vanished. She turned her mind inward. Magic answered her summons, vibrating in her lungs and the pit of her stomach. She tried not to think about how quickly she was coming to accept powers she didn't know existed two days ago.

A moment later, she found Gregory. He'd not gone far. When he finished circling the two men, he returned to her side, still invisible.

Gran took the lead, her long robes trailing behind her, quarterstaff held vertical like a walking stick instead of a weapon. Lillian still found the image of her grandmother carrying a quarterstaff a strange one. She'd dreamed last night, weird dreams about shadows lurching among moonlit trees, her grandmother swinging the quarterstaff, battling something in the shadows. Looking back at the previous two days, it was no wonder she dreamed of strange, frightening things.

Lillian followed in Gran's shadow as she entered the old mill. A short trip through a narrow hallway led to another set of doors. These opened onto a landing that overlooked the old mill's main work floor. Gran marched down the stairs leading away from the landing. Lillian lengthened her strides to match the swift pace.

They were crossing through the sawmill's old offices when she 'felt' the gargoyle drift away from her side a second time. Scouting, no doubt. He didn't go far; she could still feel him with the strange sense that hummed in her mind. They'd come to the end of the row of offices and faced a wall of windows, the glass spotted with dirt and clouded with age. The pulsing was louder here, pressing against her eardrums. She closed her eyes, feeling the rhythm with her breastbone and in the soles of her feet.

She broke away from her grandmother and the rest of the group and paced over to the nearest windowsill. Her heart hammered in time to the pulse of the drums. Like the slow disbelief of watching a car wreck, curiosity drew her forward. Condensation fogged the glass. She wiped it away. The glass was cold against her fingertips. She glimpsed white crystals and bright flecks of blue as they drifted by the window before it fogged over again.

Snow? Inside a building?

Using the corner of her shawl, she cleared the window of fog and dirt. Then blinked. No. Not snow. Tiny flecks of light swirled through the air, drifting up from a whirlpool of magic below her. Dancers were moving amid the magic—and they were not human.

Down at ground level, massive wolves, white-furred elk, small black ponies, and hounds with brown hides and tawny-colored ears shared the space with hundreds of people. They moved in time to the beat, driven in frantic circles by the pulse of the drums. A whirlpool created of living bodies. They spun and whirled, caught in the tidal pull of the circle dance.

Like the spokes of a galaxy, columns of dancers bunched closer together at the core before drifting farther apart at the edges. Those lithe figures at the center were so tightly packed together, Lillian couldn't see their features, only the pale glow of magic that surrounded them. Their swift movements sheared the magic from their bodies, freeing it to drift up like wind-blown snow.

The wild power touched Lillian on a level she didn't understand, frightening her with its seductive call.

Follow, instinct demanded.

Surrender.

Become part of the dance.

Running her hands along the wall, her fingers sought a way through.

"You might try the door," Gran said, an amused expression on her face as she pointed to a doorway a few feet ahead.

Lillian lurched into motion, intoxicated by the power. She grabbed the doorframe while she surveyed the metal stairway leading down. She hugged the railing, hoping to steady herself long enough to get control of the rioting emotions swirling through her mind.

The gargoyle came to Lillian, pressing his body against her back. Peace, love, protection, serenity—his calming and soothing emotions swamped her, flooding into her mind from where they touched.

'I will keep you safe,' he said in his silent way.

She loved him for it at that moment.

No fear. No questions. Just unequivocal acceptance.

Her boot heels clicked against the metal stairs—she'd possessed enough common sense to leave the matching slippers the dryads had made at home, instead choosing a tall, sturdy pair of boots that would protect her lower legs from the abuses of the forest. She concentrated on the sound of her boots' heavy tread. It helped to ground her scattered thoughts.

Caught up in the power of the dance, individuals swept past her and Gregory without noticing the newcomers. A strange force tried to pull Lillian toward the center of the vast room. When it couldn't physically drag her closer, it seeped into her body. The hair on her arms rose. She shivered at the invasion. The foreign magic flowed through her blood, and then it receded. As it fled, it took some of her magic with it. She resisted. It tugged harder at her soul. Panicking, she summoned power of her own. With claws of magic, she struck out at the threat and shredded the filaments trying to steal her magic.

The vortex at room's center shuddered. The tide of power

shifted, snapping from the center of the room toward where she stood. Dancers lost their rhythm. Drums faltered. The room erupted into chaos. Cries of alarm and growls of challenge resounded through the air as more people stilled in their dance. Weapons appeared in hands as the crowd gathered itself, and as one being, it turned to look at her. Some gazes were fearful, others hostile, and a few curious.

Lillian's nerve broke. She whirled back to the stairs, ready to flee, but Gregory in his gargoyle form materialized on the stairs a step above her. He stopped her with ease, his wings blocking escape. A muscular arm wrapped around her shoulders and turned her to face the crowd. Silence claimed the room.

Shock replaced fear on many faces. They weren't looking at her. They stared at the gargoyle overshadowing her with his greater bulk. A memory flashed across her mind, of the unicorn in human form when he'd first beheld the gargoyle: a look of shock and wonder, followed by desperate hunger.

She prayed they weren't about to get torn apart by a mob desperate for magic.

"We must fix what we broke," Gregory whispered into her mind through the touch of his hands on her arms. *"This was a ceremony of sharing. Had I known what we were walking into, I might have approached this differently."*

"I screwed up, didn't I?" She glanced over her shoulder. Looking at him was better than facing the mob.

"How could you know the magic would try to gather some of your power and share it with this world?" He pushed her from behind, guiding her back toward the crowd. "Now we shall fix what went wrong and make the magic stronger than it was before."

"I don't know how."

"Follow my lead and embrace your instincts. They are there, buried under layers of my protection. Look and you will find them."

Mmm-hmm. Right. "What if I screw this up like I did with the stone ring around my tree?"

"I will keep you safe."

She doubted herself but trusted him, so when the crowd parted down the middle to let him pass, she followed close at his heels. He took a long and twisting way to the center of the room, herding the crowd back into motion. They moved for him, with him, following his subtle gestures.

He spun in a circle, the motion unfurling his wings. The glow of power spread out around him, flaring in the breeze created by his wings. Stomping his feet in a slow sideways motion, he began to move. His tail lashed in time to some unheard rhythm and drums took up the beat as magic pulsed in the air.

Lillian swayed, uncertain. But Gregory gestured and called to her with power. Entranced, she took a half-step toward him, then another. The magic in the room gathered, starting to spin into a vortex once more. Order slowly defeated chaos, and both crowd and magic moved to Gregory's silent commands.

Unable to help herself, she followed as willingly as the others. She closed her eyes and guided by sound and the magic pulsing in her blood, she began to dance a softer counterpoint to his rhythm. Swaying and whirling around him in loose circles, moving in the opposite direction to him, she summoned a second larger ring of magic around the vortex. He increased the pace of his dance as the inner ring shrunk down upon itself. She danced just beyond the outer expanse of his wings. All the women in the room, beast and human-shaped, echoed her motion.

Then the males took up Gregory's rhythm and followed his lead. Moving in opposite directions, the alternate rings of dancers spun past each other, driven beyond exhaustion or reason by the rising current of magic.

She danced so close, she could feel the heat of Gregory's body, but they never quite touched. He danced in the same manner, echoing her courtship, following her every movement until the rhythm of the drums carried him away from her again, only to return that much closer with each turn. Like a pair of binary stars, they orbited each other—glowing brighter as they expended magic.

When the rhythm of the dance brushed their bodies together, she reached out to him, learning his thoughts, communicating like he did. A sense of purpose, pride in her abilities, and that she trusted him flowed from his mind to hers. There was heat as well. She accepted it. Desire simply became part of the dance.

Magic reached a fever pitch within her. Unable to resist any longer, she stroked the warm silk of his wing membranes, delighting in the way his wings quivered. When he turned to her, she thought she saw an answering heat in his gaze.

She trailed her fingertips across his chest, over firm muscle and the slight ridge of his ribs. He caught her hand, stopping its exploration.

"Naughty dryad," he scolded, but his accompanying thoughts lacked anger. "That is not part of this dance."

"I'm sorry," she mumbled as heat flooded her cheeks, suddenly deeply embarrassed by her actions.

"Never be sorry for showing me affection, my Sorceress," he whispered for her alone. Then he tossed his head back, his wings stretching toward the ceiling, and laughed.

The magic above him shuddered. A strange humming doused all other sounds for several heartbeats until her eardrums sorted the noise out. With a low whine, the magic revved up. Teetering, it hovered on the brink of losing control, then the magic exploded out, colliding with her circle of magic. When the two powers merged, a retina-searing flash of light blinded her, followed by a clash of sound louder than thunder. Energy raced away like shooting stars. Most of the magic vanished through the walls and ceiling of the room. What remained fell like big, wet flakes of snow, except they sparkled like tiny fireworks.

A tall, elegantly boned man raised a horn above his head. He met her eyes across the distance and gave first her and then Gregory a nod of respect. She'd never seen such old eyes in such a young face. One slightly pointed ear peeked out between strands of his long hair.

"We Hunt for honor." He gave the horn a little shake. "We Hunt for duty. We Hunt for life."

"We Hunt!" the crowd screamed back.

"Ride until dawn grays the sky."

"We Hunt!"

"Let the Wild Hunt ride until the moon has long vanished." He raised the horn to his lips.

With the first blast, a haunting note sounded through Lillian's soul. The crowd roared.

"We ride!" Lillian screamed the words out along with them. Then again, a final time, hard enough to hurt her throat.

The brown-furred hounds bayed madly, yipping and barking as they darted through the crowd and headed for the loading bay doors. Outside, magic pooled in little eddies, hanging above the ground like fog. It hadn't vanished as she'd thought.

It was waiting for the Hunt. Like a moonlit path paved with white stone, magic gathered, forming into a silver road. She held her breath as people vaulted upon the backs of ponies, wolves, and elk.

Gran approached and held out a bag. "I brought these for you. Thought they'd be more sensible than what the dryads made. There's a small office through that door where you can change." She pointed at the door. "Now hurry."

Lillian took the bag, glanced at Gregory, and then with a shrug, hurried into the office and slammed the door before her gargoyle decided to come and 'guard' her. Inside, she upended the bag on a desk and got a look at what Gran had packed.

"You've got to be kidding me."

When Lillian returned from swiftly changing her clothing, she found Gran already astride a white elk, her quarterstaff balanced across her lap.

Lillian pointed at her leather pants and then plucked at the black blouse and leather corset. "All I need is a crop or wicked-looking whip and I'm ready for Halloween or a new career direction."

Gran huffed. "That's not a costume. That's real leather warded with spells. It will give you some protection from brambles and whatever other nastiness we might encounter out on the trail. But by all means, if you prefer the dress..."

"The dress with the slits up the sides? Let me think about it. Hmmm? Yeah, that's a no."

"Shall we Hunt?" Gran asked.

"Yes," Lillian replied. "Though I don't know what I'll be hunting. Or what I'll be riding." Nerves fluttered in her stomach. She glanced around. Most everyone else had already exited through the loading doors.

"We Hunt and gather the magic we summoned from the Magic Realm. And never in my lifetime have I seen such bounty as what you and the gargoyle summoned as you danced together."

Lillian didn't reply, still too embarrassed by her forwardness with the gargoyle during the dance and that her grandmother and everyone else had seen her socially awkward attempt at seduction get shot down by Gregory.

"Mount, so we can catch up with the others," Gran said with a note of impatience.

"On what?" Lillian asked at last.

"The gargoyle will make a fine steed." Gran looked at Gregory and raised an eyebrow. "And he looked willing enough to let you ride him earlier."

Lillian's jaw dropped at her grandmother's words.

While Lillian was still choking on her grandmother's innuendo loaded words, Gran urged the elk into a trot, forestalling questions.

CHAPTER SIXTEEN

*W*hen the building emptied of everyone else, Lillian turned to Gregory in time to catch a blur of shadows and light as he resumed his true form. After he dropped to all fours, he came to her side and nudged her hand with his muzzle. She held her breath, frozen in place, uncertain. At her sign of reluctance, he moved forward until her fingers rested in his mane. Then, shifting his wings away from his sides, he exposed his back so she could sling her leg over, just like mounting a horse.

She frowned at the invitation.

One week of misery, which her grandmother had called riding lessons, had been enough to convince Lillian horsemanship wasn't one of her skills, and riding gargoyle-back probably wasn't one, either. She most definitely preferred her own two feet on the ground. The horse had liked it better that way, too.

But here she was, eyeing her gargoyle's broad back with mild curiosity.

Riding bareback. At night. On a gargoyle. What fun.

Apparently tired of waiting, Gregory wrapped his tail around her waist and dragged her closer. The nervous fluttering in her stomach revved up another notch.

No other alternatives presented themselves, so she swung a leg over his back and settled in place. She gripped his sides with her thighs and knees to hold herself on. It still felt like she would fall off with his first step. To hide her trepidation, she pretended nothing was wrong as she leaned forward to circle her arms around his neck. When she stretched out along his spine, he folded his wings back into place.

His flight muscles made a nice cushion, and his back wasn't bony like she'd half-expected. Perhaps riding gargoyle-back wouldn't be as uncomfortable as she'd imagined. The heat of his body sank into her bones, and the subtle scent of gargoyle surrounded her. Her jaw unclenched, and the nervous fluttering in her stomach eased. She rested her head against his mane—it was easier than straining to look up and around. Inhaling his forest-and-musky-male scent relaxed her another degree.

"Try to find your balance," Gregory rumbled. "I'll start slow. You might remember the way of it. I used to carry you on my back when you were born into a form lacking wings." His gait changed as he moved sideways and then in circles, shifting his weight from side to side as he switched directions and speeds.

"Okay," she mumbled into his mane, "I still haven't fallen off, so I suppose that's a good sign."

Gregory changed directions sharply. She squeaked in alarm when she slid sideways. His wings steadied her while she regained her balance.

"Not funny. Warn me next time you do that." She swatted his shoulder without much force.

He chuckled, shaking her insides with the movement.

"You're enjoying this," she accused.

"Perhaps a little."

"How noble of you," Lillian drawled.

"I try to be."

She laughed. It was impossible to remain angry at him.

He lengthened his stride into a lope. She tightened her grip on his neck, not knowing what else to hold. Her death grip didn't seem to bother him, and he took off at a bone-jarring run as he zigzagged his way across the vast floor space. She curled the toes of her boots under his belly. After a few moments, her muscles grew used to his rolling strides, and she started to flow with the motion. Her lips curled up at the corners. She might get so she liked riding on the back of a gargoyle.

The gaping maw of the loading doors loomed up ahead of her. Beyond them, the strange and wild night waited. Almost clear of the building, Gregory flexed his muscular hindquarters and launched himself off the edge of the loading bay, out into the night. She'd thought he'd run fast before. She'd been wrong.

Her stomach plummeted each time his talons struck the ground. Such power. It felt like he floated in the air a brief moment between each stride. Nothing like riding a horse, more like harnessing the power of one of the big cats. Laughter bubbled up, followed by intense joy.

Gregory's long strides ate up the ground between them and the distant Wild Hunt. The night was soon filled with the baying of hounds and the cadence of Gregory's rapid footfalls.

They caught up with the rest of the Hunt on the outskirts of the forest. Spreading his wings, the gargoyle soared across the expanse of gravel road in one leap. A cry of surprise broke from her lips. Coming to the ground again, he resumed his rapid pace. She was about to beg him to fly again, but he'd already overtaken the Hunt and slowed his pace to come alongside Gran, her elk, and three silent dire wolves.

"What took you so long? Lillian give you a hard time?" Gran asked the gargoyle.

Gregory grunted in response.

"I figured she'd be more agreeable to riding if no one else was around to watch her first attempt," Gran said with a grin, then saluted the gargoyle with her staff. "Sorry I couldn't teach her more of what she needed, but she's progressing well regardless, don't you agree?"

"Yes," Gregory said as he continued to pace the elk. "Thank you for guiding and protecting her when I could not."

"I'm right here under your nose, so to speak, you can stop talking like I'm not here," Lillian grumbled. "And since I haven't yet fallen from Gregory's back and broken my fool neck, what am I supposed to be doing, exactly?"

Gran cast Lillian a sidelong look and nodded her head. "In times past, the Wild Hunt had many purposes, but now need drives us. Tonight, we'll ride the borders of our domain, guiding the magic we raised into a defense against the invaders."

Lillian nodded and glanced around. She frowned, taking note of the thinning herd of riders for the first time. "Are there fewer strange creatures—uh, strangers here than started out at the warehouse?"

"Oh, young one, you forget you're one of those 'strange creatures' now."

With a twist of her lips, Lillian acknowledged her grandmother had a point. Her new view of the world and her place in it would take some getting used to. Besides, she still felt human, didn't she?

"The Hunt separated to cover more ground," her grandmother continued. "The wards and other traps must be reset to maintain the security of the Coven and Clan lands."

"Why? What happened to the defenses?" Lillian asked, a suspicion growing in her mind.

"The amount of power you and your gargoyle summoned washed away the wards we had in place like a storm's tidal surge erodes a beach. Such bounty we had not expected, and we did not prepare for it."

"So, I screwed up again."

"No, dear. You shared a great gift with us. Do not regret it. Look there..." Gran pointed at an oak directly ahead of them, where its wide branches overhung the game trail, "... and watch."

Lillian raised her head out of the gargoyle's mane and peered through the space between his horns. Gregory and the elk came to a stop when Gran raised her quarterstaff.

With her eyes closed, Gran chanted in a low, guttural tone for a full minute before shaping it into a droning melody. Her head tilted back, and she pointed her staff at the tree. Then she uttered one final word.

The world exploded with light. Lillian jerked like she'd been shot. Even the gargoyle jumped at the bright flash and turned his head away. When Lillian could see again, she focused on the tree. It still stood, but it now glowed.

"Good God! What was that?" Even as Lillian asked her question, the glow coating the tree seeped into it and vanished until only a very slight afterglow remained. It looked like moonlight shone brighter on that one tree than it did its closest neighbor. Interesting.

"That is a ward," Gran replied as the elk began to trot again. "It will prevent lesser evil from entering our lands and warn us should something nastier come our way. Now that the magic is strong again, we will know if the ward is broken or breached. Yesterday morning, when you were attacked, the wards were weakening. I believe that's why the Riven struck when they did. They would have known tonight was the Wild Hunt, and they wished to strike us a blow before we could reestablish our protections."

"Can you teach me?" Lillian asked.

An eerie cry similar to a wolf's broke through the night's calm, but it was higher in pitch and undulated strangely. The gargoyle skidded to a halt. Twisting his head to the right, he looked off into the direction of the yowl. More of the Hunt came to a halt. Heads turned toward the unnerving call and ears tilted, listening for the faintest sound on the night wind.

A human scream rose above the sounds of heavy breathing and the wind. The gargoyle spun back around to face Gran so fast, Lillian nearly slipped off his back with the force of his turn—she would have, had his wings not caught her.

"Take my lady to safety," Gregory ordered. "Those are death hounds—beasts which don't belong here. I must kill them before they report back to their masters."

"No," Lillian protested as a growing sense of dread settled in her middle at the thought of her gargoyle going into battle without her. The flash of a remembered dream stood out fresh in Lillian's thoughts, of her grandmother swinging her staff at shadows. "Gregory, I'm not letting you battle them alone."

"You're not going into battle with me. It's too dangerous and you're not ready. I might not be able to kill them and protect you at the same time."

"There are too many. You can't go alone. We'll all come with you and face whatever these things are together." Her power stirred, uncurling within her. At that moment, she couldn't explain it, but she needed to be there with him.

"Get off!" he ordered, his voice no longer gentle. Fear for her had made it deep and thunderous.

"I will not let you fight alone." As stubborn as he, she clung to his back, refusing to let go.

He growled as he reached back and grabbed her left ankle in his mouth. With a twist of his head, he dislodged her without so much as leaving a mark on her leather boots, but all the same, she still found herself on the ground.

With a curse, she rolled to her feet in time to see Gregory bolting off into the shadows. She needed to follow him with every cell in her body. Her shoulder blades itched and ached. Fisting her shaking hands, she tried to ignore the burn of power pulsing in her fingertips. Gregory wasn't the only one with magic. She had every right to fight by his side. Fear for her gargoyle filled her belly.

"Gregory is faster. If he waited for us, more people would die." The harsh line of Gran's mouth softened. "You must let the gargoyle do what he was born to do."

But Gran was wrong, Lillian's instincts screamed. More people would die this way.

She closed her eyes and sought calm. A waft of coppery

blood-scent snapped her back to attention. She relaxed her hands and found she'd cut her palms. Baffled, she studied her nails. They weren't sharp enough to do that kind of damage.

"Lillian, hurry. Mount up behind me. We can't stay here, it isn't safe," Gran said and held out a hand.

Lillian wiped her palms on her thighs and scrambled up behind Gran.

The elk bounded away from the direction the gargoyle had taken. Closing her eyes, Lillian sought the peaceful darkness and embraced the magic that let her 'feel' the gargoyle. A faint, blurry image appeared on the back of her closed eyelids. He ran through the shadows of the forest, his movements as nimble and deadly as if he hunted under the bright light of day.

CHAPTER SEVENTEEN

$\mathcal{W}$hen deadfall blocked the trail, Gregory bounded over it without slowing. Dirt and leaf litter scattered under his feet as he ran. At first, there was only the Hunt, and then Lillian linked with him, following his progress from a safer distance. She remembered that much. Pride swelled in his heart. The emotion caused him to lengthen his stride until he was flying over the ground without leaving the earth.

Battle sounded ahead.

Cries of fear and grunts of pain drifted to him on the wind. The higher-pitched snarls of death hounds were easiest to make out, and there were far too many of them. Closer now, he heard the gurgle of a death's rattle. A moment later, the victim hit the ground with a solid smack. More sounds of death echoed through the forest.

A moonlit clearing broke the darkness of the surrounding trees, and he leaped from cover into the midst of the fight. Swiping at a death hound's exposed belly, he gutted the beast before it knew he was there. Talons, which had matured while he'd slept in stone, delivered quick death to his enemies, unlike the first time he'd fought the death hounds within the Battle Goddess's kingdom. This time, he wouldn't let anyone or anything harm Lillian.

He grabbed a beast with ginger-and-black-colored fur by the throat and gave it a savage twist. Claws raked at him, but he fought on—uncaring as long as he took out his enemies before they killed again. With a second twist, the hound's neck broke. Gregory dropped the limp weight and moved on to the next death hound.

There were several more of the beasts in the clearing, each with thick, black ruffs and varying earth-toned pelts. More arrived as he watched. They far outnumbered him, but he had a few other abilities now that he hadn't had when he was newly born. While his talons ravaged his next enemy, he released small shadow magic spells of death into its bloodstream. He circled his next opponent and dispatched it in short order.

One after another, death hounds dropped all around him. The few beasts agile enough to avoid his talons tucked their tails tight to their bodies and fled.

When no more hounds came for him, he surveyed his work. He was crusted with gore and dirt. But he was whole, unlike the broken bodies that lay scattered around, pale against the darker backdrop of blood. Some were death hounds, while others were fae he'd recently danced with.

No magic could aid them now.

Lillian's sorrow touched his thoughts, and when he wished each victim's soul a safe journey to the Spirit Realm, she joined him in silent prayer.

He was about to continue hunting for the escaped hounds when a spike of fear bled across their link and Lillian broke away. Before he could ascertain the nature of the danger, she was gone.

He roared in fear and challenge.

How had the death hounds gotten around him? He'd not detected anything near his lady's location. Frantic, he sought to reestablish the link. Panic had taken hold of her mind, and his magic slithered off her defensive mental shields without connecting. He leaped into motion, heading back the way he'd come. With each stride, he prayed to the Divine Ones he would not be too late.

CHAPTER EIGHTEEN

A man-shaped shadow blocked the path twenty feet ahead. Lillian, blinded by her grandmother's glowing quarterstaff, couldn't make out the man's features. It wasn't until Gran lowered her staff to point at the man's chest that Lillian recognized Alexander. She remembered Gregory saying some of her attackers had escaped. She'd assumed this vampire was dead since she'd injured him. But here he was—undead—and much recovered. He'd even grown his face back. Damn.

Two black-and-silver-furred dire wolves circled in front of Lillian and Gran, positioning themselves between the two women and the enemy. While they advanced on Alexander with heads low and white fangs gleaming, a wild-haired sidhe galloped his mount up and took flank. More of the Clan and Coven joined them, clustering together in a loose circle with staffs, swords, and arrows pointed at the surrounding forest.

"Name yourself," Gran challenged.

"His name's Alexander," Lillian whispered. Rage made her

voice strong, even as fear sparked to life in her blood. "He led the Riven who attacked me. He wants me dead."

"That's not entirely true," Alexander said with a shrug that stretched his suit across his shoulders. "In my defense, I said I wouldn't hurt you if you came with us, but my goodwill wouldn't last if you made me go through the stone ring. As I recall, you didn't obey."

"Go screw yourself." Lillian's fists clenched, aching for a weapon of some kind. Her crossbow or maybe one of Gran's swords. Then she'd see if he could grow his whole head back.

"How very original."

If not a sword, another rock with her blood on it would do.

The underbrush shivered behind the vampire.

Eight more of Alexander's henchmen materialized out of the forest.

Without taking her eyes from the enemy, Gran motioned for Lillian to lean closer and instructed in a low voice, "Stay with the elk. He'll try to keep you safe while we deal with this threat."

"But I can fight."

Gran shook her head, then tossed her leg over the elk's withers and slid to the ground.

"What are you doing?" Fear for her grandmother made Lillian's voice break.

"The elk will have a better chance if he's only carrying you. Don't worry about me." Gran pushed the hilt of a dagger into Lillian's hand.

Alexander chuckled. "How touching. Now, if you don't mind, I have somewhere I need to be shortly." He gestured to the shadows behind him, and more dark shapes eased out of the forest. "Bring the girl. Kill the rest."

At Alexander's words, one of the intruders started shedding his clothes. He dropped to all fours and fur burst from his skin with the sound of wet sand hitting the ground. In the time it took to blink, a massive dire wolf took his place. The shaggy black monster lunged at Gran in a blur of speed.

Gran whipped her staff around. Light raced up its length and launched from the end with a high-pitched screech. It collided with the enemy dire wolf while he was in mid-leap. Magic tossed him back against a tree trunk fifteen feet away. He fell to the ground, unmoving. Gran leveled her staff at another dire wolf.

Underbrush and saplings quaked violently as the forest erupted into chaos.

A dozen wolf-creatures raced out of the woods toward the smaller circle of defenders. The screams and grunts of battle echoed all around them. Lillian clung to the elk's neck as he lunged sideways, away from snapping teeth. But there was no escape. They were surrounded, trapped with the rest of the defenders, forced into an ever-shrinking pocket of space.

The elk danced in place, then bellowed a challenge and kicked out at an enemy. His hoof smashed into an enemy dire wolf's skull with the dull crack of bone. He struck out with his deadly hooves again. Several enemies met death under his brutal defense, but more than once, he was too slow to prevent a bite. Blood now showed dark against his white coat.

The last of the enemy dire wolves crashed to the ground as a willowy sidhe woman, accompanied by a massive waist-high hound, took up the fight. The woman cried out a guttural order to her hound. The beast turned silver eyes upon Lillian. It leaped to attack, crossing the distance too swiftly. Its long, narrow head snaked out and snapped steel-gray teeth at Lillian.

Hot breath and saliva washed over her exposed arm. But there was no pain or the sensation of tearing flesh.

The beast dropped to the ground, leaving Lillian and the elk untouched. It sat on its haunches and gazed up at Lillian with a look of confusion. The hound gave a little shiver, ruffling its ginger-frosted black fur.

"Bring down!" The sidhe woman screamed at the beast, giving it hand signals as well as verbal commands.

Again, the beast lunged at Lillian but twisted away at the last minute and returned to its crouched position.

"Bring down." The sidhe gestured frantically now. "Bring down!"

The beast snorted and shook its head, its long neck twisting to snap at its own shoulder. Then it dipped its muzzle nearly to the ground and clawed at the back of its head. Something small and white glimmered at the base of the skull. The creature didn't hold still long enough for Lillian to see it clearly, but she thought it might be a giant pearl or sliver of crystal.

"Stop!" The woman screamed commands at the creature.

With an agonized snarl, it stopped digging at its own flesh and darted off into the underbrush, ignoring the woman's calls for it to return.

"You might try obedience school next time," Lillian said as she gripped her dagger tighter.

The strange woman whirled back around. Clutched in her hands, two daggers flashed silver against the darkness. She attacked. Brutal, graceful, and fast—her long hair flowing out behind her—she covered the distance in a moment. One flash of silver vanished under the elk's belly. His bellow of pain was cut short by a second violent stab. The elk took another stumbling stride as the woman danced out of his way. Lillian couldn't explain it, but she'd felt the woman's knife sever the elk's soul from his body.

Lillian glimpsed another flash of silver and pain erupted in her shoulder. The weight and power of the strike toppled her off the back of the elk. Breath exploded from her lungs when she smashed into the ground. Shoulder screaming of abuse, she rolled to her side in time to see the woman leaping on her from above. Lillian twisted in the opposite direction and surged to her feet.

The woman stared at the knife in her hand with a perplexed frown, then back at Lillian. "Why are you not dead?" she asked as she advanced on Lillian again.

"No idea."

"She should be dead. Why isn't she?"

Lillian glanced around for a second opponent but realized the stranger was looking down at the blade in her hand, talking to the knife like it was sentient. After a moment, the woman's expression darkened, and she looked up at Lillian with a snarl.

"If the demon blade won't kill you, I'll deal with you myself." The stranger surged forward with a burst of speed.

Ancient instincts reared up within Lillian, and she used her enemy's momentum to slam her head into a tree trunk. While the woman was dazed, a Clan dire wolf leaped at her. The two opponents tumbled off into the underbrush.

Lillian's body ached and her lungs burned, but she maintained her footing, scanning the immediate area and the forest beyond for the next attack. The twang of a bowstring reached her ears too late.

Agony ripped a path through the muscle of her right arm. She screamed and pressed her hand over the wound.

An archer stood off to one side, partially hidden by night. He raised his bow a second time, but a silver-haired sidhe appeared between them, and with the flick of his wrist, he sent a small knife flying at the archer. The bit of silver embedded itself in the archer's neck. Another enemy fell. The leader of the Hunt gave Lillian a slight nod and then turned to his next opponent.

With a hiss, Lillian probed her new injury. This one was just a graze, a non-threatening flesh wound unless they poisoned their arrowheads.

A snap of a twig told her she'd have to worry about her injuries later.

While Lillian had been distracted by the archer and the Huntsman, the sidhe woman had finished off her dire wolf opponent and was advancing again.

"Well, aren't you a determined bitch," Lillian mumbled with a bravado she wasn't feeling. Fear was eating away at her strength, adrenaline made her muscles shake and her heart pound. She felt lightheaded. Where was Gregory? Please let him still live.

The Otherness within Lillian's soul, the same being to first whisper the words to claim and awaken Gregory, awoke for the second time. It looked out through her eyes, taking in the scene with a calm, cold center Lillian lacked. It reached out to touch Gregory's thoughts. He still lived.

Lillian wanted to cry with relief, but her joy was short lived. The power gripped her mind harder. This wasn't like earlier at the dance, this was primal, all-encompassing power. It wasn't asking for control, it was demanding.

Had there been another way, Lillian would have fought the power rising within, fearing it more than the enemies she now faced. But more than her life was at risk. Her family needed her. Gregory needed her.

Lillian surrendered control of her body to that Otherness.

An arrow embedded in a nearby tree trunk caught her dark power's attention. Lillian backed toward the tree.

The sidhe advanced, her daggers poised to strike. Lillian waited with her head bowed, her injured shoulder pressed against the arrow still embedded in the tree. When the sidhe lunged forward, Lillian yanked the arrow free and coated the arrowhead with the blood running down her arm in one smooth motion.

Her free hand snaked out and grasped the sidhe by the throat.

Surprise widened pale blue eyes. Lillian gave her opponent a gentle smile as she reversed her grip on the shaft and jabbed the arrowhead into the woman's eye. The stranger screamed and clawed at her face, trying to dislodge the smoking shaft. Lillian shoved the arrow deeper, then sidestepped as the woman shuddered and fell forward. After twitching twice more, the sidhe went limp. Lillian leaned down and tugged on the arrow. It grated against the eye socket before coming free.

Immediate danger over, the power released Lillian from its grip. She gasped for breath and fought against the urge to retch her guts out. There was still danger. Her family needed her. With that thought firmly in her mind, she left the shelter of the tree.

Staying low to the ground, Lillian crawled to where an

unmoving lump of white glowed palely in the moonlight. The elk's shimmer was fading in death.

She hunched next to the body and scanned the area nearby, praying she'd find her grandmother alive. But there was no sign of Vivian.

Battle still raged between the trees. Pairs of dire wolves fought to the death, and a dozen or more Riven jumped from tree to tree, dropping down upon the sidhe Huntsman and his three remaining companions.

Coppery blood-scent and the stink of burnt flesh choked her. She fought the urge to gag and forced herself to focus on the dense shadows surrounding her as a new threat wormed its way into her mind. All the muscles running along her back tensed. Glancing over her shoulder, she caught movement darting between the tree trunks. Alexander broke free of cover and sprinted toward her, his expression wild, driven mad by rage or blood lust. Three other Riven trailed a few paces behind.

He jumped into the air, an impossible leap but never made it to her position. A darker shape collided with Alexander, slamming him into nearby undergrowth.

"Gregory!" Lillian screamed. The primal power of the Otherness awoke within her again.

Shrubs shook and snapped. The crunch of twigs and the smack of flesh on flesh dwindled into the distance as the gargoyle's momentum carried the fighters deeper into the forest.

The other Riven ignored her, swarming after Gregory to overwhelm him with greater numbers.

Rage and power boiled up within her, and she felt the taint of vampire a moment before she touched their thoughts.

They planned to kill her gargoyle and then come back and finish off those still living.

No one harmed her gargoyle.

She sprang after them, rewetting her arrow with the fresh blood oozing down her arm as she ran. The deep shoulder wound still felt numb. It would awaken soon enough, but for now, adrenaline drove her onward, her pains unnoticed. Her thoughts galvanized into one purpose: kill Alexander, kill the other vampires before they murdered her gargoyle.

Gregory had died too many times protecting her.

Not again.

Rage gave her strength, and she ran, unheeding of her grandmother's calls for her to return.

CHAPTER NINETEEN

*G*regory's mouth filled with the foul taint of Riven blood and a darker power, but he didn't release his hold on the monster underneath him. The dead carcass was half his size, but true demonic magic gave the unnatural beast strength. Fear solidified within Gregory's soul.

That darkness wanted Lillian.

He'd never let that happen.

Gregory flexed his talons, digging deeper into his opponent, searching for a weakness.

The Riven heaved up from the ground and Gregory fought for a stronger grip on the foul creature. More were closing in on him. He could hear the baying of death hounds as another pack approached from the west. Precious time was slipping by. He should have been able to kill this creature with ease, but demonic-aided shields wrapped the Riven in layers of protection he couldn't breach quickly.

Two more of the Riven rushed out of the forest and

landed on Gregory's back. He speared one with his tail blade. At least the two new arrivals weren't as strong as Alexander. Flexing his wings, Gregory dislodged the other but couldn't release Alexander to kill him. The beast continued to circle him, nipping at him like a mad little dog.

When the Riven came too close, he snapped his head up and caught him under the chin with one of his horns. Blood momentarily blinded him. Alexander continued to twist, managing to dislodge Gregory's talons every time he almost had a firm grip.

Minutes ticked by as they fought until the Riven's shields were frayed and blackened. Sluggish blood now oozed from hundreds of wounds, tinting his opponent's pale skin bruise-dark, but Alexander showed no signs of weakening.

Gregory heard at least three more Riven crashing through the forest, shattering the undergrowth in their frenzied madness. When they emerged into the clearing, the Riven didn't slow, only changing their headlong course to run at him. The first hit Gregory hard enough to knock him from Alexander. While he dispatched that one, a second grabbed a wing, its claws shredding the membrane. Gregory yowled and wacked the monster in the temple. It didn't slow the creature, and the male came at him again. He caught the beast, then wrapped his hand around its skull, and flexed his fingers.

The skull cracked and his talons sunk into soft tissue. Twitching death throes took it. He was turning to deal with its third companion when Alexander landed on his back. The vampire raised his hand to strike.

Something darker than the shadows of the night glimmered in his hand, eating all the light. Gregory blocked

Alexander's strike just as Lillian burst into the meadow, a pack of death hounds snapping at her heels.

Her expression was one of rage. Blinded by her fear for him, she wasn't using her other senses. His lady didn't see the death hounds.

"Lillian! Behind you!"

Alexander struck with the blade a second time. The dagger found an opening and sunk into the flesh just below where his wings grew from his back. Shocking pain crippled one wing and then the wound turned ice-cold as the blade started feeding.

CHAPTER TWENTY

*F*our massive hound-like beasts crashed through the forest in pursuit of Lillian, but she didn't fear them. The death hounds fell in beside her. She knew them from a blurred and long-ago memory. They were hers to command. A gift from the Lady of Battles. How they had come to be enslaved by the Riven was a question for another time. She touched their minds and sent them to intercept another group of enemies approaching from the north. The beasts surged forward to do her bidding. With the new threat handled, all her focus was for the two Riven still attacking her gargoyle.

Instinct told her Alexander was the real threat—the first of his kind created here in this realm. She sprinted toward him, but before she could reach him, he raised his hand and plunged a blade into Gregory's back. Her gargoyle bellowed, twisting and clawing, unable to reach the knife. In his struggle, Gregory knocked the Riven from his back. Alexander flipped through the air, hit the ground, and rolled once. Then he lay still, face down.

Unmoving.

Easy prey. Her savage, rage-filled magic whispered into her mind. Whatever demonic power had given Alexander incredible strength was exhausted. *Kill him now*, her Otherself urged.

But greater need drew Lillian's senses to her gargoyle. Through their link, she sensed his waning power. He was dying, his life force draining away through the blade.

Alexander rose to his feet, his usual grace hampered by his injuries.

Rage uncoiled in her stomach, and two-inch-long claws emerged from her fingertips. A ruthless need flooded Lillian's mind. The monster would die for what he'd done to her gargoyle.

Power continued to expand like a long-dormant flower unfurling its petals. Her forehead burned, as did the area between her shoulder blades. But a sweet, musky scent filled her nose, distracting her from the pressure building beneath her skin.

She advanced toward Gregory and the Riven, and then studied the undead monster.

"I remember you." Her voice came out in a harsh, grating tone. "You were called Alexander."

She returned his cold smile and rushed him. His haughty expression changed to one of shock as she sank her claws into his gut. She shoved with all her newfound strength, and her hand jammed up into his chest cavity, claws digging until she found his heart. The shriveled organ pulsed with murky magic, anchoring the tainted soul in the world of the living long past its natural time.

With the sharp sound of cracking ribs, she pulled the heart from his chest. She then called a small trickle of magic and closed her hand upon the heart. After a moment, dust poured between her fingers. Alexander slumped to the ground, shock frozen on his face even in final death.

Energy coursed within her, accompanied by a newly born strength. Delicious joy spread through her veins like the finest wine as the power built. Here was immense magic fit to slay all her enemies. She would make certain her gargoyle and family were safe.

Starting with the Riven, she would demonstrate what happened to those who stood against her.

"My lady, you must fight it." Gregory's voice shook with exhaustion, but he continued. "Do not give in to mindless rage. Fight the evil in your own soul, or you will become what you plan to hunt down and destroy."

His words cut through her intoxicating magic. The rage that had fueled it melted away.

Scattered thoughts rallied around the sound of Gregory's voice, and the fog surrounding her mind cleared. She blinked and shook her head, trying to remember what had occurred. How had she gotten here? Then she focused on the gargoyle and nothing else mattered.

Moving impossibly fast, she glided over the earth and knelt by his side. She cradled his head while she surveyed the damage. A wing, shredded and collapsed over his side, hid what she sought. Gently, she pushed his injured wing out of her way and exposed the offending object. Though she must be causing him immense pain, Gregory remained docile under her hands.

Now she could see the wound clearly. A ridge of stone spread out around the dagger. After she urged Gregory onto his stomach, she laid two fingers on either side of the blade. Even without touching the metal, its evil burned cold against her skin. With her free hand, she stroked Gregory's muzzle and whispered nonsense to him.

His skin quivered at her touch.

"Easy," she whispered as she closed her eyes and rested her cheek against his back.

Breath still hissed between his lips, rapid and panting. The throb of his great heart slowed. Touching him, his thoughts flowed to her.

He would turn to stone, try to heal, but it was doubtful if he would ever wake again in this Realm. He couldn't heal in time to save her. The ones of darkness would hunt her down and either kill her or use her.

The gargoyle's despair swamped Lillian.

"Easy, big fellow. You're not dead yet, nor am I." She grasped the dagger's hilt and pulled. The blade didn't come free. She applied more pressure while she braced a hand against his back. Gregory grunted, but the blade refused to shift.

Magic uncurled within her blood and flowed into her mind. She paused at the foreign sensation of her magic whispering knowledge into her mind, and then, after a moment of hesitation, she listened without question.

Narrowing her eyes, she turned her thoughts to the blade. There was a sense of presence, a self-awareness to it.

"I know what you are. If you don't stop feeding and

release my gargoyle, I will consume you." She pushed her thoughts ahead of her as she leaned down to glare at the blade, forcing it to listen and become aware of her and the danger she represented. "If my gargoyle dies, I'll destroy you. I'll take you apart until your soul is bare before me. Then I will torture you. When I am finished, I shall remake you and drive you into the hearts of your masters. This I promise."

The demon blade shivered and leaped free of Gregory's flesh. It embedded its tip three inches into the ground next to her. The dagger vibrated for several seconds before it stilled.

She paid the blade no more mind. Instead, she pressed her hand against the wound. For now, there was nothing she could do for his physical injuries, but she sensed the greatest danger was his lack of magic. He'd been bled out magically. She hadn't a clue what she was doing, but her magic stirred again, calming and guiding her panicked thoughts as it sorted through her memories.

Clear as if she heard the tale anew, she remembered the story of how the dryad queen had saved the gargoyle after he'd been wounded by demons. The queen had healed the gargoyle by sharing her magic through blood. And after Lillian and her hamadryad had been injured that day in the grove, Gregory had healed her, but he hadn't said how at the time. Now she thought she knew. He'd shared blood with her. If Gregory's blood could heal her, then it stood to reason hers might restore him. And tonight, she was full to brimming with magic. It still churned below her skin, calling for her to release it.

"You can save him," it whispered.

If her magic-laced blood were the best chance she had to save her gargoyle, she would give as much as required.

Dabbing at her bloody wound, she winced. Her fingers came away bright red. When she held them up to his mouth, his nostrils quivered, but he didn't go for the bait. Instead, he turned his muzzle away as he curled tighter into himself.

"We can't. It's forbidden," he said into her mind, his mental touch feeling much weaker to her.

"Forbidden?" She snorted. "I don't care as long as it will heal you." Rocking back and forth with his head in her lap, she tightened her grip on his muzzle and guided his nose to the wound on her arm. He was too weak to fight her, but he wouldn't lick at the blood running down her arm either. Well, she wasn't going to take no for an answer. She stuck her fingers in his mouth. "Take a little taste. That's it. Just a bit more."

As she'd hoped, he wasn't able to resist, and his tongue lapped at her bloody fingers. Growing stronger, he sucked on them and then sniffed his way up her arm. He pushed the torn fabric of her sleeve aside and licked at her wound to clean it. Her magic rushed from her into him, draining her. But she didn't care. She'd do anything to save her gargoyle.

As more and more of her power spilled into him, her mind became foggy. She drifted for a time.

Gran and the other surviving members of the Hunt found her there, holding the gargoyle's head in her lap as she fed him her magic. Gran's expression was a strange mix of fear and relief. Instinct told Lillian to keep what had happened a secret until she understood what was going on. So, she didn't tell them about the death hounds... or other things.

What other things? She asked herself as she scrambled a moment for an answer. None came. Her memories were unclear, chaotic, and sprinkled with holes.

The Riven's blade still glittered darkly beside her. There was something important she should remember about that, too. As with her other memories, it was like someone had come in and stolen them while she'd healed her gargoyle.

More of the Hunt arrived as the minutes slid past. Sable and Russet entered the clearing. Seeing the downed gargoyle, they hurried to Lillian's side. Sable offered to share some blood with the gargoyle to help him heal. Lillian nodded, and let each of the dryads share blood and magic with Gregory.

When he started to stir awake, she leaned down and made a show of kissing him on his broad forehead, and then made eye contact with each of the dryads in case they didn't understand her claim.

CHAPTER TWENTY-ONE

$\mathcal{T}$he wait for Gran's pickup was worse than Lillian imagined. Sitting helpless and cursing the Riven did nothing for Gregory, but at least it made her feel better knowing she was going to do them harm. The power which had reared up within her soul was receding, but it wasn't gone. She could still feel the potential as it simmered below the surface.

Gregory reclined on his haunches, his legs folded under him and his wings limp at his sides. Even though he lay quiet, with his head resting on her lap and his eyes closed, he wasn't asleep. His ears twitched at every sound, on the alert for danger even in his weakened state.

Lillian blamed herself for his injuries. Had she not distracted the gargoyle, he might have defeated Alexander without getting injured himself. She looked up while she continued to stroke Gregory's mane. More members of the Hunt had arrived and now stood guard at the edge of the clearing.

Gregory huffed out a loud expulsion of air in a very horse-like fashion. He lifted his head, and his ears swiveled forward.

The rumble of her grandmother's truck reached her ears a moment before its headlights cut through the clearing. Blinded, Lillian shielded her eyes with one hand until her vision adjusted. Stiff muscles complained about the cold, damp ground when she stood.

The truck skidded to a halt next to her. Lillian lowered the tailgate, and then turned to help Gregory. He was already on his feet and making his way to the truck. He moved like a joint-sore old man on a rainy day, but he doggedly limped his way over and heaved himself into the truck bed. Lillian winced at how much that leap had to have hurt him. She climbed up after, being as careful as possible so as not to jar him any more than could be helped.

There was precious little spare room in the back of the truck, and Lillian settled cross-legged in one corner, braced her back against the cab, then patted her lap. Gregory lowered his head, cautious of his horns. With a sigh, he closed his eyes again.

The ride back took twice as long, but thanks to Gran's driving, they were saved from the worst of the potholes. Lillian thought she might cry from happiness when the truck turned into their driveway. Soon she and Gran could tend Gregory's wounds. While the deep knife wound was the most worrisome, she didn't like the raw-hamburger look of his shredded wing. God, he might never fly again.

As the truck rolled to a stop, Jason appeared and opened the tailgate. Gregory sighed and gathered himself. His legs shook with each step, and she wanted to help, but there was nothing she could do for him. Instead, she shadowed him, encouraging him along as best she could.

Gran hurried ahead of them and vanished into the house. Lillian stayed by Gregory's side while he made his painful way up the back steps, through the kitchen, and into the living room. She would have stopped there, but the gargoyle limped on up the stairs. Lillian followed him until he collapsed next to her bed.

An array of first aid supplies were already laid out in orderly rows at the foot of her bed. Gran held a plastic squeeze-bottle of sterile saline in one hand and was reaching for a roll of cotton when Lillian came alongside. "How can I help?"

"Blankets to keep him warm and something to rest his head on."

Lillian nodded and hurried to grab a pillow off the bed. She placed it under his head with gentle care and then went in search of clean blankets. When she came back, Gran was already cleaning some of Gregory's wounds.

The older woman mumbled to herself as she probed the wound at the base of his wing joint and then examined the rips in his wing. "I think our gargoyle got banged up right and good, but he should recover." She patted Gregory on his shoulder and smiled. "Besides, you're too stubborn to stay wounded for long. Too much evil out there that needs killing, if I know you."

Gregory snorted, but his laugh turned into a grunt of pain.

"Easy there," Gran said. "Cleaning your wounds will hurt. A lot. And I don't want to risk giving you something for the pain that might cause a reaction. You ready?"

Gregory nodded in agreement while Lillian shook her head. No, she wasn't ready to see her gargoyle in pain again. She still couldn't banish the image of him twisting, writhing in agony, unable to reach the dagger embedded in his back. Nausea rolled through her stomach in a hot wave. She ignored it and placed her hands on either side of his head.

At the contact of skin on skin, she linked with him like he had when she was showing him her language that first day. Pain. He ached everywhere. But his lady's small, cool hands soothed his throbbing headache, and her scent calmed him. If he had to be injured, this was the best he could ask for. Though he shouldn't have allowed himself to be beaten so severely. Embarrassment tainted the link.

Lillian broke away from their mental link. "Oh, Gregory. It's not your fault. I didn't listen to you. My foolish wish to fight by your side could have cost you your life. I'm so sorry."

"Not your fault," he whispered. His words were cut short by a hiss of pain when Gran syringed saline into the knife wound.

Lillian held him and shared in his pain as Gran worked. Time dragged by.

When finished, Gran ordered one of the hovering dryads to bring water and then make broth for Gregory. Lillian's world narrowed down to her injured gargoyle. She didn't know what to call him. Friend. Ally. Protector. He was every-thing to her, and that scared her.

When Sable came with the bowl of water, Lillian took it from her and tipped it to Gregory's muzzle so he could drink without straining himself. He lapped thirstily. She worried he would make himself sick, but he finished the bowl, rolled onto his side, and fell asleep on her carpet without any ill effects. She knew so little about him. That would change as soon as he was well.

CHAPTER TWENTY-TWO

*N*ight advanced toward dawn. Everyone else had sought their beds long before, and now the house was quiet. Lillian sat on the floor next to Gregory with her back braced against the foot of her bed. They would have moved him, but no one wanted to risk waking the gargoyle. She smoothed her smaller hand over his and admired the finger-length talons. Yep, disturbing a sleeping gargoyle could be bad for one's health.

They had left him on the ground and covered him in blankets.

Since it hadn't seemed right sleeping in a bed when he was curled on the floor, Lillian sat with him. By chance, she witnessed the oddest thing.

He was healing.

She could see his flesh knitting together until the shallowest of his injuries looked like old scars, and the worst of the damage—the knife wound and his shredded wing—seemed at least two weeks old. Whether he healed because it was a gargoyle's nature to recover quickly, or he mended faster than usual because she kept in physical contact and shared energy with him, she didn't know, but she was ecstatic at the signs of his recovery.

Now that she knew with both heart and mind that he was on the mend, other things started to encroach upon her consciousness. She stank. For the second time in as many days, gore coated her skin, and her hair was matted in rotting Riven blood and other nasty substances she didn't want to think about.

She left the gargoyle asleep on the floor and made her way over to her bathroom, shedding the remains of her leather outfit as she went. She adjusted both showerheads for complete annihilation and cranked the water as hot as she could stand. Then she stood and let the steaming water soak the crud from her body. Touching it or fouling a sponge with the crap just seemed wrong. When the water ran clear, she slathered herself in soap.

She was on her hair's third shampooing when she noticed a big, black shadow waiting on the other side of the shower's glass partition. She twitched and bit back her scream—well, mostly. A tiny yelp escaped before she locked her jaws. Then she just stood there, frozen, muscles tensed, her pulse racing, fear and embarrassment battling for dominance within her.

Hell in a handbasket! He'd nearly scared her half to death.

She was still shaking in reaction when their gazes met and locked together.

Then, even without the touch of skin on skin, his thoughts flowed to her, broadcasting both his overwhelming regret that he had scared her, but also his need to be near her, eager for the solace he felt in her presence.

He needed her. His Sorceress—his oldest confidant and companion. His other half. He needed this simple, innocent intimacy. It wasn't sexual for him. It was something else, something deeper.

Lillian did not fully understand, but as her initial fear melted away, replaced by mellow warmth and a deep unquestioning trust, she decided she didn't need to understand this. She just needed to accept their special link for their wellbeing.

Knowing that her overprotective guardian would never harm her lent her a sense of confidence she hadn't expected. Her lips curved at the corners as he continued to wait in his silent, demanding way for her to make up her mind.

She opened the first glass partition, pushing it back until it clicked softly against the wall. It was the only sound in the room beside the splash of water. Gregory waited silently while she opened the other side.

Another shy smile curved her lips. "When Gran renovated the master bath to include the biggest walk-in shower I'd ever seen, I thought its sheer size was obscene. Somehow it doesn't seem so big now."

Her mind must have snapped and gone to a different place where modesty no longer existed. Was she going to be insanely embarrassed about this in the morning? Probably. Did she care about that now? No. Not in the least. Not when her gargoyle needed comfort so desperately that she could sense it without touching him.

Lillian moved as close to her showerhead as she could, and he still had to squeeze in order to fit. He didn't complain. Getting rid of rotten vampire blood must be a high priority for him, too. She smiled. He didn't even crowd her very much.

"This should be awkward," she said as she applied her soapy sponge to his back. "Embarrassing. Blush-inducing. But it's not. Why? Is... is this love?"

Several seconds slid by without an answer.

Since he never said much, his silence didn't upset her. She shook her head and switched to washing a gore-splattered wing. He flexed it so she could better reach the dirt. A slow grin spread across her face at the ease with which they fell into a routine. Being with him felt as natural as brushing her hair.

"No."

When her mind absorbed his belated answer, it felt like a kick in the gut.

"No?" she prompted and continued to scrub the membrane between the stout bones so he wouldn't know how much that one word hurt. Or how foolish she now felt.

He paused for a long moment. Then words poured from him. "Love is the mingling of souls. A powerful emotion. And if we were like any normal souls, then yes, love would be a good word for what we share. Yet we are different. We share one spirit—a single soul between us. Like the Divine Ones, who were once one entity who chose to split into the Mother and the Father to better understand itself, we are one being in the Spirit Realm, but two outside of that place. What we share, that eternal link, is more profound than mortal love."

His words were shocking but also like balm to her wounds. What he said should have been outlandish—and it was—but his words fit. She more than loved him. He was a part of her. Her other self. They had known each other for an eternity. She now knew the reason she'd been drawn to him even while he'd slept in stone. Smiling, she soaped up his mane.

"Gregory."

"Yes?"

He sounded hesitant, almost fearful, and her heart turned over in her chest, expanding with emotion at his vulnerability. Poor thing. He was as lost as she in this world. "I don't fully understand it. I've only known you two days, but you mean so much to me." She was going to say more. She needed to say more, but the words wouldn't come.

He sighed, the contented sound rumbling over the noise of the water. "You are my world, my reason for existing. I will do all in my power to keep you safe."

"And I'll try not to make your task any harder than it already is." She ran the sponge down his back while he ducked under the showerhead and rinsed the soap from his mane. When he came back up for air, she had a bottle of conditioner at the ready. His doubtful expression told her she was walking on thin ice, putting lily-of-the-valley-scented girl products on his hair. "It will make the tangles come out easier. Trust me, when I'm yanking a comb through it, you'll appreciate this."

He sighed again but let her continue. With the dirt and gore washed away, and his hair clean and tangle free, she surveyed her work. It was the most natural thing in the world to reach under his wings and fold her arms around his waist as far as she could reach.

The skin of his back was warm and slick. His wings shifted, trapping her between them. The scent of forest and male enfolded her in a blanket as soothing as his silky wing membranes.

Seeing the pale line from the knife wound, she stretched up onto her toes and kissed the scar. "That we share one soul explains so much. You are a part of me. At first, I was terrified by the link between us, thinking it was an enchantment or our power drawing us together. Later, I thought it was the awareness the dryads spoke of. And I very much wanted whatever was between us to be more than just a chemical reaction. I wanted something deeper, more meaningful... because it already was for me."

There, she'd spilled her heart. She waited with her eyes closed, barely daring to breathe.

"Each lifetime, it has always been so for me, as well."

She sighed with contentment.

Just standing there, holding him, made her mindlessly happy. When she was with him, she felt complete. Now she knew why. They shared one soul.

She nuzzled that area where his wings attached.

His skin was warm, his scent indescribably wild and male.

Gregory shifted, a rumbling purring sound escaped him as he turned in her arms.

After that deep purr subsided, only the sound of running water reached her ears. He said nothing as he stared down at her. When the silence between them became awkward, she peeked through her lashes. He was watching her with intense heat. There was nothing platonic in that look. She couldn't hold his gaze and glanced down.

Oh... he was... oh my.

What was she doing?

Still, her gaze lingered a moment longer, until she forced her head up and looked off to one side. She cleared her throat. "I should... go towel-dry my hair. You... uh. You can finish up in here." The long-absent blush returned with a vengeance, and she bolted from the shower. She tripped in her rush but caught herself against the sink. The door of the vanity slipped out of her hand with a bang. She tore it open again. When she tried to get a towel, the stupid thing pulled several of its friends along with it. She left the mess on the floor and scooped up two before she fled to her bedroom.

CHAPTER TWENTY-THREE

By the time Gregory exited the bathroom, Lillian was clothed in a floor-length nightgown and housecoat, her hair dry, with the blow-dryer cooling on her nightstand, but she still didn't have her emotions under control. They were an unruly riot she didn't know how to sort out. While she brushed her tangle-free hair, she watched him out of the corner of her eye. When he hesitated, she gestured for him to come closer. He still didn't move.

"Gregory, come and sit. We need to talk."

Without a word, he came to stand before her, head bowed.

She cleared her throat. "About earlier, I owe you an—"

"I did not mean to frighten you," he cut in.

"You didn't frighten me."

"You ran."

"I wasn't afraid."

His brow furrowed. "Yet you ran away."

Lillian sighed. Damn, he was like a bloodhound with a scent. "Yes, I did. And I'm sorry. I was surprised and mishandled it. I'm an idiot. Give me an honest threat, and I'm game for battle, but toss me into an embarrassing situation, and I turn tail and run, every time. Not something I'm proud of, and I'm sorry." She reached for his hand and pulled him down to sit on the bed next to her.

"I'm glad you were not afraid," he rumbled.

With a smile, she began to pull the brush through his mane. He turned to give her better access. In the end, she sat on her haunches behind him. She was working up the nerve to ask him one question that burned brighter than the rest when he turned and looked at her with dark eyes full of knowledge. She was touching him. Of course he already knew what she was going to ask. She folded her hands in her lap and prayed for composure. The question lodged in her throat and didn't want to come free. After three more tries, she got her voice working.

"Do you want... I mean... clearly, you're mature... with needs." Lillian winced at her word choice and had a sudden urge to whack her head against a wall.

"What occurred earlier isn't something I'd normally let happen," he explained. "My control is usually better, but after all that ensued tonight, the power of the dance riding us, then you feeding me blood—both acts are very similar to courtship, and I reacted."

Lillian sobered at his words, her reaction far closer to disappointment than relief. He wasn't actually interested in her. She was just a warm, willing body, and she'd been all over him—literally. What a mess. She scrambled for something to say to him, something to throw him off track so he wouldn't know how his words hurt.

"What I'm trying to say is... if you want to spend time with one of the dryads, go ahead. You seem to think you need to guard me every waking moment, but you should take some personal time, too."

"Personal time?"

She didn't dare look up at him. "If you want to take one of the dryads as your lover, you should."

Another long silence followed. She started to worry at her robe tie.

"There is one I want." He said the words like they were dragged from his soul.

"Then go to her and find what solace you can. You have my blessing." The lie tasted bitter on her tongue, but it was better than shackling him with the truth. He was so loyal; he'd forgo his own needs if he thought it would make her unhappy. In this case, a small lie served the greater good— even if it was gnawing at her heart hard enough to dampen her eyes. "Go, be with your chosen one."

"I already am, silly dryad. How can you not know that? You've felt the depth of our link." He shifted. The bed rocked as he moved. Coffee-dark eyes bored into hers a second before he embraced her, drawing her against his chest. He hid his muzzle in her hair and drew on power.

Eyes closed, she shivered at the delicious sensation. There was a moment of great heat, and the world shifted around her. When she opened her eyes, she was lying on her back with him sprawled over her.

Gregory, now in human form, leaned toward her, a look of tenderness on his face. She turned her head at the last moment, and he landed a kiss on her jaw instead of her lips. His miss didn't seem to upset him, and he nuzzled her neck, inhaling her scent. Warm fingers stroked her breastbone. "You are the one thing that both calms and arouses me, my greatest and most forbidden desire."

Panic slammed her heart against her ribcage. He had said 'forbidden,' hadn't he? She needed some answers. It was hard to think with him nuzzling his way along her neck and his nimble fingers working loose the tiny row of buttons running down the front of her nightgown. He was entirely too distracting, but she gathered her thoughts. "What's forbidden, and why?"

He jerked like her words were a bucket of cold water.

"This." His expression turned sober. A moment later he jumped from the bed and began to pace around the room. "I..." He let the sentence die as shadows thickened, hiding him.

"No. Don't go. Please, answer my question. What's forbidden?"

"My love for you—my desire—it is forbidden." His disembodied voice floated to her from a different corner of the room. Even invisible, he still paced back and forth.

Times like this made her wish she could go invisible, too. But now she needed answers. "Go on, I'm listening."

"I haven't told you everything. I should have, but I was afraid." His voice shook, and she could hear the torment within his rumbling tones.

"Gregory, I know you withheld information when you said we shared one spirit. That very confession tells me there has to be more that you haven't told me, so much more." Lillian stood and walked in the direction she'd last heard his voice.

"And I'm not so naive that I don't see how much it hurts you to keep things from me. Talk to me. I promise I'll try to understand, and even if I don't understand it all, I'll still accept it and you."

He continued to pace, his feet padding softly against the carpet. His voice now came to her from near the bathroom door. "We are the Avatars of the Divine Ones."

He said it like those eight words explained everything.

A smile tugged at her lips. While he might not be the most forthcoming of creatures, at least she'd pinpointed where he stood. "You're going to need to explain what that means."

"As their Avatars, we can wield their power. That same power always wishes to reunite and create, but we are forbidden to join outside of the Spirit Realm, for it is too dangerous. Any child we birthed would be more god than flesh."

"I can see how that could be a problem." The scent of gargoyle was stronger in the northeast corner of the room.

"Duty was enough for us in the beginning. But over the eons, each time we were reborn, we came to crave a closer link, like what we share in the Spirit Realm. More so than we had any right, we encouraged each other to deeper love. While the Divine Ones forbid us to mate with each other, we sometimes found orphaned younglings to raise. Or one of us would seek a mate elsewhere and bring the child back. Over the last few lifetimes, we couldn't even do that because something had changed." He paused.

With her hand outstretched before her, she encountered his warm skin before she could see him. After a moment, the shadows hiding him receded and she found him still in human form, standing with his back braced against the wall, eyes staring unseeing at the floor. The need to hold him, to comfort him in whatever way she could, had her moving closer. She embraced him before he could bolt again. Then with an arm around his waist, she urged him back toward the foot of the bed. "Talk to me."

He took a great, shuddering breath and pulled her against his side as they sat on the end of the bed. "Six lifetimes ago, I had chosen a gryphon mate and was guarding the young when you came and dramatically claimed all of them as yours. And then, five lifetimes ago, I nearly killed your mate. You were a dragon, as was your mate. If he'd been of a more fragile nature, he wouldn't have survived."

"I was a dragon?" Lillian interrupted. While she *did* want to learn about her past, she was more interested in distracting Gregory from his melancholy. "Guess that would make me bigger and stronger than you," she said with a lopsided grin.

"Superior size didn't offer your dragon mate much protection from my wrath."

Lillian's smile wilted. So much for a lighter mood. "We chose mates in an attempt to resist the deep love growing between us when we were flesh and blood, didn't we? But it didn't work, because jealousy got in the way."

"Yes, and after those two disastrous events, we wisely never tried again. We could do nothing but endure. If we weakened, even for a moment, and came together as lovers, it would lead to our deaths. The Divine Ones would have no option but to hunt us down. And there would be no rebirth this time."

She rested her elbows against her knees. "I'm so sorry Gregory. If I'd known, I'd have..." She paused when she realized she didn't know what she'd have done differently. She didn't remember who she had been. But in this lifetime, he was in pain, and she wanted to help, but if what he said was true, and she had no reason to doubt him, he could never be with the one he loved. She couldn't make the leap to picture herself as the Sorceress, his beloved. "I'm sorry."

"Why? You couldn't have changed anything."

"No, but if I were your Sorceress, then she'd understand and share in your pain. You wouldn't be so alone." Her throat tightened. She'd only known him a short while, but she was already certain Gregory was the noblest being she knew. If anyone deserved a bit of happiness, it was him. She wasn't the Sorceress he remembered, but perhaps she could still give him something he craved. Her fingers traced a line over the curve of his shoulder, down his arm and along the inside of his forearm.

"If I understand the restrictions correctly, it isn't that we must remain chaste. Instead, we must ensure we never have a child together." She caressed his side, and he shivered at her touch. The contrast of warm, soft skin over hard muscle stirred a great many longings. If there were any justice in the world, she would be free to give him what she sensed he most wanted—the love of his Sorceress and a child by her. But if that was forever denied him, perhaps she could give him something more than a few forbidden kisses. And if she was honest with herself, she'd wanted him since she'd first sensed the tenderness within his soul, wanted to touch him, to hold him within the protection of her arms while he was vulnerable.

He rumbled something indecipherable in her ear and then sat stiffly beside her.

Oh, he had picked up on her thoughts. Her cheeks warmed.

"Gregory, I'm not familiar with the world you came from, but in my world, there are things I can do to ensure I don't get pregnant. There are protections we can use... or ways to share pleasure without the risk of a child. I mean, if we both decide that is the path we wish to take... once we get to know each other a little better." She paused and glanced up to his face, knowing her own was burning a bright red.

"Protection?" In human form, his astonishment was all too easy to read by the way one eyebrow arched nearly to his hairline. His expression made her blush hotter. Unable to maintain his gaze, she ducked her head.

"Yes," she cleared her throat, "Please don't make me show you the visuals. Remember about awkward conversations—I might bolt."

"I doubt whatever your world has invented will work in this situation. We are Avatars, and as such, we carry the potential of creation within us. The two sides of our power yearn to be together and create. Nothing your world could possibly create could holdfast against that power."

He stroked the side of her jaw and on down the column of her throat to rest his palm between the swell of her breasts. His fingers feathered lightly against her skin. Her lids fluttered shut at the heat his touch aroused in her. Warm breath caressed her face a moment before his rumbling voice broke over her.

"If we tried to come together as lovers, our magic would ensure fertility—we must never give our powers that opportunity. It would be disastrous for this world and all others near it." He got up and began pacing again. Between one stride and the next, his human form vanished, and he was all gargoyle again.

Mortification burned hot in her soul. She plucked at her robe as she smoothed out the wrinkles, welcoming a distraction so she wouldn't have to look up at him until she had her hormones under control. She'd just tried to seduce her gargoyle—again.

Another thought occurred to her, and anger awoke. "How could the Divine Ones be so cruel?" She folded her arms across her chest. "And their rules are pure bullshit. We're not allowed to have a child because the child would be too powerful. Yet we're so fertile that birth control won't work. If we're not allowed to reproduce, why the hell not make us infertile? Or disinterested in sex? I don't understand why these Divine Ones would do this. Is our loyalty being tested or some shit like that? 'Cause if they reward their loyal servants with that kind of shit..."

"It's not like that," Gregory replied as he came to stand in front of her. "The Divine Ones only ask us to endure what they themselves endure. All of creation stretches out between them, and if they were to reunite, it would unmake all they have made. To overcome this problem, the great God and Goddess use our mortal bodies to bear their children. They infuse us with their power and spirit, then in a moment of fire and ecstasy, we die as the Divine Ones birth their newest child into the Realms."

"Holy shit! That's supposed to make me feel better about all this?"

"It's a great honor."

"Fire and death. Some honor."

Gregory sighed with annoyance and bumped her thigh

with his tail. "You only say that because you don't remember the pleasure..."

"Death..."

"A happy occurrence for us. Death only means that we return to the Spirit Realm and become one being once again. And we always carry the knowledge that we will be reborn again one day."

Lillian frowned. "How many times have these Divine Ones knocked us up?"

"Such disrespect." Gregory chuckled. It was the first sign of humor she'd seen from him all evening. When he had himself under control, he continued. "While our duties to the Divine Ones are many and varied, they have only honored us with their greatest gift twice in this present era, once for the Shieldbearer, and once for the twins, the Lord of the Underworld and the Lady of Battles."

"I'm sorry, Gregory. I'm not angry with you, and I promise I'll try to accept the whole Avatar thing. What you need is your Sorceress of old." Leaning forward, she wrapped her arms around his waist and pulled him closer so she could rest her cheek against his chest. She needed him to know she wasn't scared of him. "And now, for the first time, I've been born in the form of a dryad. That makes it a little more difficult for you, doesn't it?"

"Yes, but I don't care. I will fulfill my duty to the Divine Ones."

"Got any idea what that is this time around?"

"Hunt down evil."

"And?"

"Destroy it."

"You've certainly got a one-track mind. I mean, do you have any specifics?"

"No." He exhaled, then leaned in to sniff at her hair. "But I've found evil here, so I'm in the right place, for now. Once we've defeated these Riven, we can return home, destroy the blood witch, and learn what the Lady of Battles has been up to. Even imprisoned, she's been busy." He settled upon the bed next to her.

After a few moments, his muzzle dipped close to her neck. Before she could say anything, his warm tongue brushed under her ear. He pushed her robe off her shoulder as he nuzzled her, his eyes half-closed.

She wasn't sure if he was aware of his actions. A warm weight bumped her hip and settled in her lap—his tail, the tip flicking gently. She brushed her fingers along the bladelike end. He allowed a few caresses, and then his tail slithered out of her grasp and wound its way around her waist.

She frowned.

Touching him had already gotten her into enough trouble for one night.

Forbidden, forbidden, forbidden, she chanted to herself, then said aloud, "Okay, so we're a little weak in the planning department, but for what it's worth, I've got your back. And now that I know the rules, I think I can play along. Kill the bad guys, preserve the Light, no-contact bed sports, return home, and do nasty things to this Lady of Battles. Got it."

The bed shook, and she glanced at Gregory. He was shaking with silent laughter. "Yes, my Sorceress, those would be the rules."

A yawn snuck up on her. She blushed and apologized. "It's been a long day. If you don't mind, I think I'll go to bed now."

He nodded and unwound his tail from her waist. She immediately missed the warmth. The other side of the bed dipped under his weight as he crawled in. Lillian watched his progress with an arched eyebrow.

"Ah... with me being a dryad and all, aren't you tempting fate a little?"

"Perhaps," he rumbled, on the edge of sleep. "But I crave contact or at least closeness after being locked in stone for so long. Besides, how does a person react when they are denied what they want most?"

"Oh, they crave it all the more... so you're saying this and stuff like the shower, it's okay?"

"Yes. As long as we don't take it too far." His voice held an edge of sadness, and he glanced off into the distance with an unfocused look.

After she turned off the bedside lamp, she mulled over the sadness in his tone. Of course, he probably remembered an earlier time when his Sorceress loved him and knew enough not to tempt him. Her poor conflicted gargoyle. She really was going to do better.

The soft sheets caressed her legs, and she burrowed deep into her pillows with a contented sigh. Even though her eyelids were heavy, she blinked them open. Gravity wanted to pull her toward the depression where Gregory's weight made the bed sag. She let it.

When she was snug against his side, she reached out and touched his face. Cupping his cheek, she whispered in his ear, "I'm sure your Sorceress loved you as much as you loved her." She placed a chaste kiss on his forehead, between the deadly horns.

"Yes, she did." The essence of sadness echoed in his voice.

Lillian snuggled into him and combed her fingers through his mane. She kept up the motion until his breathing evened in sleep. "Rest well, my gargoyle. I'm sure she'll love you again like that one day." She curled her body against his, hoping the contact would sooth away any nightmares. "I think she already does."

CHAPTER TWENTY-FOUR

*S*he stood in the shadow of twin obelisks, their massive girth nearly twice the dimensions of an ancient oak tree's base. The pillars of polished onyx framed a view of open sky. Below, a narrow valley stretched down and away from her. Starting about a third of the way down the mountain's east side, greenery softened the stark slopes and increased in lushness near the bottom. Several hundred feet below, a wide river cut a twisting path through the valley floor.

Some of the tallest mountain peaks reared up through the clouds. The entire scene reminded her of dark boulders poking up out of the foam-dotted crests of rapids. It was as beautiful and breathtaking as anything she might see on earth, but the twin suns and teal-colored sky were unique to a different land, far from the place she now called home. Yet she knew this place from recent dreams, and a more disturbing memory from long ago, when she was still a child.

With newfound fear gripping her, she turned away from the view of the valley and stepped between the two great obelisks. A sprawling temple-fortress of polished black onyx reared above her head. It sat *midway up the slope of what had once been the proud pinnacle of an extensive range of mountains. To either side, smaller peaks flanked the temple's mountain, their rounded, stony shoulders showing their age. She remembered the name of this mountain with its crown of vapor: The Dark Mother of the Ridge.*

Tall, elegant columns made of the same dark stone as the obelisks marched up the side of the mountain until they came to the gate of a great, sprawling city carved into the ancient bedrock. Flanking the giant gate were two statues. Each identical. The huge statues depicted an elegant lady wearing armor and a long skirt. She was poised over an armor-clad warrior, her sword stabbing down into her victim. Lillian suppressed a shiver at the expression of fierce joy on the stone woman's alien face with its too-large eyes and sharp angular features. She glanced away.

Steep, garnet stairs emerged from the base of the city's main gate and cascaded down the side of the mountain like a blood-red water-fall, adding to the soul-chilling feel of the place.

The heavy, black velvet of Lillian's skirt brushed the steps as she made the long walk up to the Battle Goddess's fortress. The garnet steps were polished to such a shine that she caught glimpses of her reflection upon the stone's surface. Had she not witnessed her own face, she might have thought she'd somehow stepped into someone else's dream, for this vision was too extraordinary for her brain to have borrowed the images from her mundane life.

A black, leather harness hugged her waist and hips. The weight of a sword and scabbard swung against her leg with each step. A breast-plate of deep burgundy matched the stitching of her skirt. The strange garb felt both familiar and foreign at the same time, just like the dream itself.

This was not the first time she'd visited this place in a dream, and like the other times, her body continued the journey to the city without her control or consent. Clammy sweat trickled down her back. Lillian was a passenger in her own body—a puppet, nothing more.

Her feet carried her through the gate and beyond, into an eerily empty city of more black and red stone. At last she came to the entrance of the temple with its simple post-and-lintel archway, a maw of darkness at its heart.

Against her will, her feet carried her through the archway and deeper into the temple.

As she walked farther into the empty fortress, she heard the rattle of chains being drawn tight. Her journey ended at a great hall and another magnificent set of stairs. Though this one was much shorter than the one leading up a mountain.

The soft rustle of fabric on stone and more rattling of chains flowed down the stairs from the temple entrance above her. Lillian wanted to turn and run, but instead, her body dropped into a deep bow.

"My special one," a voice like the wind, eternal and strong, whispered from the darkness beyond the temple's second, smaller archway. "What news do you bring me?"

"Great Lady," the thing controlling Lillian's body replied, "the gargoyle has awakened from his stone sleep."

"At last. I had not planned to wait this long. Do not make me wait longer still. Bring him soon so I can continue my work."

"You will not have long to wait. It is as you thought. He is still loyal to me, even though he suspects I carry darkness within. I shall bring him to you when I have made him mine in all ways."

"Good. Continue to serve me well, and you shall be greatly rewarded."

"You are ever gracious. I will not fail you." Lillian straightened.

"Go, before the gargoyle awakes..."

CHAPTER TWENTY-FIVE

*L*illian awoke with a jolt, the last remnants of a dream scattered even as she tried to grasp them. Heart pounding, she reached for Gregory and found his side of the bed empty. There was something important she needed to remember so she could tell him. But whatever the dream had revealed vanished within seconds, leaving her with nothing more than a sense of foreboding.

"A meaningless nightmare," she mumbled to herself. "You idiot."

Of course she'd had a nightmare. No wonder with all that happened last night. A night of magic and awe turned to one of death and carnage. Gregory could have died. Her mind shied away from the memory of the battle. She wasn't ready to face that yet.

It was for the best the gargoyle was gone since her rational mind had slipped into gear at some point during the night, and now, in the light of day, she could hardly believe she'd invited him into the shower with her, and then allowed him to sleep in her bed. Again.

She tossed the covers back and headed into the bathroom to dress. While she pulled on clothing, she went over the events after the battle and concluded she must have been high on magic when she'd whispered that she loved him. Crazy-ass thing to say. She didn't know who or what she was beyond what others had told her. Before she took up the responsibility of a lasting relationship, she needed to know who she was, what she wanted, and what she would become.

A nightmare was the least of her worries.

Once she had dressed, she emerged from her room into the hall and froze in place. A group of five slender, pale-skinned men with very pointed ears acknowledged her presence with deep bows while she stood thunderstruck. The alert intensity of their gazes and the fluid way they moved reminded her of martial artists. If that hadn't been enough for Lillian to guess their natural occupation, their weapon belts and tunics with the emblem of a silver stag adorning the heavy forest-green silk would have been enough to scream "soldier."

She wanted to call them elves but scoured her brain for memories of the Hunt. Ah, her grandmother had called them sidhe. After one more lingering glance at their ethnic garb, she mumbled a hasty hello before hurrying on down the hall. Soft footsteps followed in her wake.

If she was not mistaken, Gregory had enlisted some new guard dogs. As if the unicorn wasn't bad enough. When she found her gargoyle, she would enlighten him about certain niceties, like discussing his plans with her before implementing them without her knowledge.

She increased her pace and was about to glance behind to see if the sidhe were still following when Sable opened the door of the guest room. Her eyes widened when they met Lillian's.

Sable bestowed Lillian with an elegant bow.

Alrighty then. Lillian must have crossed into an alternate reality if Sable was willing to show her such respect. "Care to tell me why you and those men bowed to me?"

"We all felt the power you and the gargoyle summoned. Rumors are flying like bees in a clover field. Some speculate you and the gargoyle breached the Veil between the Realms and drew on power directly from the Magic Realm. Instead of just gathering up the Veil's cast-off power." Sable raised an eyebrow in question. When Lillian didn't confirm or deny her statement, the dryad continued. "Regardless of the truth, anyone who requires magic to survive will cluster to the gargoyle with the hope he will allow others to make the journey when he leaves this realm."

"Sorry to spoil the anticipation, but they'll have a long wait ahead of them, since I don't plan on being driven from my home by the Riven." A tiny, hummingbird-like creature whizzed by Lillian's head as she came around the corner, heading for the stairs. "Was that a fairy?"

"No, it was a hummingbird."

Lillian glanced sidelong at Sable. "Do I even want to know?"

"It's a familiar."

"A little small, isn't it?"

"The size of the familiar doesn't matter."

Lillian thought about her eight-foot overly familiar

gargoyle. "After last night, I'm not so sure. Gregory's better in a fight."

"Better at other things too, I imagine."

Lillian scowled in Sable's direction. The dryad was already making her way down the stairs. She moved like she floated. With a snort of disgust, Lillian tromped down the stairs in pursuit. By the time she reached the bottom, the frustrating dryad had already disappeared. She continued to the kitchen.

The essence of gargoyle permeated the kitchen like a magical scent. Dark-shadowed forests and rich, damp loam mixed with the sweet fragrance of sun-warmed meadow grass and something purely male. She inhaled a deep lungful of the pleasant aroma. Her mind flashed back to the night before when they'd indulged in a few pleasant—and apparently forbidden—touches. With a shake of her head, she cleared her mind and told her hormones to behave. There would be none of *that* going on in her grandmother's house.

As if thinking of her grandmother summoned her, Gran materialized at her shoulder.

"Sweetheart, I'm so glad you're looking better today. I would have come up to let you know the council has been arriving all morning, but Gregory said you were still asleep. Do you feel up to meeting the council?"

"I'm fine. It was Gregory who took a blade in the back."

"I know, but you were so upset. I worry. I think your gargoyle is there if you want to talk to him." Gran pointed off to one empty corner. "Gregory said to tell you he's much recovered and slept very well. Who would have thought an old rug would be so comfortable?"

Lillian blushed and mumbled her excuses. She escaped in the direction of the invisible gargoyle. But when the *zing* of a mild electrical current flowed over her skin, she skidded to a stop.

"All is well. That was only my ward." Gregory's voice rumbled over her as his breath caressed her ear. Heat swirled through her belly.

Whoa, she told her hormones, then turned in the direction of Gregory's voice. To her mild annoyance, he remained invisible. "A ward to do what?"

"To repel the others for now," he replied. "I don't know if I can trust the Fae Council yet. And while I have an obligation to protect you, I may need the council's help to hunt down and destroy all the Riven. Not even one can survive, or it will be able to start infecting other creatures. After today, I'll know better which councilors I can trust."

"I'm sorry. I've been nothing but a burden."

"Never." Strong fingers curled around her arm and a second wave of tingling energy flowed over her skin.

When she looked to the gargoyle, he was visible, but the rest of the room was foggy, like an out-of-focus picture. "Are you going to teach me this trick any time soon?"

He didn't dignify her question with an answer, but it didn't bother her as much as it should; she was already distracted by something of greater interest. Her gargoyle was in human form this morning, and she wondered if his wounds would show up better on human skin than gargoyle hide.

She skimmed her eyes over his bare chest and then the rest of him, looking for scars or bruises. There weren't any. And still, she stared. It was impossible not to with that virile body on display.

Dang, her gargoyle didn't play fair. "You still haven't

grasped human dress code—as in you *should* wear clothing in public."

One dark eyebrow rose, and he smoothed a hand over his beaded loincloth, then adjusted his armbands. "I understand enough about human clothing to doubt its comfort. My attire serves me well."

"Ornaments are not clothing." She shook her head in exasperation but sobered a moment later. "You're recovered? Really?"

"I'm recovered," he said as he scanned the kitchen behind her.

When she cleared her throat, he looked back at her quizzically.

"Turn around. I want to check the knife wound."

"I'm fine. There is nothing to see."

"Not a debate."

In case he pretended he suddenly couldn't understand English, she grabbed his left shoulder and tugged until he turned. She viewed his back with its smooth, brown skin, perfect except for a shiny vertical line just below his right shoulder blade. So close to his spine.

She laid a hand on the scar and gently probed the area around it for signs of heat or swelling. It looked to have healed well, but she couldn't forget it had nearly killed him. The image still haunted her when she closed her eyes.

Stretching up on her toes, she pressed her lips against the pale mark and circled her arms around his torso. Memories of the previous night returned. Unable to help herself, she slid her fingers up his chest until she found the throb of his mighty heart. Sighing, she rested her head against his back and began counting each beat. This was the sound of life, peace, and home.

She might have spent half the day listening had his deep rumble of pleasure not startled her into releasing her hold. She stepped back just as he turned to face her, his eyes full of dark heat.

Apparently, she wasn't the only one remembering last night. She couldn't maintain his gaze and stared at her hands.

"Thank you for everything you did last night." His voice still held a heated quality to it. "I'm glad the Sorceress will one day love her gargoyle again." A finger under her jaw guided her head up.

"Shit. I thought you were asleep," she growled.

"I can still hear and understand while I'm in a light sleep."

"Not fair. You're like Super Gargoyle. Your wings are even cape-like."

He laughed, the deep tone raising gooseflesh. "And you are a strange little dryad."

"Thanks, I love you too." She hoped gargoyles understood sarcasm.

"I know." Gregory shifted back to his true form with a blur of light and shadow, then rested his muzzle on her head.

So much for sarcasm. Her mind switched to more pressing topics. "Why has the council come?"

"They must make a decision."

"About?"

"Us," he rumbled into her hair.

"I don't like the sound of that."

CHAPTER TWENTY-SIX

*L*illian stood in the meadow's center, her redwood towering at her back. She idly petted the soft needles of her hamadryad while she waited. Gran had directed the council to meet at the center of the maze, saying some of the more reclusive members would feel more at home protected by the labyrinth and sheltered by the tree. More likely Gran chose the spot for the gargoyle's sake. The shadows could hide him without him having to go invisible and break his promise to Lillian. She had never met such a creature of opposites. Fearless, yet shy; soft-spoken, but brazen. She found his core personality intriguing and could overlook some of his quirks, such as his aggressive, overprotective tendencies. A grin tugged at her lips.

She and Gregory had arrived early because he wanted to check the wards on the grove again. While the gargoyle worked his magic, she decided to try her hand at some dryad magic she'd overheard Sable and Russet discussing.

With her bare toes digging into damp earth and embraced

on either side by low-spreading branches of her hamadryad, Lillian closed her eyes and sought the forest lurking beyond the manicured gardens of her grandmother's spa. Magic answered her wish, and the presence of the land touched her mind.

It was there, waiting to reclaim the cultivated grounds and return them to a natural state. The forest called to her, wanting her to merge with its vast expanses. She focused her mind and, on closer examination, found the spirit of the woods was connected by water, like blood vessels within a body. Creeks meandered into streams, and her mind followed those subsidiaries as they made their way into fens and rivers, then finally to lakes. She flowed south with the water, toward Haliburton Forest. While not tame, that forest lacked the size and wild abandon her heart craved. She sought east and north, to where the smaller track of woodland butted against the mighty Algonquin.

We are here, the trees whispered. *Join us. Be one.*

"Lillian, it's time to come back."

The voice intruded upon her link with the land, and she tried to push it away.

"My Sorceress, return to me."

A tongue slathered her cheek, and Lillian returned to herself with a sputtered exclamation. "Ugh. What the hell?"

Gregory was holding her upright—her own legs felt like rubber. He nuzzled her again, licking at her neck.

"Gregory, have mercy." She pushed at his shoulders, attempting to look serious, but the effect was spoiled when he licked her cheek again. She burst into giggles. When she got herself under control a moment later, she asked, "Okay, what happened?"

"You do not have the training you need, that is what happened." Each word came out clipped.

Not good. He sounded pissed, which meant he was scared.

"I'm sorry," she whispered. "I overheard Sable and Russet talking yesterday while I was getting ready for the Hunt. Dryad magic sounded so easy and natural. I'm tired of knowing nothing..."

"We will talk of this later." Gregory's ears swiveled toward the entrance of the maze. "I hear the others coming. Please, do not call on magic until I have time to teach you some basic rules."

Lillian concluded Gregory didn't lie very well. Yes, the others were coming, but that's not why he didn't want to talk about magic. Every time she wanted answers about magic, he evaded her questions. "Okay. I won't use magic again."

She lied better than her gargoyle.

From her position under the shade of her redwood, Lillian surveyed each of the council members as they emerged from the maze. Two young girls arrived with Gran, one to each side. Gran led them to the picnic tables next to the stream.

On closer inspection, Lillian realized these were not children, but delicate, four-foot-tall women. Each wore a simple but elegant cream robe tied at the waist with a golden rope. The taller of the two had mottled brown-and-white hair, not from age—this was a pattern. The brown-and-white layers ran horizontally. The other woman had the same style of hair, but it ran to tan and brown. They gazed around the meadow, their jewel-bright eyes immediately drawn to the redwood at meadow's center.

At the sight of the majestic tree, the taller one made a soft cry, and what Lillian had thought were bangs lifted from her forehead into a short, spiky ruff. "Look how much the hamadryad has grown!"

"Yes, yes. We'll talk more about that later. In the meantime, eat." Gran gestured at the food laid out on the tables and then headed in Lillian's direction.

When she reached Lillian's side, she smiled and nodded toward the others arriving. "I figured I'd tell you a little about each member as they arrive."

Nodding absently, she studied the next person to enter the maze. He was the man she'd seen leading the Hunt the night before. "Okay, they're getting ahead of you. The two short women, who are they?"

"Hyrand and Goswin are sprites. They are mother and daughter and represent the lesser elementals of the Clan. Both have been members of the council for decades. All the council members are allies, but some are less dangerous than others. You can trust Hyrand and Goswin." Then Gran nodded to the taller silver-haired man who stood looking at the tables with disdain. "That is the sidhe lord, Whitethorn. I doubt that's his real name. I've known him for many years, but he doesn't trust easily." Gran gave a little shrug. "Even in this realm he is powerful and holds the Clan and the Coven together by sheer strength of will. Do not offend him or challenge him in any way. While he and I may not share an unending attachment, in the past we have always gotten beyond our differences of opinion. At the very least, he deserves respect. He has given up much of his power to protect our people."

"Got it. Don't piss off the big, pale one."

While they'd been conversing, a small, black horse eased out of the maze's shadows and into the light. At first, Lillian wondered if this was the sidhe lord's steed. Then it turned to look at her with glowing, yellow eyes like they burned with an internal flame.

"Ah, the pooka has arrived. Good."

Lillian studied him a moment more. Something about him caused a shiver to race down her spine. "I can already tell he isn't one of the friendly types."

"Like many of the old ones, the pooka took the greatest joy in the Hunt when it was untamed. He will not even gift us with a name we can call him by, so we call him the pooka. Though he likes the naiads and the dryads more than some of the other species, so you might get him to open up."

"I don't think I'll be striking up a conversation with him anytime soon."

"Ah, here comes Greenborrow."

Lillian tore her eyes away from the pooka and noticed an older-looking man hovering in the shadows of the cedar walls. With one hand he was petting the maze, in the other, he held a massive club. A raven perched on his shoulder and a giant wolf walked at his heels.

"I hope he's friendly. What's he doing to my maze?"

"Oh, likely admiring the thickness. A little pride on his part. He planted this hedge for you many years ago. Greenborrow is a leshii, a forest lord. Another of the old, powerful ones—much diminished now, but don't let on."

The leshii ignored the others gathered around the picnic

tables and made straight for Gran. His taupe-colored tunic was without a belt, like he'd lost it at some point and couldn't be bothered to find another. Bare feet covered with dust and grass stains added to the newcomer's wild-man look.

"Well, so this is our fine, young dryad. I saw you and the gargoyle at the Hunt last night," Greenborrow said, then slapped his thigh. "I've never seen such power. Magnificent. Your gargoyle, he's here?"

"Yes," Lillian paused, realizing Gregory had drifted off somewhere. "He was just here."

"Oh, never mind, dear. He's over by the pooka." Greenborrow pointed behind her.

Lillian turned. Her breath hissed out in surprise. The pooka was behind them, less than ten feet away. Gregory stood on all fours, his wings mantled in aggression as he faced off against the black pony.

A streak of white blurred between the tree trunks and the unicorn skidded to a halt next to the gargoyle. Both equines eyed each other with disdain.

"I don't think they like each other," Lillian remarked.

"No," Gran replied. "Two stallions seldom get along. And Gregory... well, he doesn't trust anyone, and the pooka has a nasty enough history it probably sets alarms a-ringing in his head, I imagine."

"To put it mildly," Greenborrow added, his accompanying laugh echoing across the meadow. Both stallions turned toward him. The leshii inclined his head to the unicorn and then the pooka. "If you two misbehave, I'll see what I can do to discipline both of you." He ran his hand along his club, caressing the wood. "Anyway, I wish to talk with Hyrand and Goswin. It's been entirely too long since I last chatted with the lovely sprites. Good day, ladies." He bowed and then wandered away.

"I like him," Lillian declared.

"Old Greenborrow is a good sort, but like all his kind, he has a dual nature. Be certain to always be on his 'good' side."

"I'll keep that in mind. By what I've seen of the Clan and the Coven so far, I don't think I want to witness his bad side."

Gran smiled. "If he had a bit of ambition, he'd be the Clan's leader. But he doesn't. Though he has the loyalty of more people than Lord Whitethorn, Greenborrow is loyal to the sidhe lord, so it all works out, for now."

"Is the wolf at Greenborrow's side a dire wolf? They seem smaller in the daylight."

"No, it's just a wolf. Last night, the dire wolves lost their prime alpha pair—think a High King and Queen. The prime alpha pair rules over all the packs. Now all the North American packs will unite and compete until a new alpha pair is chosen."

Lillian barely had time to nod before Gran launched into her next introductions.

"Ah, here comes Mardina." Gran gestured at the woman entering the meadow.

The one called Mardina was of medium height, and with her alabaster skin and blue-black hair that flowed past her shoulders, she drew the eye. Her hair was held back out of her face by two long, silver combs. She ran a hand through the locks, smoothing the wind-tossed strands back into order. If it hadn't been for the deep gray under her eyes and her strange robe, she would have been beautiful. Gray and sea-foam white, the robe was flimsy and frayed and looked more like a ragged bank of fog than clothing. It floated and swayed around her body like it was caught in some unfelt breeze.

"Mardina is a banshee."

"Oh." Lillian mouthed the name, testing it. "Is she friend or foe?"

"Mostly friendly, depending on how pure one's soul is. Now—" Gran cleared her throat and chuckled evilly, "—if she were to run across a murderer or rapist... then she might not be so nice."

More movement at the entrance caught Lillian's eye. Sable entered with Lillian's brother.

Jason held a metal toolbox at arm's length like it might bite. He went directly to the picnic tables without a word of greeting to anyone. After he placed the box on the center table, he tossed back the lid and frowned down at the contents. One by one, the others gathered around the table came to look within the box. No one reached to touch whatever was inside. By their expressions, Lillian envisioned a severed limb, or a mummified cat stuffed within the confines of the toolbox.

"It's here. We should begin." Without glancing at Lillian, Gran marched over to the picnic tables and seated herself at the center table.

Gregory appeared at Lillian's shoulder, and she instantly felt complete.

"Guess it's our turn," Lillian muttered as discomfort enveloped her in a nervous sweat. Gregory shadowed her steps. Briefly, she wondered what they looked like to others— two very different beings moving as one across the dew-dampened grass.

CHAPTER TWENTY-SEVEN

*L*illian arrived at the table as the pooka leaned over the box. He tilted his head and one bright, yellow eye fixed on the mystery item within the toolbox. His lips curled back from his teeth, and after a quick sniff, he jerked his muzzle away with a snort and a shake of his head. His glossy, black skin shivered like he was being attacked by invisible flies.

Unable to stand the mystery, Lillian leaned forward until she could see inside the box.

The knife lay within.

The knife that had tried to kill her gargoyle.

"You," she hissed and snatched it out of the box. Her grandmother shouted, and Whitethorn made a motion to knock it out of her hand, but the gargoyle blocked them with his wings. She glanced first at Gregory and then back at the knife. She turned it over in her hand. A dark, reddish-brown stain soiled the smooth mirror surface of the blade. Gregory's blood.

Rage tensed her muscles, and her pulse pounded in her ears. This was the thing that had tried to take her gargoyle's life. Power bubbled up from within Lillian, fed by the wrath until it simmered in her blood, lending her muscles strength. She laid the knife flat on the table and pressed her hand over it until the table creaked with the strain. She held her power back, letting it build. When it spiked, she channeled it upon the knife. *Destroy it*, she whispered to her magic.

A bright flash like a bolt of lightning blinded her. Sparks danced across her vision. She blinked. When her sight returned, she looked down where the blade had been.

It was still there. Perfect. Untouched by her magic.

A growl tore up from her chest.

The amount of power she'd summoned should have reduced the knife to ash. Yet there it lay. She leaned closer. No, it was not wholly untouched—the blood was gone.

Without the visual reminder of Gregory's near-mortal injury, Lillian's turbulent power and consuming wrath slowly dissipated. Taking measured deep breaths, she calmed, her heart resuming a reasonable pace.

With her power's abandonment, she collapsed back onto a chair and rubbed at her temples to ease the tension. Weakness descended upon her body a layer at a time as the seconds flew past. A clawed hand settled on her shoulder. Before she could look up at Gregory, he began to share power with her.

"I'm sorry. I know I promised I wouldn't use my power, but I wanted that *thing* destroyed for what it did to you." Lillian rested her cheek against the back of Gregory's hand.

"*Shh... I know,*" he whispered into her mind through his touch.

"Well, that was fascinating," Greenborrow stated. The leshii leaned closer and waved his hand over the blade.

A good six inches of empty air stretched between the steel blade and his flesh. And Lillian could still feel how the blade sucked the magic through the air, weakening the old fae.

Greenborrow retracted his hand. "Interesting how a lowly dryad can hold a demon blade and not have it consume her, and yet all I have to do is stand close enough to the thing to feel it draining me," he said, his tone offhanded like he was commenting on the weather.

His remarks stirred the others at the table out of their shock. Multiple conversations erupted at once. The hum of discussion buzzed around the table for several chaotic minutes. Gregory flicked his wings in annoyance, then issued a deep, barking challenge in his own language. The verbal debates dwindled to silence.

The sprite, Hyrand, was the first to gather her courage. She inclined her head in Gregory's direction. The gargoyle nodded.

Hyrand bowed her head in thanks, then looked to the leshii. "Greenborrow, are you accusing Lillian of carrying darkness in her soul?"

"Nothing so serious, my dear." He glanced at Gregory. "Just saying it's interesting is all."

Hyrand didn't seem convinced, and she studied Lillian from under her lashes until Lillian became uncomfortable. The sprite cleared her throat and continued as if she chose her words with care. "I would hear how you stopped this blade from destroying your gargoyle."

"Gregory was injured by the Riven. It was my fault the

monster got in a lucky shot. My magic reacted to save Gregory's life."

"And the Riven, he just stood aside and let you do this?"

"No, of course not. He was already dead by the time I reached Gregory's side."

"Yet you said you distracted the gargoyle and the Riven got close enough to stab him. You did not say Gregory killed it. So, the gargoyle dropped before he killed the Riven?"

"Yes," Lillian blurted before she could stop and think.

"What happened to the Riven?"

"I don't know, everything happened so fast. It was all chaos and death. Gregory was injured. I panicked. I think I ran at the Riven. I must have had a weapon with me because the next thing I knew, I was at Gregory's side and Alexander was dead."

Greenborrow interrupted. "The Riven was torn to shreds. Gutted. His heart missing and half his ribcage spread out across the grass. Tell me, what kind of bladed weapon does that?"

"I don't know." She shook her head, more to deny the existence of a void in her own memories than in response to Greenborrow's question. Gregory leaned down and rested his chin against her hair, saying in his silent way not to worry. It didn't work. She trembled, and her hands shook like she'd been in a car accident. "Why does it matter? He was evil, and now he's dead."

"Exactly. He's dead. A dryad has no hope of killing a Riven in a one-on-one fight. But if that dryad is something rarer than her sisters, and she could draw magic directly from the Magic Realm, well then—that is one sorry Riven."

Silence thickened like fog on a crisp autumn morning.

"I have magic. I don't really know anything about it. Heck, I didn't even know about it until a couple of days ago. I certainly don't know how to use it. That I have magic is no secret. You all saw the gargoyle and me raise magic for the Hunt. So maybe I did use that power to kill a Riven. So what?"

"But," Greenborrow continued, "that's my point. We saw the remains of the Riven and felt the echo of the magic used to do the damage. That was not dryad magic."

Lillian fisted her hands against her thighs. "First, I am a human, and then I'm not a human. Next, I'm a dryad, and now I'm not a dryad. What do you think I am?"

"I didn't say you weren't a dryad, only that the magic used wasn't dryad magic."

"My gargoyle can string together better sentences. Say what you mean or leave me alone."

Gregory tightened his hold on her shoulders. "The leshii is older than the others, and his memories run deeper. He recognizes what we are or has—as you would say—put two and two together."

"Huh?"

Greenborrow clapped his hands together. "Ah, I'm right! How delightful! I've been dying for an adventure."

Gregory's tail lashed; a sign he was faced with something he'd rather leave untouched.

"The time for secrets is over. I have tested everyone here; there is no new darkness on any of your souls." Though he had paused and looked at the pooka and the banshee when he'd said 'new' darkness. "I will share a truth with you." Gregory's voice rumbled over her head, darker and more sinister than she'd ever recalled hearing. "If you want the truth, stay. But you shall never repeat this to anyone outside of this meadow—you will not be able to, for my weaving will steal your words. After you've heard what I have to say, if any of you try to harm my lady, I will steal more than your words. I will escort the betrayer to the Spirit Realm myself. Stay or go, the choice is yours. I will give you a few minutes to decide among yourselves."

Even immortals could be shocked into silence. Lillian didn't take comfort in that fact, though.

After his ultimatum, Gregory turned and marched over to her tree. He merged with the shadows to await the council's decision. When Lillian realized all the faces had switched from following the gargoyle to staring at her, she lost her nerve and bolted after the gargoyle.

She probed the shadows until she caught him, then locked her fingers around his arm. "What are you doing?"

"Giving the truth."

"Like the stuff you told me last night about our history?"

"Yes."

"You didn't make me swear some kind of death oath."

"No. Why would I?"

She clenched her jaw. His clipped answers were scaring her. "If we're going to trust each other, you need to fill in some details."

"What I reveal will be more than I've told you." He sighed. "While I have not lied to you, I have not told you the full truth. I hope you can forgive me."

Gran came over to them before Lillian could ask what he was talking about.

"The others are in agreement," Gran said with a glance over her shoulder at the other tense-faced individuals waiting at the picnic tables. She frowned and Lillian wondered if Gran was annoyed that Gregory hadn't told her everything up front. If so, Gran wasn't the only one.

After a moment, Gran schooled her expression and continued. "We agree to Gregory's terms. If there is a secondary danger to us beyond the Riven, then we need to know what it is and how to protect ourselves."

The gargoyle bowed his head in acknowledgment and followed Gran back to the table. Lillian trailed after, unsure if she wanted to hear what he'd kept secret.

Gregory didn't sit. He seldom did, but now he stood unmoving like he'd grown roots.

"As Greenborrow already guessed, I am not *just* a gargoyle and Lillian is not *just* a dryad. She is the Mother's Sorceress, and I am the Father's Gargoyle Protector. We are the Avatars of the Divine Ones, born to fulfill their purpose, to maintain the balance and hunt down evil intent on upsetting that balance."

The silence was so complete, Lillian would have heard a hummingbird if one flew across the glade at that moment. She stepped up next to Gregory and placed her hand in his. He glanced sideways at her and nodded his head. "Lillian does not remember who she is because I stole her memories."

Lillian's mind blanked at his words, too stunned to function. White noise filled her ears. It took her a few seconds to realize it was the buzz of conversation she heard. The other fae creatures at the table were shouting questions. She shouted louder than the others. "What? You... you stole my memories?" She jerked away from Gregory. Horror opened a hollow in her gut, which betrayal quickly filled with bitterness. "Why?"

She had trusted him. All this time he'd been responsible for the void in her mind where her childhood memories should have been.

Everyone at the table fell silent.

"I could not trust you because of where I found you," he admitted.

"Yesterday, you told me you rescued me from my abductor, the Lady of Battles. You saved me from whatever she had planned."

"I said I had rescued you from her, not that she had abducted you. And I'm not even sure if I've thwarted her plans."

"What are you talking about?"

"A gargoyle stays in his mother's tree for ten years before he is birthed fully mature. A dryad carries her daughters for only three. When we were both eight, I emerged from my mother's tree early, so I could rescue you from the Battle Goddess's domain, the place where you had been conceived, born, and lived for eight years."

Conceived. Born. Not kidnapped. His word shook her soul like felled trees crashing to the ground.

He continued, unaware he was trampling her fragile sense of truth. "From the time of your birth, and perhaps while you were still within your mother's tree, you were shaped to become a tool for the Lady of Battles, training with her captains to one day lead her army. I escaped with you and then, too weak to escape her hunters in the Magic Realm, I came here."

"Oh my God. You couldn't trust me," Lillian said as she thought of something worse. "You were afraid of me, of what the Lady could make me do."

He didn't answer her right away, and that was enough to start a chill crawling up her spine.

"The Lady of Battles might have been using you as bait to lure me to her. Once she had us both, she may have planned to make us serve her by threatening the other. I don't sense any evil upon you now. When first I found you, there was a dark taint, but here in this place, far from the demigoddess's influence, you may have managed to purify yourself."

She heard the doubt in his voice. "But you still haven't given me my memories back. You're afraid."

"I can't risk this world until I know for certain what she did to you. Please understand."

Lillian grabbed the edge of the table to stop her hands from trembling while she calmed the churning in her soul. It made sense now. Gregory hadn't betrayed her. He'd done what he could to protect her. But not just her—everyone else, too. If she weren't such a fool, she'd have seen that sooner. They were two halves of one soul—she could only imagine what keeping this secret had cost Gregory. Placing her hand in his, she touched his thoughts and projected her understanding and thanks, and then intertwined their fingers.

"How will you find out if I'm a threat, and how will you deal with it if I am?"

"We need time." He squeezed her fingers and then turned to the others sitting at the tables. "If I am given time, I think I can heal whatever was done to my Mistress. In a way, being trapped in this realm was a blessing. The Lady of Battles cannot reach into this realm from her prison and likely has no idea what happened to the Sorceress. As long as we stay here, I think Lillian will be safe. At least for a little while."

He paused with a long look directed at the silver-skinned

leader of the sidhe. "For the first time in many, many life-times, I find myself in need of allies. I cannot defeat the Riven if I'm too busy protecting Lillian from both the Clan and the Coven. I must put my trust in you here today. Know I will fight your enemies alongside you if you agree to continue to shelter Lillian."

Another silence stretched by, longer this time than the last until the banshee pushed back her chair and stood. "Why should we help you? For all we know, you too have been corrupted. For that matter, your precious mistress might even now be corrupting you. You claim you don't know what happened to her. How can you ask us to protect her when you don't even know how dangerous she is?"

"We'd already be enslaved if the gargoyle was corrupted." Greenborrow rapped on the table. "I say we give the gargoyle what aid he needs, and then we accept his aid in turn. We grow fewer with each year. How much longer can we go on if we will not work together?"

With a nod, Whitethorn stood. "You both have good arguments. I say we give the gargoyle our aid but make certain the Sorceress is no threat."

The banshee's gray eyes turned stormy. "How will you be certain of her innocence? If this was as easy as you make it sound, I'm sure the gargoyle would already have done this. Yet he, one of the greatest spellweavers in all three realms, has not done this. Why?"

Greenborrow chuckled. "Because the poor fellow hasn't been given two free minutes to rub together, methinks. That, and it's not a task he'll be looking forward to performing."

The gargoyle grunted in way of answer; his "yes" to all things nasty.

Lillian swallowed hard as nervous sweat made its way down her back. That she might be evil scared her, but the thought of losing Gregory because of that evil was far worse. She needed to know.

"I'll agree to this if it will prove I'm not a threat." Her rushed statement turned several heads. Before they'd talked about her like she wasn't there, but now each eyed her like a snake studying its next meal.

Not an improvement.

Whitethorn nodded, his lips forming a hard line. "Then, with the gargoyle's aid, we shall bind your power and read what resides within your soul."

"No!" Gran cried. "She's too young, and she doesn't have the mental discipline needed to survive without being damaged. She'll go into shock. She could die. Let the gargoyle and me give her the training she needs to prepare."

"We can't risk the wait," Whitethorn said. He looked to the gargoyle. "We do this tonight if you want us to shelter her while you deal with the Riven."

Gregory glanced down at her, his dark eyes turbulent.

Surprisingly, Lillian's own soul was suddenly serene, fear a distant thing. She didn't fear death. This was a battle, and she never ran from a challenge. Her only concern was for Gregory and her family.

She rested her hand on his shoulder and squeezed.

"It's okay. We need to do this. I need to know. I couldn't live with myself if there was something evil slumbering within me and it harmed those I love because I didn't do anything to stop it."

CHAPTER TWENTY-EIGHT

*T*he unfamiliar feeling of worry gnawed at Gregory's stomach all the way back to the house. If Lillian knew what binding her power and reading her soul involved, she wouldn't have agreed so readily. After a quick discussion, the council decided the house would be the best location. It was familiar and more defendable. Gregory pinned his ears against his mane. By that, the council members meant they would have a better chance at containing Lillian if something went wrong. A low growl built in his throat; he clamped his teeth to prevent its escape.

Some other sign must have given him away because Lillian stepped closer until her arm brushed his. "It's all right, Gregory. You said I lived in our enemy's territory for years. If it's as nasty as you implied and I survived it, I must be tougher than you think." She skimmed her fingers down his arm until she laced them with his. "And I understand why you had to take my memories—you had no choice. I was just a little taken aback at first, but now I understand why you did what you did."

"You lived because the Lady of Battles wanted you for some purpose. That is why you survived." Even as he said the words, they lacked the harsh edge he'd strived for, and his ears relaxed. He whispered a prayer to the Divine Ones, thanking them that Lillian had forgiven him for stealing her memories.

"Then I am tough because I survived whatever she did to me. Can you deny I stand before you with my mind intact and my heart beating?"

He sighed with exasperation even as a grin tugged at his lips. "Yes, you are a tough little dryad. But it doesn't stop me from worrying."

"I know." She squeezed his hand.

While they talked, they had entered the house and arrived in the living room. Lillian looked around at the other fae. "Now what?"

Vivian stormed into the room, the older woman's fierce expression focused on Whitethorn. "You can't toss me out of my own house. If we're going ahead with this foolery, then I'll be at my granddaughter's side."

"The ceremony's rules are clear. There will be no family present." Whitethorn's tone was as unforgiving as Vivian's stubborn streak.

"Fine," Vivian replied. "She isn't related by blood. I'm staying."

Whitethorn *did* look ready to toss Vivian out of her own home, Gregory decided, but the fae kept his composure.

"No. You are bound by the rules the same as we all are. We cannot change them just to suit our own needs. Go. I will keep you advised as to the gargoyle's progress and our findings."

"Gran," Lillian said. "I must do this. It will be easier if you're not present." She stepped away from Gregory, her hand sliding from his. Immediately, he missed the contact. With an act of will, he focused on the tension in the room.

Vivian's knuckles whitened against her staff. After a count of ten seconds, she relaxed her fingers. "Fine. But I will be near if you require me."

"Thank you." Lillian hugged her grandmother. Gregory had a surprising urge to embrace the older woman for her protective streak, too.

Vivian released Lillian, then caught Gregory's eye. Her look told him to kill anyone who attempted to harm her granddaughter. He nodded in silent acknowledgment.

Sable came up next to Gregory. "I'll help Lillian get ready."

"Thank you," Lillian replied.

He touched Lillian's shoulder and sent thoughts of peace and comfort. She smiled, broadcasting love back at him before she broke contact and followed Sable.

Gregory called the shadows to him and vanished to make his own preparations. He would need more power if it became necessary to overwhelm Lillian's shields. No matter how much he didn't want to face the possibility, the evidence pointed to the fact that she was a host to dark magic.

Closing his eyes, he began summoning magic, drawing chilled power directly from the Spirit Realm until his skin took on a patina of frost.

CHAPTER TWENTY-NINE

*S*o far, the ceremony had been pleasant enough. It began with a purifying bath, the hot steam scented with lavender oil and sage. When Lillian finally exited the bathroom, she found Sable had lit candles in the four corners of the bedroom. A small fire burned in the fireplace. The air was heavy with sage, sweet grass, and cedar. The heat, low light, and fragrances helped Lillian relax. At least she'd gotten over her initial fears—mostly. Some still fluttered annoyingly at the edge of her consciousness—like what she would do if there were darkness inside her.

Might it not turn Gregory against you? The small internal voice of her conscience nagged at her like it had since Gregory first told her why he'd taken her memories. She pushed that worry away. She'd already covered every possible disastrous outcome a hundred times.

While there was the possibility of losing him and everything she cared about, she imagined it was a slim chance. Gregory loved her too much to give her up. Or at least, he loved his *Sorceress* too much to allow the Lady of Battles to win.

A breeze flowed in through an open window. The singing of frogs and the scent of night filled her bedroom and relaxed her further. With nothing else to do but wait, she stretched out on top of her comforter and worried at the drawstring of her pajamas. When she caught herself fidgeting, she folded her hands across her midriff and stared at the ceiling.

A soft knock at the door startled her from her worries. She sat up and tucked her legs underneath her. "Come in."

The door pushed open, and Gregory entered. He paused when he caught sight of her on the bed. His look traveled the length of her, lingering in some places longer than others.

Warmth suffused her and tension fluttered in her belly. The door opened more and the pooka trotted in after Gregory, followed by Greenborrow, Sable, and Hyrand. Heat died and the nervous fluttering in her stomach turned into a rock

All Lillian knew about the ceremony was that Gregory would peel her shields away like the layers of an onion until her soul was bare to him, so the others would be able to read her thoughts. Sable had made it sound like the binding of the magic would be done with only Gregory present, which didn't sound so awful. But magical binding sounded a whole lot less appealing with an audience.

With her best impression of a serene mask, she continued to watch Gregory. It was a better alternative than looking at the others where they'd lined up at one end of her bedroom. The gargoyle sat on the edge of the bed, and after glancing down, he leaned in closer and tucked the blanket from the foot of the bed around her.

A throat being cleared alerted Lillian that the others were no longer conversing among themselves. Whitethorn was standing off to one side, his lips pursed, and brows furrowed. Apparently, he wasn't overly patient.

"I'm as ready as I'll ever be. Let's get this over with," she told Gregory.

Gregory nodded, and Lillian tried to relax while she waited for the gargoyle to do his thing.

The thought had barely crossed her mind when chilled magic blanketed her. "Ah! Cold. What the...?"

"Magic from the Spirit Realm. The strongest weapon I can call upon."

"Well, it's damn cold. I thought I was supposed to relax. How can I do that with my knees whacking together and my teeth trying to rattle loose from my jaws?"

"Try," he rumbled.

"Right—oh." She broke off as his fingers settled on her temples and massaged the tension away with a firm touch. He moved back into her hairline, massaging her scalp. Caught up in the mild pleasure, she missed when he started filling her with that cold power. Its chill lessened as she adjusted to the invasion. "Okay, this isn't so bad."

The words had barely left her mouth when the chill intensified, and his magic reached into her mind and tried to claw the first layer of tissue from her brain. She screamed. Her eyes flew open as her heart jumped into gear. She batted at the gargoyle, but she could have been slapping a statue for all the reaction he showed. Screaming had no effect on him, but she didn't care and drew another breath.

Warmth caressed her ear. *"I'm sorry."* He leaned back, his

breath coming in pants. *"I'm sorry, beloved. Forgive me. Do not fight me."*

"What the hell? I—"

The pain engulfed her in another flow of icy lava. A whimper was all that emerged. His talons of magic and power slashed across her mind. She arched off the bed, struggling with everything in her. She punched him under the jaw and clawed at his bare shoulders. He took the abuse as if he didn't feel it. Leaning his weight against her, he pinned her to the bed so she couldn't fight him. With a tearing sensation in her mind, another barrier shredded under his attack. The pain receded into numbness. She floated above the pain, praying she would not fall back into her body lying upon the bed. Surely that was death. Where the hell was her magic when she needed it?

"Lillian, don't call your magic. Please don't fight me." His voice shook. "If you call your magic, it will repair your shields... please... I cannot do this to you again."

The agony in his dark timbre pulled her back into her body. To her surprise, there was no blinding-sharp pain eating away at her brain. She looked beyond the barrier of her mind, out into the world. Gregory hunched next to her. Pain etched across his face, a tattoo of his horror. Dampness streaked his cheeks. Shocked, she reached out and gathered a tear on her fingertip.

"Oh, Gregory, that hurt you as much as it did me, didn't it?" she asked as she fought to get her breathing under control. "I knew this wouldn't be pleasant from your reluctance. I'm sorry I was such a wimp. I'll do better." She laid her hand along his cheek. *"I love you."*

"I know." He covered her hand with his own and curled his

fingers around hers. When he turned her hand, so the palm faced up, he leaned down and placed a kiss upon it. Then drawing her hand to his chest, he rested it against his heart. The steady beat of his pulse surged under the skin and bone. *"The rest of this will be easier."*

"If something happens and you find I am one of darkness, do what you must, but know I'll love you regardless. You are a part of me."

He touched his forehead to hers. "We are one, always."

With his words, she felt his magic flood over her, sweeping thoughts and worries away. He went deep into her mind, pulling at her memories as he hunted. To her surprise, his presence in her mind wasn't an invasion. He belonged there. A half-smile curled her lips as he delicately leafed through her thoughts.

Minutes eased by, one after another until she lost track of time, and still, he did not find what he sought. The sensation of his mental hunting stilled, and he pulled away. She was about to ask what was wrong when a wave of darkness reared up and rolled across her consciousness. She blinked and yawned but was unable to fight off the intense compulsion to sleep.

"Surrender, my lady. Know what peace you can find in sleep."

She blinked sleep-heavy lids. The last thing she remembered was Gregory's troubled expression.

CHAPTER THIRTY

*G*regory watched the rise and fall of her chest and prayed she would be all right. He'd put her to sleep as soon as he'd sensed the trap. When she was deeply under, he summoned his magic and flowed back into her mind. He had no idea what form the trap would take, so he slid his consciousness into her body a bit at a time, fearing to trigger something until a part of his soul was with hers, where he could help her fight it.

He sifted through her recent memories, mildly surprised how much she already trusted him, even though she did not know him. Further back, he encountered the night of the Wild Hunt—*the awe and sense of rapture when they danced together and summoned power from the Magic Realm. Then her joy turned to horror as he fought the Riven. The glint of a knife in the moonlight descending toward her gargoyle.*

His first clue came with the wash of her raw emotional reactions. He turned them over in his mind, examining them. He'd felt her possessiveness toward him before, and a small part of him took pleasure in her reaction, but now he witnessed a different side to it—ownership, not love.

That was not how his lady thought of him. He moved to the next emotion, her rage. He'd been hurt in battle before. Once the Sorceress had sent a mountain crashing down into a valley where a demon army was amassing.

But the rage she'd felt on the night he'd been stabbed was fueled by a love twisted up with possession. She'd raged that someone had dared to harm *her* gargoyle, and she'd wanted to cause equal pain upon the enemy, to rip and tear into them and shred what remained of their dark souls. She'd grown talons, and with a strength she shouldn't have possessed, she'd smashed the Riven's ribcage and destroyed its heart. Then the demon blade had recognized a darkness greater than itself and obeyed her wishes and released *her* gargoyle.

Gregory shook free of her thoughts, and with a sinking feeling realized when he was in danger, she surrendered to a new dark and bestial part of her soul—a part he'd never known in all their lifetimes together and a part that clearly thought of him as hers. This was the Battle Goddess's work. But what could it mean? Lillian had killed evil to protect him many times in the past. What was the purpose behind making her more protective of him than she already was? The Lady of Battles had plans layered upon plans, and Gregory needed to dig deeper to find the root of this.

He sought a childhood memory. One before she came to this world...

A child of seven, she stood on a battlement, looking up at the teal-colored sky with its weak sun casting meager light upon the forests below. Small demons and lost spirits wandered among the trees.

She debated attempting to sneak into her father's prison, but

Mother would be angry if she did. Besides, she was due at her next lesson. This one was to learn the weaving of invisibility like her father could summon. And that would be a handy ability, especially if she was going to sneak out of this place before her gargoyle matured and came looking for her. She wouldn't let the Lady of Battles have him. The gargoyle was hers, after all, and no one else had the right to command or enslave him. Only she had that right. She was Mistress.

Gregory broke away from the memory.

Even as a young child, Lillian had known what the Lady of Battles had planned. But by trying to twist the Sorceress's love of him into something evil, the Lady had created a fatal flaw in her plan. Lillian would allow no one else to use him. Lillian's childhood memory had made that clear.

Darkness had corrupted the foundation of what they were. While this news was unwelcome, it was still something within his power to heal, if given time. But there must be more—the Lady of Battles was thorough, intelligent, and completely competent. Twisting Lillian into something of darkness would only be the tip of her plan.

Gregory returned to the memory where Lillian had ripped out the heart of the Riven. She'd done it with talons. Another clue. The Sorceress wasn't gifted with shapeshifting, yet she'd grown claws.

Since he and the Sorceress were so closely linked, if the Sorceress learned to shapeshift, she might naturally take another shape he'd find even more appealing than a dryad. He envisioned Lillian with a thick mane, long tail, and graceful wings.

His blood surged at the image.

With a mental curse, he halted his line of thought. There was one excellent reason why the Mother had made it so the

Sorceress could never shapeshift. Best not to even think about how his Mistress would look given a gargoyle form. Death waited down that path.

Surely that wasn't the Battle Goddess's plan. There were easier ways to kill him and his Sorceress than inciting the Divine Ones to a rage and having them burn their Avatars to ash. Once roused, there was no stopping or hiding from the God and Goddess.

Gregory's skin shivered with cold even as his heart raced. No, the Lady of Battles would gain nothing by stirring her parents' ire and having them seek out the cause of all the trouble. And then the Lady of Battles would have a greater problem than being caged in her prison.

Gregory slid deeper into Lillian's mind, merging with her soul. He needed to find what else the dark goddess had done to her, but her thoughts and memories pressed upon him from all sides, warm and peaceful, distracting him from his purpose. This felt like home—that vaguely remembered time in the Spirit Realm when they were one soul.

With some regret, he turned his attention back to the internal dangers lying dormant upon her magic and soul. After sifting through her younger memories, he encountered a tight knot of something foreign. He poked at the mass, and it quivered and slid sideways away from him, seeking shelter in other memories.

At last, an anomaly that did not belong. It tasted of a foreign power, of blood magic, and something else. A second spirit. Gregory examined his find with growing horror. The Lady of Battles had enslaved another soul and embedded it within Lillian. It grew within his lady like a parasite.

He swam after it and chased it down a second time. The foreign consciousness tossed another barrier between them.

He wove a net of magic and cast it around the second spirit. Focusing, he stripped a layer of its protective magic away, only to reveal another layer underneath. Evil hit his senses with its unclean taste. This was no regular soul, but a demon soul—an evil seed that would grow into one of the powerful, higher-level demons.

If he'd fought it within their home Realm, Gregory had no doubt he would win. But here in the Mortal Realm, his options were limited, and the demon was protected within Lillian's body. If he wasn't mistaken, it was feeding on her power, growing stronger with each passing day.

Lillian shivered as a wave of unease coursed through her. Her heart rate spiked, her breath becoming labored. She thrashed like in a nightmare. If she physically flung him off and broke the link between them now...

Cursing, he disengaged from Lillian's mind to control her body. Dryad scent, the silk-soft warmth of skin, and his own heady desire swamped his senses. Grunting, he admitted that sometimes he hated having a flesh and blood body.

Fighting for control, he mentally shook himself, then took a firmer hold on Lillian. At least the umbilical of magic between them remained strong, unharmed by her brief fit of wakefulness or his break in concentration.

He poured his consciousness back into her body and met with resistance. The demon soul had been busy the few moments Gregory had been distracted.

The darkness uncoiled within Lillian, expanding and building defenses as it fed on her magic. Gregory attacked her

link to the Magic Realm, hoping to starve the demon into
defeat.

Magic surged and Gregory realized he was already too
late. A dam broke within Lillian, unleashing a river of magic
upon him. Helplessly, he was thrown back into his own body
by the torrent.

The demon soul continued to call power as it expanded its
spell outside Lillian's body.

CHAPTER THIRTY-ONE

*G*regory raised his head from the pillow of Lillian's hair and inhaled a steadying breath, hoping to calm his racing heart and gather his thoughts. It had the opposite effect. He brushed the back of one hand against her cheek. Her eyelashes fluttered but didn't open. As a precaution, he whispered a spell so she would slip deeper into slumber. Then he forced his attention away from Lillian long enough to glance around.

A pale, nebulous power dripped down the sides of the bed and gathered in an ever-spreading pool on the floor. After a moment, the shimmer intensified and began a purposeful crawl up the north wall of Lillian's bedroom. What he'd first thought was a spell to loosen his hold on her mind was something of greater concern.

His own magic answered his call with a skin-tingling rush. All his senses were riveted on the foreign spell and claws extended from his fingertips, poised to rend anything the hostile magic might summon. The silver flames crawling up the wall now flickered with the look of true fire. The mass seethed and heaved like wind-blown grass, and then with a bright flash, a window opened into another place.

The teal-colored light of the Magic Realm illuminated a vast, circular room with a raised dais at the center. Occupying the dais, two massive thrones, carved of dark rock and polished until they resembled black glass, overlooked the rest of the room. Instead of a back wall, a series of stone arches allowed in light and provided a majestic view of white-capped mountains set against the backdrop of a cloudless sky. Presently, the thrones were as empty as the sky, yet by the shimmer of the polished stone floors, this room was well cared for.

From the corner of his eye, Gregory caught movement. He'd forgotten the Fae Council members were still in the room with him. Whitethorn approached the magic window. He had a sword in one hand, point forward. With a blur of motion, he slashed at the image. The blade bit into the unseen wall behind, raining chips of plaster and white dust down across the floor.

The reflection to the other world rippled like a stone had been tossed into a still pond.

Blessedly, it was only an image and not a real gateway. When Whitethorn eased back to his original position a few steps in front of the other councilors, Gregory caught his eye. "Get out of the line of sight. The less this new enemy knows about our alliance, the better. Let them think Lillian and I are alone."

Whitethorn's expression darkened, but he nodded and signaled the other immortals out of sight. The sidhe bowed in Gregory's direction, then vanished as quickly as the rest.

Gregory stared at the door Whitethorn had used a moment more. At least he had some allies, even if they were reluctant ones.

Lillian thrashed upon the bed, fighting his compulsion to sleep. She made a soft exclamation and sat up next to him as she shrugged off the last of his sleep spell. After she took in her surroundings, including the new wall, she focused on him again. Her expression remained serene. A faint smile played across her lips. "Durnathyne, my Hunting Shadow, let me handle this."

The use of his old name startled him enough that she slipped by him and was half off the bed before he'd realized she was moving. He leaped into motion and repositioned himself to keep her behind him, fenced in between his outstretched wings. He held her in place with his tail for good measure. "Stay behind me. Your protection is my duty."

"For once, let me protect you. You'll find these enemies don't play by your rules, my beloved," Lillian said. She didn't fight him but remained behind him with her one hand resting on his back. "The demon soul the Lady of Battles grafted upon me thought it was under attack. It tried to summon help, but it exhausted itself. We are lucky it is not yet mature. Now I am in control, and I remember everything. Let me deal with this. Please."

"But I must—"

"Protect your Mistress?" she asked, sounding sad. Then she pressed a kiss to the muscle of his shoulder as if in apology. "Always the noble protector. I think we've taken our disguises too far and you have forgotten we are equals in power."

The click of boots on stone tiles drew Gregory's attention

back to the image still rippling against the wall. Two columns of heavily armored guards marched into the room from opposite sides, converging upon the center dais with its raised thrones. Tall spears bristled above their heads, and they wore helms shaped in the image of horned demons and snarling beasts. If he'd had doubts about their allegiance, their surcoats with the black dragon against a red field quickly banished his misgivings. These were the Battle Goddess's creatures.

The black-clad guards positioned themselves in a semicircle directly in front of the viewing window, then froze in place. Silence, thick and heavy, pressed all around Gregory. He strained his ears. At first, he heard nothing, and then a soft scuffing sound teased his senses.

A ripple went through the line of soldiers as they raised their spears and thumped the staves of dark wood against breastplates. Again, Gregory heard the sound. Louder now. Boot heels striking stone.

A man of middle height stopped a few paces in front of the viewing mirror, his black and crimson armor polished until it glistened like blood and wet shadows. Gregory noted the armor looked to be composed of thousands of individual scales, and he wondered if it was grown and not made. At the man's side, a small, graceful woman waited with her head bowed. A delicate chain peeked out from the flowing sleeve of her gown. The silver links glittered in the dim light, but abruptly vanished into gloom a few paces behind the woman, like they had been severed with an axe.

Something about the shadows caught Gregory's eye, diverting his attention from the leader to the small woman. It hit him then, a shock so profound he recoiled back a step.

Behind him, Lillian smoothed a hand across his shoulder in a subtle caress.

"Easy, my gargoyle," she said, pitching her words to carry like she intended for the new arrivals to hear. "When you rescued me, you were not the only gargoyle there. They needed to practice capturing and holding one of your kind before they attempted to capture you, my pet."

At the mention of another gargoyle, the small woman with the manacled wrist gave the chain a tug. The shadows parted and a gargoyle materialized on the opposite side of the viewing mirror. He sidled up next to the woman and licked at her hands before bowing his head low. Then he settled at her feet. Like a loyal dog.

Gregory's stomach heaved. He looked over his shoulder at Lillian and whispered along their mental link, *"Is this to be my future?"*

"Not if I can help it, my love." Lillian's voice filled his head. *"Play along with me if you do not want to become their slave for real. As long as they think I'm winning you over to their side, they will not go to the trouble of coming here. They'll assume I'll bring you home to them once I've had my fun. Gregory, please play along no matter what I do. I promise not to shame you in front of the others. You have my word."*

Lillian's thoughts were as shocking as her hands sliding under the obstacle of his wings and around his sides in a gliding caress. Her fingers traced along the ridge of his tensed muscles.

"You're playing a dangerous game," he cautioned.

"I like danger," Lillian said, her breath disturbing his mane and tickling his neck.

Her tone, so like the Sorceress of old, warmed him. Then

her hands shifted lower, her thumbs hooking under the top edge of his loincloth. And *that* wasn't anything like his old Mistress.

"Greetings, Commander Gryton," Lillian said while she draped herself along Gregory's back.

"Daryna." The man in the black and crimson armor raised his visor and nodded in her direction, though he didn't take his eyes off Gregory for long. "Our Lady will be pleased you've finally decided to contact us. Where have you been?"

"The Mortal Realm, as you already know."

The face looking out of the shadows of the helmet was human enough. Though that meant little. A number of creatures could pass for human at a distance. Considering this one's location, Gregory doubted he had any human blood.

"When you called your gargoyle and escaped, I have to say, we expected the worst."

"He woke early, sensing where I was and rushed to my rescue." Lillian paused to smile at Gregory over her shoulder before returning her full attention to Gryton. "I wasn't yet old enough to control him and he would have taken me back to Lord Death and destroyed all our plans. I knew I had to do something, so I convinced him our only avenue of escape was through the Veil to the Mortal Realm."

"A risk," Gryton countered.

"Yes, but it worked. He had to turn to stone to heal from his injuries."

A rumble of threat built in his chest and when the armor-clad man took a step forward, Gregory released a glass-shaking growl.

Lillian laughed, then with surprising speed, she stepped

around him and pushed him back until he collided with the edge of the bed.

"Easy, my Durnathyne. They're no threat to me." Lillian turned her attention back to Gryton. "My gargoyle has always been protective, but now he's added handsome males to the list of things he doesn't like me near."

"He's fully matured and already yours?" Gryton questioned, doubt clear in his raised eyebrow.

"Yes. As I said, I continued to work on his conditioning while he rested in his stone form."

"Good, you'll have no problem bringing him home now."

"He'll follow me anywhere. However, I'm not coming home yet."

"Do not make me retrieve you."

"You won't have to. But why do you think I have not contacted you since coming here?"

Gryton sighed and glowered at the woman holding the silver chain. "Because you were a rebellious young fool. I blame your dryad mother for allowing you too much freedom."

Gregory studied the woman. So, this was Lillian's mother. He glanced between the woman and the chained gargoyle, wondering.

"Perhaps you have cause to think me rebellious. I'm not coming home until Gregory is completely mine. Once he is, I'll return and serve the Lady of Battles as she wishes. But Gregory is mine, and he'll take orders from only me. I don't share. And I won't share the responsibility of his training and conditioning either."

"That is the talk of a traitor."

"If our Lady has a problem with how I choose to serve, let her judge me."

Gryton tapped a finger along one armor-clad thigh. "Why did you contact us, if not to say you were returning home?"

"Two things. Have you checked your armory lately? You'll find you're missing a demon blade—and no, I didn't steal one as I ran. But if there is more than one missing, I'd like to know how many, since a Riven tried to kill my gargoyle with one. And in this magicless realm, he came closer to death than I wish ever to see again."

Gryton swore and turned to glower at someone just beyond the window. "Your cursed blood magic is running amuck. You said the demon blades would help you control the rogue Riven."

A tall, slimly built woman with long brown hair walked into the frame. "I said it *might* help me regain control of them, but no spell works as it should in that realm."

Gryton huffed, looking like he'd like to take the woman's head. Gregory recognized the blood witch from the last time he'd faced her in the Battle Goddess's kingdom and would have cheered the commander on, if only to see the universe rid of a blood witch.

The witch merely shrugged off the commander's glower. "The Riven shouldn't be an issue for Daryna. She already knows enough blood magic to control them."

Daryna laughed. "And waste my magic in this power-starved land? Tearing out their hearts is easier."

"Dangerous, though," the witch said as she cocked her head, studying the Sorceress in a way Gregory didn't like.

His Sorceress just gave the witch a shrug. "As far as I can see, the only threats to my gargoyle have come from the

Magic Realm. A pack of death hounds now serves the Riven. Who sent them?"

The blood witch laughed, a clear tone of delight. "Commander Gryton thought to use them to spy upon you."

Daryna glared at Gryton. "They tried to eat my gargoyle."

Gryton scowled at Lillian. "All the more reason you should return home to the Magic Realm."

"Are you actually saying the Lady's domain is safer?"

He grunted. "I prefer my assets where I can protect them. Until you and the gargoyle are fully mature, you are both vulnerable. The Lady of Battles will be angry if you're foolish enough to get killed. She doesn't like having to start over. And I don't like having to deal with an angry goddess. It's not good for one's immortality."

"I'm perfectly capable of protecting myself and my gargoyle. The Lady made certain of that. Now, back to my requests..."

"Fine. What request?" His tone was indulgent, but Gregory was certain it was an act.

"First, no more interference. Second, since you've sent demon blades and death hounds, you must have found a way to travel here, I'd like my mother and father to come. It wouldn't hurt to have another gargoyle around to deal with the Riven while I finish taming mine. And no doubt, my mother has advice to help tame a gargoyle."

"I thought you said he was already yours?" Gryton paused and narrowed his eyes at Gregory before returning his attention to Lillian. "You don't sound as confident now."

To anyone watching, Gregory hoped he looked appropriately tamed by Lillian's power, his body language docile—the willing victim. While lying wasn't one of his strongest talents, he'd certainly been honing that skill a great deal of late.

"Oh, he is mine. I just wanted to know some of my mother's secrets." Lillian trailed her fingers down Gregory's chest in a slow, leisurely descent. At the caress of her fingertips against his sensitive skin, his pulse picked up until it thundered in his ears, and he no longer had to fake the "willing" part.

"Fine." Commander Gryton waved a hand as if that would make Lillian stop touching Gregory. "I don't need to witness any dryad and gargoyle mating habits. I'll send your parents to you within a moon's cycle, then I want you back within the season. You *will* report your progress once every fortnight until you return."

"As you wish." Lillian bowed her head in the stranger's direction. "I will expect mother's arrival soon. But until then, I have other plans." She pushed Gregory back on the bed, and he felt her touch his magic. Before he knew what was happening, he was shapeshifting into his human form.

Gregory allowed Lillian to press him into the bed. She trapped him with her slight weight more surely than a rockslide. Her lips caressed his, and he closed his eyes, concentrating on boring things—like mending harnesses and polishing swords—while standing in ice-cold water.

Lillian chuckled and nipped at his lips.

"Nice try. Let me know how that works for you."

She broke off the kiss and looked over her shoulder at the enemy. "Goodbye for now, Commander."

A moment later, the magic feeding the viewing mirror dwindled to a trickle. The images of the other world quivered, and then shattered into a hundred grains of light and misted away into nothing.

"I'm sure Gryton didn't buy my little deception. He will send my mother sooner than expected," Lillian said, then nibbled at her lower lip in a way Gregory found interesting. "I doubt she'll be alone."

Gregory struggled into a sitting position, trying not to dwell on how soft and warm she was, or how much he liked her weight pressing against him. Instead, he snatched at the first question that came to mind. "Why did you ask for your parents?"

She let him up, then sat on the edge of the bed. "I had to do something to pacify Gryton's suspicions. He wouldn't expect me to ask for help if I had something to hide. Besides, I want to rescue my father. He's been a prisoner all my life. Even as a child, I wanted to help him."

"And your mother? What of her?"

"My mother was born and raised there. That life is all she knows. While she serves the Lady of Battles, she isn't evil."

"Anyone in service to the Battle Goddess opposes the Light." He drew a deep breath. At least in his human form, without her dryad scent affecting him like a drug, he could almost think clearly.

"You don't know everything about the politics there. Those who serve the Lady of Battles do so because they see her as a lesser evil."

He schooled his features into a neutral expression. He wanted to hear her words without his reactions influencing them.

"Not everyone within the Lady's domain is evil. At least

not compared to the demons which have been allowed to spread unchecked since the Twins went to war."

He tilted his head to one side and remained silent.

Lillian crossed her arms. "These are not the lies the Lady of Battles tried to feed me. Many in her armies started out serving the Divine Ones but made mistakes along the way until they couldn't face the Light. When the Light shunned them, they sought a life elsewhere. And the Lady of Battles will give shelter to any who will serve her in her fight against her brother."

"Your words sound reasonable. I'll agree with some of what you say, but it doesn't mean they can be saved."

"I'm not the Lady's tool," she said in a voice tinged with anger. Then it softened. "At least not yet."

"I know."

"And I'm not defending Gryton or his kind. I just wanted you to understand some of them didn't have a choice. This wasn't a life they chose. They were forced into it by circumstance. Some still honor their ancient duty and guard the Veil between the Realms, preventing more demons from escaping from the Void. We may be able to use that to our advantage one day."

"Very well. I will keep that in mind," he mumbled, his mind already focused on the next problem. He did some quick math. Time was faster here than in the Magic Realm, but even then, he might only have days before Lillian's mother came, trailed by her pet gargoyle. "Do you think your mother can be reasoned with?"

"My mother loved both my father and me in her own strange way, but she is loyal to the Battle Goddess. My father was prisoner, not willing subject to the Lady of Battles, but I think he still loved my mother. That was when I was a child. I don't know what has changed while I was here."

His stomach churned. No matter that it should have been impossible to change a gargoyle's allegiance; it had been done. And if it could happen to one gargoyle, Gregory wasn't arrogant enough to believe it couldn't be done again.

With Lillian sitting on her bed, watching him through her lashes, he didn't doubt he could be swayed from the Light if he didn't guard against it. It would be all too easy. He thought he knew how the other gargoyle's protective nature might have been used against him. A dryad surrounded by enemies would be something vulnerable in need of protection. Lillian's father had probably thought her mother was a fellow prisoner.

Gregory would do anything to protect Lillian. He wasn't certain he'd have fared any better than that other gargoyle.

A warm hand cupped his cheek. Lillian tilted his head until she was looking into his eyes. "Durnathyne, I'll not let what happened to my father happen to you. Our love isn't a weapon for the Lady of Battles to use against you." She came to her knees and placed her hands on his shoulders. "That's why you need to put your spell back on my mind. By blocking my memories, you inadvertently halted the Lady's handiwork."

"I don't understand." There was so much he didn't know, and he didn't like feeling helpless.

"Everything you've speculated about is true. You were right when you thought of it as my bestial side. She created me to grow and transform into something greater than a dryad. Whatever I become, I fear I'll be far more dangerous to you. Like a seed, this poor, tortured soul needs me to call on my magic to grow. She feeds on my emotions, my deep love for you. And on my ancient knowledge, growing stronger until one day she will consume me—or twist me into something so different, I'll wish I didn't remember anything."

Lillian paused, her expression no longer serene. Fear slithered along their link. "Your wards upon my memories blocked the demon's memories, too. And the lack of magic in this realm inhibited its growth. Until the last few days, the demon soul slept, but now she remembers her purpose. I'm running out of time. I don't know what to do to save us, but I can't let her harm you."

Gregory couldn't watch her struggle, and he gathered her to his chest. He tucked her head against his shoulder and rocked her gently. "I'll find this dark seed and dig it out."

The tension leaked out of her smaller frame, and she relaxed against him. "My Durnathyne, you can't. The Lady of Battles expects something like that. If you try, the demon soul will trigger a spell woven of the blackest of blood magic, killing us both, as well as anyone with the misfortune to be too close. But it will not stop there. It will deliver both our souls to the Lady of Battles, and she will begin again. You must find another way to disable the demon soul. Wrap it in so many layers of magic it can never escape while I live. If that fails, you must take me to the Lord of the Underworld; he will prevent my spirit from being recaptured by his sister. I think my half of our soul would die if I harmed or enslaved you. Promise you'll surrender me to Death's mercy once we return to the Magic Realm. I don't want to become the Battle Goddess's creature."

No! His soul rebelled at the thought of handing her over

to the Lord of the Underworld. He'd be sealing her death. It would be like killing her himself.

"I'll need your help," Lillian continued. "The Lady of Battles will have built traps to prevent me from seeking her brother."

"I can't," he growled as he crushed her against him. "Ask me anything else, but please don't ask me to help you die. I won't do it."

She continued to run her hands along his back, soothing, pleading for him to listen. "For now, you must put the block back on my memories and my magic. That will give you a little more time to try to find a way to stop the darkness growing within me. But if there is no cure, you must take me to the Lord of the Underworld before the demon enslaves us both." She leaned into him and rested her head against his chest, over his heart.

His hand shook as he reached to stroke her hair. He wanted to cry or rage—anything to ease the cold horror pumping through his veins. "Please, I can't do what you ask."

"Shh." She placed a finger across his lips. "Everything will be fine. The Lord of the Underworld will free my soul to return to the Spirit Realm, and then I'll be reborn again. We'll not be parted long."

"No." Changing his grip on her, he sought her lips to stop her flow of words. He projected his ancient love for her and his more recent desire until she returned his kiss with heat. Small, almost purring sounds escaped her. Molten fire shot through his veins at the sign of her pleasure. He flipped her onto her back, pressing her into the bed. She melted under him—warm, willing. He shivered at the soft caress of her fingers along his skin, intensely aware of her body pressing against his, how she spread her legs, so he fit perfectly between her thighs. Gods, he wanted this, needed the other half of his soul.

"Hmm." She turned her head, breaking the kiss.

He growled in frustration.

"Durnathyne, no." Lillian's breath came in uneven gasps. "The Lady wants us to get lost in our passions, but we must never forget our duty."

It took him longer to gather his own scattered thoughts. "You talk of duty and yet ask me to help you die." He buried his face in her hair, refusing to look at her. "My duty is to protect you. If I break that oath, then I no longer serve any duty. Nothing is more forbidden than what you ask."

"All you need to do is help me find the Lord of the Underworld."

"No." He pushed himself up and leaped off the bed, catching the corner of the nightstand in his hurry to escape her words. It teetered for a moment, then clattered to the ground, drawers spilling across the floor. Uncaring, he continued backing up until his back hit the wall behind him. "Don't ask me again. I'll have no part in your death. I'll block your memories and do what I can to block your use of magic. I'll find a cure, no matter what. I'm not going to let you die because of the Battle Goddess's manipulations. Death will claim us one day, but not like this."

"Easy. It's all right. I'll not ask that of you again." The Sorceress patted the bed. "Come back to me. I want to hold you for a little while before you make me forget."

A small smile curved her lips as he inched back toward the bed. Her expression softened more, and she motioned him to come closer. Uncertain of the wisdom in getting within touching distance but wanting to be near her too much to care about the outcome, he glided the last of the way to her side and eased back onto the bed. A moment later she curled into him, and her arms came around him. It was a fragile peace. One he was terrified wouldn't last.

"I love you," she murmured against his shoulder. "Let me have this one, perfect moment. After I fall asleep, block my memories."

He held her until her breath evened in sleep, then he summoned his magic, placing the wards upon her mind one layer at a time. When he was finished, he reverted to his gargoyle form and buried his muzzle in her hair.

"I love you too, my Sorceress." Surely his heart was shattering, it ached so much. The overwhelming need to show her how much he loved her threatened to strip him of his reason, and yet he was afraid. His simple words of love didn't begin to encompass what she meant to him. He couldn't fool himself anymore. He no longer served the Divine Ones first and then the Sorceress—he served her above all else.

As a restless sleep came to claim him, the last thing he dwelled on was what to do if he couldn't find a cure for her. Her death was not an option, not for him. A small, selfish part of his soul planted the seeds of a solution.

Perhaps he could bargain with the Lady of Battles— become one of her army in exchange for Lillian's freedom. If what Lillian said about the Lady's army guarding the Veil between the Realms was correct, he might be able to become one of them without completely betraying himself, or what it meant to be the Sorceress's Protector. He closed his eyes and rested his head on her breast, listening to the throb of her heart until sleep claimed him at last.

CHAPTER THIRTY-TWO

*L*illian awoke to find Gregory hogging all the bed. The damp heat of his breath washed over her shoulder where he'd buried his muzzle in her hair. If she could feel that, she supposed she wasn't a ghost, so she'd survived whatever he'd done. She felt no different than before. There was no river of memories flowing from the depths of her mind like she'd half expected. All those lives he'd alluded to; why couldn't she remember her past?

But with him spooning her, his wings warming her better than an electric blanket, she could forget her worries for now. She listened to the throb of his heart as she lay tucked safely in her nest. With her head resting on his bicep, she had a clear view straight down the length of his arm. Every few seconds, his fist would clench and his talons flex. She raised her head.

He growled and twitched in his sleep, in the grip of a nightmare. When she turned toward him and rested a hand on his chest, it calmed him, his twitching and struggles lessening.

"Easy, Gregory," she soothed. "I'm here. There's no danger."

Curious, she lowered her shields and reached for him with her mind, and like the few times she'd done it by accident, his mind opened—his thoughts and emotions sweeping into her. After a moment, she sorted through the chaos until she found the source of his nightmare.

Last night unfolded in his thoughts. His guilt over causing her pain, the triggering of the trap on her soul, the window to another world, his love intertwined with bone-deep, shameful desire—his every worry and fear replayed within her mind. And then the horror of hearing her other self say she wanted him to help her die if he couldn't find a cure.

"Why, that selfish, sanctimonious bitch." She stroked Gregory's mane until he calmed. "How dare she put it all on you? Heal me or kill me. What kind of bullshit is that? My poor gargoyle. No wonder you're having nightmares. That's a horrible thing to ask." Lillian mulled over the situation. She still didn't have her old memories back, but after what she'd learned from Gregory, she didn't think she wanted to be that person, anyway.

Apparently, she was evil.

She expected to feel something. Great sorrow, fear, mind-numbing shock. Something. Anything. But there was nothing, not unless being monumentally pissed off at her "older self" counted. Then, slowly, a greater concern crept into her consciousness. What if that wasn't her old self at all? What if it was the demon soul testing Gregory's resolve?

It didn't really matter if it was the demon or Lillian's older self, the problem was still the same. Sooner or later, something was going to take her over.

"Fine. I'm evil. I'll deal with this, somehow. You won't have to," she told the sleeping gargoyle. Leaning forward, she kissed him on the forehead between his horns.

Then, deciding she'd better get up before he figured out she'd learned some important details he'd planned to keep from her, she scooted out of bed. A shower and proper clothes were the first order of business, followed by coffee. Maybe by then, she'd have come up with a plan so Gregory wouldn't have to make choices that would destroy him.

Hell, a chainsaw to her tree might solve everyone's problems, but she doubted she'd be able to accomplish it with the gargoyle and the unicorn always on guard—not to mention, she'd probably pass out at the first cut.

CHAPTER THIRTY-THREE

*T*he bathroom door's hinges creaked as she opened it. Lillian winced at the jarring sound. Gregory bolted upright on the bed, his surprise and confusion evident by his pointed ears and flared nostrils while he took in his surroundings. Calming, he extracted himself from the sheets and eased off the bed. He turned his back to her and tidied the sheets.

"Morning," she said. Her greeting sounded more cheerful than she'd intended.

He returned her greeting after a short pause. Brushing her damp hair out of her face, she narrowed her eyes. If she hadn't known what had transpired last night, she would have just thought he was still half asleep. But she knew better. Gregory couldn't tell a lie to save his life. With his back to her, she couldn't read what was written on his face. But if she could see, she thought she'd see shame and embarrassment.

She cleared her throat and prepared to lie. "Since I'm still alive, I assume everything went well."

"Yes, you passed the test to everyone's satisfaction." The gargoyle returned her lie.

"Then I think I'll go hunt up some breakfast for us." She smiled, a stiff-muscled expression, just in case he happened to look her way. "I'll be in the kitchen when you're ready."

He nodded and vanished into the bathroom. As far as she could tell, he still hadn't detected her lie, which just reinforced how out of sorts he was. He could normally detect a lie as easily as she could draw a breath.

She fled, leaving behind the gargoyle and the room full of deceit.

Downstairs, the living room was empty, but murmuring voices drew her toward the back of the house. When she reached the kitchen, Gran and the pooka stood close together, deep in conversation.

Gran looked up. Her expression flashed from worry back to her usual jovial look so fast, Lillian nearly missed the slight change.

"I saved you some muffins, and there's fresh coffee," Gran said as she gestured absently at the kitchen counter.

While Lillian mechanically took a bite out of a muffin, the pooka edged closer to her. His equine eyes, while not friendly, were less hostile than she remembered. Had she been better at reading body language, she'd have said the pooka wanted something.

"Come walk with me. There's something I want to tell you," Gran said, interrupting Lillian's thoughts about what a pooka might want from her.

Lillian allowed herself to be herded out the sliding door and onto the back porch. A warm breeze beckoned her to walk the maze, but she needed to know if Gran would lie to her. "What is it? Did I fail the test? Are the others going to try to harm me?"

Gran's eyes widened, surprise warring with displeasure. "No one will harm you, and while some of them are not satisfied with all they learned, we have more immediate concerns."

"There *is* something amiss with me."

"Not to cause you more worry, but do you think you'd still be here if you harbored evil within you? I'm sure the gargoyle would kill you himself if he thought you evil. The Clan is more concerned by the vast amount of power at your command, and your lack of training to control it."

"Then I'll be careful not to draw on power when Gregory can't help me control it." Lillian's stomach soured at Gran's lies. Her family knew what the gargoyle had tried to hide. She wanted to crawl away somewhere deep and dark.

"While you and Gregory rested, the rest of us have been finalizing our plans. If the Riven want a fight, we'll give them one. The dire wolves think they've found one of the daytime lairs of our enemy. We'll take some of the Pack and check it out. I want you to stay here. There are enough wards on this land to protect you and the other dryads while we're away."

Lillian nodded. "What about Gregory?"

"If he can bring himself to leave your side, I imagine he'd like another chance to take out some Riven."

Gran's words didn't ease the tension in Lillian's shoulders where fear had lodged along her spine. Sweat dampened her palms. She rubbed them along her jeans. Her fingers felt stiff. After a moment, she'd started rubbing the base of each nail and realized they were itchy and aching like she'd grabbed a fistful of poison ivy—or like the time Gregory had been injured, just before she'd blacked out.

Gran continued to speak, but Lillian no longer heard. Something rose within her, an alarm flaring within her mind. Lillian opened her mouth, about to say she didn't want them to go without her when the ground shook. Nearby birds erupted into flight.

An inhuman scream split the air—high, eerie. Fast on its heels, the low-rumbling growl of a dire wolf joined it. The growl too was cut short, ending in a yelp. Like a river in a flash flood, a wave of power broke across Lillian's skin. She grasped at the magic, but it slithered between her fingers and raced away. But a familiar scent lingered.

"What was that?" Lillian jerked her head in the direction the commotion emanated from, then turned to look at her grandmother.

"Jason!" Gran cried, her eyes wide, her features reflecting her horror. "That was a witch's staff being shattered. The Riven have Jason."

Such cold rage looked foreign on her grandmother's face. Before Lillian had a chance to react, Gran was pushing her in the direction of the house.

"Go," Gran ordered. "It's a raid. They're attacking the wards. Get to the house and tell the others. I'm not letting them take any more of my family."

A protest died on Lillian's lips. Gran was already running toward the unseen danger, unarmed. Every cell in Lillian's body screamed to follow her grandmother, to challenge whatever had invaded her home and taken her brother, but reason prevailed. She'd need a weapon first.

She turned toward the house just as an immense black shadow skidded to a stop at her side. Gregory was on all fours, Gran's quarterstaff clutched in his jaws. He spat it out so he could speak.

"Get on my back, I'll take you to the house. My wards there will ensure your safety. Once you're safe, I'll return for Vivian."

"No! Go help my grandmother. I'm fine."

"I can't leave you. And I won't take you into battle with me." He butted her in the stomach like he could physically herd her to safety.

Lillian gasped and stumbled a few steps before she caught her balance. "I'll go to the house, but you need to help Gran rescue Jason. She said the Riven were attacking the wards. If they breach the defenses, I'll be in greater danger." While she held Gregory's gaze in a battle of wills, three dire wolves, each carrying a sidhe on their backs, ghosted past. "If you go help Gran and the others, you'll be protecting me, too. I'll follow your progress through our link. Please, Gregory."

More cries echoed across the meadow, now accented by the ring of metal on metal.

Gregory snarled and pushed her toward the house once more, then he picked up the staff and bolted off in the direction Gran had run. He spread his wings as he ran, each of his bounding strides covering a vast amount of ground. Within moments, he'd overtaken the dire wolves and vanished into the distant tree line—one shadow among many.

Lillian turned and ran back to the house. She hadn't said she'd stay there. Besides, she needed a weapon and a way to track the Riven. Somewhere hidden in the house was the perfect tool for the job. She just had to find it and coerce it into serving her.

CHAPTER THIRTY-FOUR

The gardens outside the house were silent, the emptiness a strange contrast to the death-cries and blood-scent of battle she experienced through Gregory's senses, where he battled over a kilometer distant. Lillian slowed to a walk, and with some regret, shut down the flow of sensations coming from her gargoyle. But she kept a light touch on their link in case he was injured.

She glanced around the gardens again, this time searching with something other than her eyes. Magic stirred, flowing out from her, seeking dangers. She sensed nothing between her and the house. Within her home, she detected a spark of magic. Another dryad? Probably, judging by the forest-scented magic, but there was another source of power coming toward her.

She cocked her head as her ears strained. The drumming of hooves grew louder a few seconds before a black pony emerged from around the magnolia on the east corner of the house. Even from that distance, the pooka's bright-yellow eyes caught her attention.

Unafraid, she held her ground as he skidded to a halt in front of her. Of all the Clan, she'd not expected to find the pooka still here. She would have pegged him as a lover of death and chaos, battle and bloodshed his sweetest joys. But then again, perhaps it somehow made sense he'd be the one to stay behind. He wanted to return to the world of magic with a desperation the other fae lacked. And since she was the pooka's ticket home, Gregory probably didn't have to coerce him into the role of a bodyguard. Very well. She had a use for him, too. Actually... he'd fit her plan nicely. She didn't want to risk an innocent.

"You here to play the bodyguard?" she asked.

"So it would seem," he whispered into her mind even as he turned his attention in the direction of the combat, *"Though, I would have enjoyed a good battle."*

Lillian's attention followed the direction of his gaze even though she could feel what was going on from the gargoyle's thoughts.

The battle was joined—he and Gran had caught up to the rearguard of the enemies. They fought back-to-back, holding their own, but were unable to break through the guard and go after Jason's captors.

Anger and frustration fueled Gran's magic, and she dealt blow after blow with her quarterstaff. Gregory was ruthless, decapitating, gutting, and maiming with each strike of his claws or tail blade. But for every enemy they took down, more came out of the forest to continue the battle. The Riven were like the Hydra—take one head and two more came out of nowhere, ready to bite.

The pooka raised his head and lipped at the breeze. *"They fight well. I would bring your grandmother with me into the Magic Realm if she would come. There she could realize her full power—and a full, long life. Not like these short quarter-lives the Coven experience here."*

"Now is hardly the time to think of that."

"What else would you talk about while we await this battle's outcome?"

"How about why we're standing here talking instead of doing something about the enemies invading our land? You must hate having to stay behind."

The pooka shook his head and snorted, and then trotted in a half-circle around her. *"It is of no consequence."*

"Gregory commanded you to stay with me, and now you can't enjoy a 'bit of fun,' I'm guessing," she countered.

"The gargoyle didn't trust the single-horned fool to protect you."

Lillian nearly grinned at the rivalry between the pooka and unicorn.

He bobbed his head, ears swinging back. *"The dryads are good at misleading and confusing a trail in the forest, but they are no warriors. I stayed to protect you—from nothing. I sense no evil nearby."*

Lillian nodded agreement, though his statement wasn't entirely true. She sensed a great darkness very near, rearing up within her own soul now that Gregory was in danger again. Perhaps a darkness greater even than the Riven. "I don't plan on sitting and doing nothing. Can I count on you to aid me with a little task?"

His ears swiveled forward.

"As a reward, I will take you through the Veil." She called her magic and reached out, running a hand along his neck.

His skin shuddered at her touch, but he leaned into her caress, butting his muzzle into her stomach. He tilted his head to the side as one yellow eye rolled to study her.

"To which kingdom?"

Ah. Smart pooka. "Do you really care as long as it gets you away from this place?"

His tail slapped his rump, and he pawed at the ground.

"No," he said at last.

"Then serve me well, because I am a Power and those under me shall be rewarded."

He bobbed his head once more and fell in line beside her when she resumed her walk to the house. There was one other thing she still needed.

She'd been able to keep her true thoughts from Gregory by giving him random images of her wandering through the house, pacing and worrying with the other dryads while they awaited news. It had worked so far, but now she'd have to work fast to stay ahead of the gargoyle. If he caught her before she completed her plan, he'd get hurt.

She didn't want to see him or anyone else get hurt because of her. Everything was her fault. But she was about to make it right.

Lillian continued through the house until she came to the attic's stairs.

The air at the top was thick with dust and heat from the afternoon sun beating on the south side of the roof. She navigated the clutter on the floor and followed the fresh tracks in the dust. Far back in the east corner of the big attic, she found the old cedar chest. Worn and discolored with age, it didn't look like much, but it was solid. Its metal hinges and lock glistened with fresh oil. She ran a finger along the domed lid, sensing her gargoyle's magic. The sturdy padlock would slow most normal modes of entrance.

But the faint blue shimmer that flared when she touched it was the chest's primary means of protection.

An ancient memory awoke. She closed her eyes and reached inward. Power welled up from within. It overflowed her body and spilled out onto the chest. Directing the magic was easier than she thought. When she judged she'd poured enough onto the lid, she imagined it digging in—digging deep, past the shimmer of blue warding, into the grain of the cedar.

Opening her eyes, she looked down upon the chest and curled her fingers into a claw. Her hand still hovering above the chest, she made an upwards jerking motion. The lid issued a deep groan of strained wood as it gave way. Three chunks of old cedar planking flew out and away from her to slam into the rafters and bare walls. Silence returned. Leaning forward, she glanced into the shadowed bottom of the trunk. The demon blade glittered dully.

She snatched up the dagger. Its hilt was chilled, and the blade vibrated in her hand. It projected its eagerness to draw on blood and death.

"You will serve me," she told it with a single-mindedness to match its own.

It shivered in her hand, its agreement ensured.

There was no doubt in her mind.

CHAPTER THIRTY-FIVE

*H*er crossbow bumped against her back with each of the pooka's strides, but that couldn't be helped. Speed was more important than comfort. The black pony's pace blurred the forest into vague shadows all around Lillian. While he galloped full out, he slowed enough that the sharp turns and twists in the trail didn't throw her. She was lucky. Had he been less mindful of his rider, her meager skills probably would have failed her. Her grand plan of self-sacrifice would have ended then and there.

"This is far enough," she shouted over the whistle of the wind in her ears and the thunder of his hooves.

"As you command, great lady."

When the pooka slowed, she unwound her hands from his mane. He eased into a trot, picking his way through the forest. Birds chirped, hopping through the canopy high above. A squirrel perched on a branch overhanging the trail, its tail wagging in aggravation. The peace of the forest did not soothe her. She tried to relax by drawing in deep breaths.

She managed to unclench her fists, but no command from her mind could loosen the tense muscles along her shoulders and lower back.

A weight at her side reminded her of her decision. The demon blade bore more than a physical weight—its malevolence dragging on her soul. Even sheathed, she could still feel its pull, its will working away at her mental shields. But she now knew how to fix that. Memories from another time were resurfacing with each use of magic.

Drawing the blade, she held it at eye level a moment, turning it this way and that, looking for the runes her memories said would be on such a blade. Oh, yes, there. Close to the hilt, two finely etched symbols. Only two.

Death. Thief.

Simple. Effective. All the demon blade needed. It had no other purpose, only to bring death by stealing life energy.

Until now.

She lowered the blade and brought its tip down against her other palm. A quick, short pull and blood gushed up to stain the blade. A brief sting, a cold drawing sensation, and the demon blade began to feed in earnest. She let the blade drink her power for a few seconds more.

"*Enough.*" Her thought rang with power. The demon spirit in the blade stilled and listened to her. Its uncertainty and curiosity came across the blood link. While she had its attention, she touched a thumb to the first rune.

Thief.

The word rang with power.

Steal life. She touched the second rune as she thought it.

Bring death.

A third rune of power burned itself into the demon blade.

And serve only me.

The dagger bucked in her hand, fighting the command, but it was no match for her power. It calmed, then turned its attention to her. Waiting. Wanting to hunt and kill.

"*Soon,*" she promised. *"But first, tell me where your brothers wait."*

It did not tell her in words or show her images as she had hoped, but it did answer her, linking with another of its kind somewhere to the north and west of her position. Like she did when she wanted to know where her gargoyle was, its magic tugged at her mind, urging her in that direction.

She glanced at the pooka. He'd remained still throughout the whole ritual with the blade, but now he rolled a white-ringed yellow eye back at her, his skin shuddering.

She grinned at the pooka. "Shall we make like thieves, steal our enemies' lives, and bring them death?"

"Yes."

CHAPTER THIRTY-SIX

They rode in silence as they headed in the direction the demon blade urged. No more birds sang or flew between the trees, nor were there any squirrels or chipmunks or other creatures of the forest. The animals sensed the same thing she did. As she rode nearer, the stink of evil hit Lillian full in the face, thickening until she could almost taste it on her tongue. She liked the scent no better than the wildlife did.

Had she a choice, she'd have fled the area, too.

"We're almost there," she told the pooka.

"Good. If that wretched Riven stench gets any worse, I will let you walk the rest of the way, great lady."

Did all the beasties have overly sensitive noses? She grinned. At least it made her like the pooka a little bit more than she had before.

Thinking of sensitive creatures summoned an image of her gargoyle, and her smile faltered. He hadn't yet found out about her plan.

Her throat constricted at the thought of his panic when he did, and then later for the guilt he'd experience.

He would see it as his failure.

The idea of his grief was nearly enough to make her turn back. Almost, but not quite. She wouldn't let any more innocents die because of her. And, as big, scary, and ancient as he was, her gargoyle was an innocent. She would not let him become a victim.

If the Lady of Battles got her hands on him, she would do all in her considerable power to make him into her creature.

A change in the pooka's gait drew Lillian from her thoughts. They had reached their destination. She unslung her crossbow and loaded a bolt. Her plan didn't actually involve using the weapon on them, but it was better to have it at the ready just in case her plans went to shit.

The forest opened into a small clearing, created when one old tree had collapsed and taken down another of its neighbors. Standing in the center of the meadow, five men awaited the pooka's approach.

To call them men was perhaps inaccurate. A faint power, laced with the scent of Riven, wafted off the nearest one. He turned his head in her direction, but made no other move, his stillness unnatural. The pooka hadn't tried to hide his approach, so she wasn't expecting to sneak up on them, but these five looked like they knew she was coming.

"Mistress," the blade whispered in her mind. *"They knew I was tracking them."*

"You told them I was coming?"

"Yes, so that we might begin the hunt."

"You have done well."

It was probably best she not surprise them, as she

doubted they took being surprised at all well. She wasn't ready to die yet, not until all the rest were in range.

The pooka halted a few feet away from the closest Riven, but he jerked his head back toward the forest and snorted. A dire wolf padded out of the trees, his pace slowed by the added weight of a rider.

The newcomer was another pale-skinned fae. This one was short and boyish-looking, but the glint in his eyes told Lillian this was no child. Evil emanated the strongest from him. It was a lesser version of what slept within her soul.

"I assume you've come to trade for the male?" the demon boy asked in sweet tones.

"My brother lives?"

"Yes."

She'd been certain he was still alive but hearing he still lived unlocked something in her heart. She could do this. "If you free my brother unharmed, I will come with you willingly. No tricks."

"Very well."

"Where is my brother?"

"He is elsewhere. We'll take you to him, and then you can watch as he escapes."

"Agreed."

"Then come." He gestured at the center of the little circle where they stood.

She nodded and dismounted. The pooka followed her as closely as her gargoyle would have. But she didn't feel safe.

"My friend will carry my brother to safety." By the sound of the pooka's tail slapping his rump, he wasn't happy with her volunteering his services, but he didn't disagree either, so she had his agreement.

The four older-looking men took a few steps apart, making room for the pooka inside their circle. The demon boy stayed close to Lillian. When she and the pooka were in the exact middle, the four strangers each drew a demon blade from their belts and held them aloft.

When the first started to chant, Lillian cringed.

Her skin crawled with the power rising from the ground.

Dark and twisted, it swirled around her and the pooka until she wanted to gag. She tried to block out the chanting as it rose and fell, making her ears ache with the strain to understand what they said. The chanting increased, peaking like a wave's crest, and then the men plunged their daggers into the ground. The world went black.

CHAPTER THIRTY-SEVEN

Gregory patrolled the battlefield and dispatched anything that still moved and reeked of evil. He snarled at a broken Riven as it tried to crawl away into the shadows to hide and heal. Never again. With a thought, his magic surged up and burned the creature to ash. He whirled away and moved to the next. He was dispatching another when Vivian called out to him and gestured behind. He turned in the direction Lillian's grandmother pointed. Sable and the unicorn raced toward him.

If they were here instead of guarding Lillian...

He froze, his earlier joy at dispatching evil gone.

The thoughts of his lady were still in his mind. She worried over a steaming cup of tea while she paced the kitchen, awaiting his return. Had he been thinking clearly, he'd have realized the cup of tea would have long gone cold. But he hadn't been blessed with clear thinking since he'd first come to this world.

She had lied to him. Lied to protect him. He shook his

head, his mane flying out around him as horror and rage broke something within him. It was too much to contain; it would tear his soul apart. He roared his anguish.

The fae and dire wolves froze in place. Some sent anxious looks in his direction. Vivian said nothing, just stared at him with a look of shock and horror. She didn't need to say anything. Her expression said it all. She had just lost two grandchildren to the Riven instead of one. He reached out to her mind and her despair hit him, slamming into him with a force as great as his rage.

"When you find the demons, kill them all," she whispered. "Let none of them escape." Her voice broke. "So, shall it be."

"So, shall it be," he echoed in his thoughts.

He tensed his hindquarters, bunching the muscles, and sprang into motion. When he was running at top speed, and the trees were shadows and the ground a blur, he unfolded his wings and leaped. His wings slapped the air, lifting him further from the ground with each down sweep.

By the time he found Lillian, it would be too late. Far, far too late. He had failed her, again. There would only be blood, vengeance, and death when he reached the end of his flight.

CHAPTER THIRTY-EIGHT

*B*lackness. Like a wet and moonless night, darkness encompassed Lillian's entire world. A wrenching sense of dislocation. Endless falling through nothing. A void. No sense of direction. No soothing forest. Not even ground to stand upon.

Sound returned in waves, fading then strengthening. The pooka snorted a challenge. Her own breathing came raspy and panicked.

Between one blink and the next, the sun warmed her skin again.

Lillian lay upon damp ground, the sky overhead was a bright blue with the occasional fluffy cloud. To judge by the color of the sky, she was still on Earth. She sat up and glanced around. The trees were of a familiar type, but instinct said she was elsewhere, Gregory a long way off.

Thinking of him allowed Gregory into her mind. *"Lillian! Don't do this. Use your power and fight them. Escape."*

"I'm sorry, Gregory. I'm remembering. This is the only way to stop

the demons and kill the darkness within me. The Lady of Battles does not share. When the Riven use their death magic to steal my power, the Lady will destroy them as I die."

"Please don't do this. I'll find another way."

She dragged in a steadying breath, nearly a sob. *"Oh, Gregory. I can't be the Lady's slave, and I won't let her use me to enslave you. This is the only way."*

"I just need a little more time."

"Only the Divine Ones can help me now. Goodbye, my soul." Lillian closed her mind to Gregory, and he was gone. It was the hardest thing she'd ever done. He didn't understand. Not yet. Perhaps one day he'd forgive her.

She forced thoughts of Gregory from her mind and looked around.

Wherever she was, she was in another small clearing with no obvious path or game trail leading in or out. A small stream was the only landmark. It cut through the glade before disappearing into the shadowy tree line at the north end of the meadow. The demon boy was walking away from her, toward the stream.

"We have traveled far." The pooka sounded fearful.

It couldn't be a good sign if one of the monsters was afraid.

Secretly, she was relieved they had relocated. It would take Gregory longer to hunt her down. And she needed as much time as possible.

"This way." The demon boy gestured toward a stream at the far end of the clearing. Lillian obeyed, and the pooka paced her, his ears pinned and his head high. He shied when they approached the stream.

The stream seemed normal enough upon first glance until

she noticed the yellowing grass along the bank and the wilted marsh marigolds, which looked like they were turning to slime. She felt it then, the weight of mortality. Death in its purest essence flowed along with the waters of the stream. The sickly-sweet odor of disease wafted from the slow-moving water. Other signs of stress marked the route the stream took. The brown of dead grass flanked the stream in wide swaths. Along the northern edge of the glade, the evergreens were blackened, their needles dropping when the breeze plucked them from their branches. It was an eerie sight. Like all the color had leached out of the world.

"What could do this?" she asked the pooka.

"You ask me? I haven't been to the Magic Realm in many, many centuries. Perhaps you should ask that question of yourself. It is a working of great magic. Close kin of yours, maybe?"

"Thanks for the help."

"Always happy to help one of the Avatars."

She could almost taste his sarcasm. *"You're an ass."*

The demon boy led them deeper into the woods. More dead trees to her left outlined the meandering path the stream cut through the forest. After walking for another ten minutes, she spotted a cabin through the trees. Dire wolves stood as silent sentinels among the trees.

Four of the dark-furred wolves ghosted out of the underbrush to flank her and the pooka as they made their way to the cabin. One dire wolf paced so close his fur brushed her arm, but he seemed unaware of his surroundings. She glanced sideways at him, studying his milky eyes. If she'd had more time, she would have tried to free him from the demon's influence. Now all there'd be time for was a swift death. She hoped.

When they reached the cabin, half the guards remained outside with the pooka, but the others followed Lillian within. Inside, the main room was covered in thick carpeting. Two bent-willow chairs and a sofa with a crocheted throw sat in front of a vast mantle. A fire burned in the fireplace, chasing away the chill of the spring dampness. It was a lovely cabin, and for a moment she grieved for the ones who had lived here. Surely, they were dead. But they would be avenged as soon as her brother and the pooka were safely away.

The demon boy continued to the very back of the cabin to a small bedroom. Within, her brother lay trussed up. He turned pale when he saw her. A gag prevented him from speaking, but the fear and grief in his eyes needed no words. Jason blamed himself for her capture.

"It's all right, Jason. You're going to leave with the pooka. He'll get you to safety." She knelt on the floor next to him. He was shaking his head back and forth. Lillian placed a hand on his shoulder. "It'll be over soon. Don't worry about me. This is my fault, and I'll make it right. I'll follow when I can." She turned back to the creature pretending to be a child. "Release my brother."

In case he decided to change his side of the bargain, she drew the demon blade across her wrist while summoning the magic of the Spirit Realm. And like the time Gregory had done it, cold filled the room, causing her breath to fog in the air.

The demon hissed and leaped back. "You promised no tricks."

She laughed. "A demon complaining about deceit—how ironic. Don't worry. It's just a precaution. Stick to your side of the bargain and all will go well. If you don't..." She let her sentence die but reached outside to where the pooka waited and whispered her plan into his mind.

"Once you and my brother are far enough away, I'll see if I can kill everything in a two-kilometer radius."

"Your brother and the pooka are free to go." The demon boy bowed to her, then straightened and took a step back toward the door. He made no move to bolt, so she turned her attention back to Jason. She had planned to give him her crossbow, so he would have a weapon, but there was rebellion in his eyes. Time for a new plan.

"Please tie my brother to the pooka's back. I doubt he'll go willingly."

"As you wish." The boy gestured and two demons wearing adult bodies picked up Jason and carried him out to the pooka.

The black pony was nervous, but still waited where she'd left him. He could have fled. He had the power, yet he stayed.

"Thank you."

When the pooka approached the cabin's porch, she leaned over the railing and laid her hand on his shoulder, sharing some of her power with him, strengthening him for the return journey.

"Run fast, swifter than death. I'll give you as much time as I can. Please try to save my brother."

"You never planned to return to the Magic Realm."

"No. I plan to return to the Spirit Realm—and somehow, I don't think that is where you want to go."

"Traitorous dryad." He snorted and pawed at the ground, his yellow eyes gleaming with rage.

"Your loyalty will be rewarded. Tell Gregory it was my wish that

you make the journey with him when he returns to the Magic Realm."

"And if the gargoyle doesn't listen?"

"He'll honor my last request."

"You're certain?"

"Yes. Please tell him not to grieve. I'll meet him again soon."

The pooka bobbed his head.

She stayed in the cabin's doorway, watching as the demons bundled her brother onto the pooka's back. A yellow eye rolled back toward her. She nodded her head, and the pooka bolted into motion.

She tracked the pooka long after he was out of sight. He wasn't followed, but she continued to stare at the trees where he and her brother had vanished for long moments. Each minute she stalled the evil ones, bettered the chance her brother had of escaping.

At last, she handed her crossbow to the demon. She no longer needed a physical weapon.

Fear was absent, and a strange thing was unfolding within her. Each time she'd called on magic, a small portion of her memories returned. Fragmented and chaotic, they were no help yet. But if the evil ones took too long to do whatever they planned, better possibilities might present themselves.

"Bring her," the demon boy ordered.

Two male dire wolves, white eyes foggy and unseeing, approached her with their heads down, tails held limply behind them. She wondered once again what the demon child had done to them to make them serve. Her magic flared, and a memory surfaced of her gargoyle father looking out over a battlement, listless, head hanging.

She'd been a small child, four or five at most, and seeing

her father like that had saddened her. He'd been "disciplined" after he'd tried to escape with her. She remembered her mother had been upset with the captains for resorting to soul-binding magic.

Trap a soul so that it could not gain strength from the Spirit Realm or a living body, and it would weaken. A weakened soul would, in turn, undermine rational thought, making the person more biddable. Her mother had called it one of the darkest forms of magic.

And the same spell—or a similar one—had been cast upon the two dire wolves approaching her. She moved away from the porch, allowing the big wolves to herd her toward the east side of the cabin. They continued to guide her until she was blocked on one side by the small creek.

Death magic rose from the water's surface like fog, seeking and smothering life as it encountered it. She strengthened her shields another notch, even though the magic hadn't been able to do more than brush along the curve of her shield before being repelled.

The demon child said nothing as it trailed along behind Lillian. She maintained a brisk pace, wanting to stay ahead of the demon. It sidled up next to her, perhaps sensing her unease. Then it tried to take her hand like a child would. She inched closer to the stream.

The scent of death wafted upon the breeze. But underlying that stench, there was a sweeter smell. Honeysuckle. And something else similar to sandalwood. Memories stirred.

A sense of peace, like returning home after a long life.

Impossible.

She took a deeper breath. Yes, she was certain. The Lord of the Underworld was near.

But how could that be? He was imprisoned in his own temple. Both Twins were by the duality curse. One sibling couldn't walk free while the other was trapped. The Lady of Battles was still imprisoned. Lillian knew it in her heart—and yet she sensed the Lord of the Underworld near.

The death magic flowing from the water was deadly, but now it lacked the stench of evil. Strange. She tried to piece together the memories that told her why the magic in the water was dangerous but not evil, and they slipped away.

They entered the forest once again. Nothing living remained. Everything was dead. She mourned the trees and the wildflowers. Even the moss was dead.

"It didn't like our tinkering and lashed out," the demon said. "It killed a good half of us before we could get out of its range."

"What didn't like your tinkering?" Whatever "it" was, if it had killed half of these little monsters, she wanted to help it kill the other half.

"When we sacrifice you, it will be more biddable," the demon called over its shoulder as it skipped ahead. It giggled and vanished around a bend in the path.

She swallowed against the bile rising in her throat. Touching the demon was the only way to know for sure if it had possessed a child or merely shapeshifted to look like one. She didn't want to get close enough to find out. Better not to know.

The footing became treacherous as the path narrowed. Boulders and rocks showed through the eroded soil like the bones of the earth. With her eyes on the rocky ground, she didn't see she'd emerged into a new meadow until she finished climbing up the leaf-littered slope.

She blinked several times and still she didn't understand what she saw. Trees laid broken and splintered like a hurricane had exploded out from the middle of the meadow. Branches and trunks were tossed haphazardly to form a dam of wooden shrapnel along the outer edge of the newly and violently cleared crater. At the center, someone had erected a monolith. She didn't know what else to call it. It looked like a sword, a massive, twenty-foot sword. A giant's weapon. By the way the point was embedded in the rocky soil, it looked like something had stabbed it down into the earth with a great deal of rage.

Its blade shimmered, eerie in the dim light. And if she was to approach it and run a finger along its blade, it looked sharp enough to cut off her hand. She shivered. The death magic was stronger here at the source.

Memory returned.

No, she'd been wrong. This great weapon didn't belong to a giant. It belonged to a god. Memories from past lives unfolded, triggered by the sight of one of the Lord of the Underworld's four swords.

In the memory, she and Gregory had returned victorious from a battle and were bringing a dangerous artifact back to the Lord of the Underworld for safe keeping. They'd bowed at his hooves, and he had towered over them, his horse's body topped with a four-armed humanoid torso and a jackal-like head.

In another life, she'd not thought him strange—but now, all she could think was that he looked like a love child between Anubis and a centaur. He had horns and a flowing mane like a gargoyle, and she remembered Gregory had once said all gargoyles called the god of death their master. If this creature wasn't fearsome enough on his own, having to walk between his four massive swords before kneeling at his hooves would have cowed most anything.

However, that time she and the gargoyle had nothing to fear from the Lord of the Underworld. He'd greeted them like friends, and she supposed they were. Being the god of death was a lonely duty, and like the gargoyles, he'd spent his existence alone.

"It rests, dormant as far as we can tell," the demon said in its child's voice.

Memories faded and she returned to the present. She still faced the massive sword.

The sword complicated her plan a bit.

"It may have used up its defenses, but we're not risking ourselves on a guess," the demon said. "But the sword *will* recognize you as the Goddess's avatar. It won't consider you a threat. And then we'll use your blood to forge its new allegiance."

She didn't need to be told what their next step would be. They'd command the sword to tear a hole in the Veil between the Realms, and more demons would flood into this land. The Clan and the Coven would be the first casualties in the war.

And then there would be no one left to protect the humans of Earth.

CHAPTER THIRTY-NINE

*L*illian let them herd her toward a dead tree, one of only three still standing within sixty feet of the sword. The demons were careful to go no closer to the weapon. *Come on Lil, you can do this. Act the helpless victim. Pretend you don't have the knowledge to protect yourself. How hard can that be?*

With jerky motions, they tied her to the tree's blackened trunk, using a bit of nylon rope to secure her. The occasional anxious glance over their shoulders said they didn't trust the sword's serenity. She didn't either.

An insubstantial current of magic swirled past her ankles on its way toward the sword. The great weapon siphoned power from the land, reclaiming some of the magic it had spent in the first attack. She didn't think the demons sensed what it was doing, or she doubted they'd still be so close. Lowering her shields, she opened herself to the magic coiled within her soul. A small trickle welled up and flowed across her skin. She directed it into the ground. None of the demons looked in her direction. They were too busy erecting a circle of stones for their spell casting. Or rebuilding one, perhaps? Yes. That looked likely. She'd come to them sooner than they had planned.

Maybe she'd have time to give the sword enough power to return to its master. She dared not let her captors use her blood to remake the sword. Nor could she risk the sword falling into the hands of the Lady of Battles. There was no telling what damage the dark goddess could do with one of her brother's weapons.

Lillian opened the part of her soul connected to the Spirit Realm. A cold rush of power filled her. She guided it into the ground, one slow, measured bit at a time. With her head bowed, she looked up through her lashes in the sword's direction. The massive blade continued to feed.

Fifteen minutes crept by, and the demons still hadn't noticed her silent rebellion.

This wasn't so hard, she mused. All she needed to do was give the sword enough power to return home before the demons came to slay her. However, there was one weakness in her plan.

If her own demon soul awoke before she was ready, it might enslave her and the sword, and then return to the Lady of Battles with a grand prize.

She glanced at the stone ring. Unfortunately, demons possessed strength and agility greater than a human, and the ring of stones circling the central altar was nearly complete. Lillian didn't think her enemies would lavish much time on other preparations once the last stone was in place.

Frosty power filled her body to the point of pain, but still, she held it in check. Long minutes crept by as she gritted her teeth against the burning pressure. When she could hold no more, she released a great flow of magic into the ground. With the crisp smell of winter, cold air rushed away from her in an enlarging circle, caressing the grass and kicking up a delicate scattering of dust as it raced away.

A dire wolf eased out of the trees to the west of her position. He raised his head and sniffed in her direction. Uh-oh, perhaps the demons were nose-dead, but the wolves weren't. Before she choked off the flow of magic, the dire wolf barked, a high-pitched sound of warning.

At the alarm, Riven rushed from the trees as if the dead forest spat them out. Forty, fifty. Far too many. Instinctively, she pressed her back into the dead tree.

"Stop her!" the demon boy yelled. He was on the opposite side of the meadow, sprinting toward her.

"Oh, what the hell." She unleashed another wave of magic. The sword drank her power, swallowing it faster than she'd thought possible. *Go*, she willed it. *Go home. Please.*

Not enough power, it whispered into her mind.

She dropped her mental shields to speed up the transfer of power, and Gregory was suddenly in her mind, his grief and rage buffeting her. She blinked and then realized he'd been there the whole time, but she'd been so focused on the situation that she'd blocked him from her consciousness. Now there was only one way to protect him. She showed him what was unfolding while she shoved all her recent memories at him. The number of enemies, their plans to force the sword to serve them and tear a hole in the Veil between the Realms, and all tactical information about the meadow. Then with that done, she sent one last message. *"Gregory, you mean everything to me, and I'm sorry to cause you pain."*

Lillian turned her thoughts from him to the task at hand as she forced her connection to the Spirit Realm wide open. Power flowed through her. She screamed as a wild current tore through her thoughts. Her vision blurred, and then cleared in time to see a demon standing in front of her, his arm raised, the silver glint of a blade in his hand. Pain exploded in her shoulder and a second scream tore free of her chest.

CHAPTER FORTY

The world below streaked past in a blur as Gregory winged closer to Lillian. He was almost there when her thoughts came to him, flowing across his own. His wings faltered. Shocked, he grasped at her thoughts as he leveled out his flight.

Her thoughts flooded his mind with the knowledge she'd gathered. The demons. The sword. Their plan to invade this Realm through the torn Veil. The Riven had been planning a rebellion long before the first one hitched a ride to this realm with him.

He smelled evil carried on the breeze and overlaying that odor, the distinct scent of the Lord of the Underworld.

Gregory was almost there. Hope filled his numb wings and burning lungs, and with renewed strength, he sped toward his other half.

Another image of the enemies flashed through his mind. A demon with a dagger poised to strike.

Despair engulfed him. He'd hunt the demons down, find

the deepest abyss in the Magic Realm, and imprison them with their own dark magic until all they would know was unending torment. And it wouldn't be one-quarter of the pain he'd feel for failing Lillian.

Lillian's fear washed across his mind, her agony resonating within his soul. He roared one short, sharp howl, echoing her pain.

CHAPTER FORTY-ONE

*L*illian awoke, a hot, wet agony slicing along her stomach. Had they stabbed her with a branding iron? She gritted her teeth and looked down. She was naked, her abdomen a red ruin. Blood soaked her bare legs. A second, smaller ember of fire gnawed at her shoulder where a demon blade was buried—probably the same dagger they'd all but gutted her with.

A whimper escaped. Her breath came quick and shallow. She'd been prepared for death, but not this pain. A swift death. She'd been too naive.

She didn't remember the demons moving her, but a slab of stone propped at an angle now supported her back. She hung from her bound hands, her shoulder joints so taut something would dislocate if she moved even a little.

Blood covered the stone, running down its surface in rivulets. Jagged little flashes of light sparked at the edge of her vision. She wasn't going to pass out, not yet. When she closed her eyes, she could sense Gregory near. His thoughts were no longer crisp but muffled by whatever the demon blade was doing. Or perhaps it was from losing so much blood. She was weakening fast.

Just not fast enough.

Gregory would arrive in time to watch her die and then he'd get himself killed. He'd died for her so many times in the past; he deserved to live this time. While she couldn't will herself to die faster, perhaps she could find another way to defeat them. Lillian had hoped the demons would trigger whatever trap the Lady of Battles had laid on her soul when they stabbed her, but Gregory must have done something to keep her demon soul from waking. Now the stupid magic couldn't even kill her properly.

Focusing proved difficult, but she gathered her thoughts and began picking at the tight knot of coiled memories and magic at her core. There must be something there she could use. She just had to get to it.

Blood continued its slow descent. It circled around her ankle and dripped off her bare toes, and still, Lillian dug deeper into her memories. Then she found what she sought, a tether linking her demon soul to the Lady of Battles. Lillian followed the path, reaching, stretching, seeking until another powerful and fearsome being acknowledged her with a caress like lightning across her skin.

"My child," the other said as a malevolent power snaked through Lillian.

A mild surge of relief escaped Lillian in a giddy laugh. The demons turned puzzled eyes in her direction, but she didn't care if she'd given herself away. There was nothing the demons could do to stop her. Power poured from her and flooded out across the meadow. Fog rose from the earth, shifting and flowing into thick ropes that wove themselves into a billowing tapestry. The mist solidified and became a silver-edged window, like the time Lillian had spoken to Commander Gryton, but this one was much larger.

The Lady of Battles reclined on the garnet-colored stone steps inside her temple. She raised her head, and then came to her feet with the soft rustle of fabric and the rattle of chains. With the deep-red stairs and the polished-black onyx of her temple behind her, the Lady of Battles glowed pale against the darkness, an ethereal creature with alabaster skin and green eyes. A delicate bare foot poked out from under the hem of her cream-colored dress as she descended the steps. Her slim-figured elegance was at odds with the blood-red breastplate and manacles encircling her wrists and ankles.

The goddess continued down the steps in an unhurried manner. Her billowing skirt reminded Lillian of sails in a strong wind, the chains disappearing into the shadows, the ship's rigging.

It wasn't until the Lady of Battles reached the foot of the stairs and knelt to peer through the shimmering window that Lillian realized her true size. The dark goddess was a giant, like a Titan of old. The individual links of the chain binding her were the size of Lillian's torso.

If she was not so far gone, Lillian would have been terrified. But terror was too great an emotion to muster now.

"What is this?" The Lady of Battles demanded, her voice booming across the clearing. "Wee little demons, do you seek to better yourselves?" Her voice grew softer and darker. "Better yourselves by sacrificing my daughter? I think not."

Lillian was so woozy, she could barely think.

"I have planned too long to let your foolish greed destroy

my work. Release my daughter, and I might let you live," the Lady said, while her piercing gaze tracked everything in the clearing. The two green orbs at last settled on Lillian. "Daughter, let me help you."

Accompanying the words, Lillian felt more of the foreign magic invade the meadow from the viewing window. The demons hissed at one another, nearly stumbling over each other in their hurry to get away. The magic continued to pour into the meadow, and then it reached her.

Lillian burned and itched. A searing agony shot through her. She bucked and spasmed with the pain, feeling as though her bones were melting and reshaping themselves.

CHAPTER FORTY-TWO

Gregory flared his wings to slow his descent while he took in a scene more horrible than he'd expected. A chaotic mix of power swirled around the meadow. But it was the essence of his greatest enemy that overlaid every other scent. Somehow the Lady of Battles was here.

"You're late," the Lady said as Gregory landed. "Again."

Gregory froze at the sight of the silver window occupying half the meadow. The Lady of Battles looked out upon the scene from the steps of her temple. In front of the mirror was a small slab of stone propped up haphazardly by another boulder half-buried in the ground. Upon the stone altar, Lillian hung suspended by her wrists. Blood dripped down the length of her naked body and coated the stone beneath. With a cry, Gregory bolted into motion, uncaring if he was about to walk into the battle goddess's trap.

Up close, Lillian was gray, and her breath came in shallow gasps. Her eyes, wide with fear, met his. He slashed the ropes tying her to the crude stone altar. She slumped into his arms.

"Go. I don't want you to die," she whispered.

"Foolish, beloved Sorceress. I can endure much, but I cannot live without you." He lowered his muzzle to her and rested his forehead against hers. This was all he could do. Hold her while she died. "I'll follow you. Soon we'll start over." He would seek out the Lady of Battles in her prison and pick a fight he couldn't win.

"No, love," Lillian said. "If you challenge her and die in her prison, she'll trap your soul as she did mine, force you to be reborn into a body she can control. That's what she wants. She tried to heal me, make me into her tool, but I'm too weak —now I'm useless to her. She needs you."

"Gargoyle, feed her some of your blood," the Lady of Battles commanded.

Tears flowed freely. He didn't care if the Battle Goddess witnessed his grief or took joy in it. He caressed Lillian's hair as he tried to comfort her as best he could. This never got easier, ever. "I have you," he whispered into her hair. "The pain will be gone soon. Let go. I'll join you shortly."

The Lady of Battles slammed her chains against the stone of her temple. "You don't have to watch her die. Share your blood!"

"It will only prolong her pain," Gregory growled at the goddess. How he wished the Divine Ones had let him destroy this creature. "There is no magic in this Realm strong enough to fix what is broken. I can feel the wound to her soul. Even on the border of the Spirit Realm, with the full complement of our power at our call, this would be taxing to heal. If you possessed even a little mercy, you would leave me in peace for this."

"Fool. Do you think I would make one of my creatures so

easy to kill? She is my pride, my greatest weapon. I made her harder to kill, not easier. Give. Her. Your. Blood. Unless you want to watch her die. Choose." The Lady of Battles crossed her arms and sat down to wait.

Gregory glanced down at his Mistress. Could it be that simple to save her? Did he care if he was playing into the battle goddess's hands? No.

He exhaled sharply as he slashed his talons across his chest, then forced her limp body to rest against his. She turned her head, sniffing. When she laid a quivering hand on his chest and skimmed her lips along his skin, he shuddered. Her warm tongue slid over the wound, and her throat worked as she drank his life-giving blood. After he forced his breathing to slow and his mind to focus, he looked for changes in Lillian. At first, he sensed no difference in her condition, and then she gasped in pain as spasms shook her body.

Before he could react, she grasped both his shoulders and pushed him back against the altar. Her lips sealed more firmly over the wound. Her throat worked as she swallowed.

Magic from the Spirit Realm thrummed through his veins, and he released it into her. He continued to pour more and more into her, as much as she would take. Her breathing eased, and her color improved with each passing moment. Recovery was swift. The wound on her shoulder was gone completely and only pale, white lines marked the skin of her belly. He stroked his fingers over the area to reassure himself.

After several moments Lillian stirred in his arms, pushing at his chest and putting a little space between them so she could lap at the blood making its way toward his abdomen. Lillian's fingers skimmed lower, making him shiver. He savored her shocking caress a few moments before he tightened his arms around her shoulders to prevent her from following the trail of blood. Lillian made a soft sound of protest, which he did his best to ignore. When she was still again, he rested his chin on her hair and watched his enemy. Thanking the Lady of Battles wasn't something he'd ever thought he'd contemplate in his life.

"Thank you," he whispered.

"You're welcome, Protector. You might return the favor by serving me..."

Gregory gently placed Lillian on the ground, then stood to face the Lady of Battles. "My allegiance cannot be bought or sold."

"Perhaps you'll come to think differently. What would you be willing to do to save your beloved Sorceress when she's carrying your youngling?" The Lady of Battles straightened from her crouch. "I think you'll come to serve me to protect them from Divine wrath. You'll have no choice. What a splendid addition to my army you will make, both of you."

"I will not serve you."

"Fight me if you wish, but I'll still get what I want in the end. Wouldn't it be better to come to me willingly? You could fulfill your deepest and oldest wish—to be with your Sorceress and reciprocate the deep love you share."

Gregory shook his head. "I won't serve you."

"We'll see how long you last." The Lady of Battles chuckled. "I think you'll find my daughter has an aggressive side. One of the traits I instilled in her. Oh, she's overly protective of her gargoyle, too." Chains rattled against each other as she leaned forward suddenly and gestured at something behind Gregory's shoulder. "Beware!"

Distracted by Lillian's feeding and the Battle Goddess's startling admission, he hadn't heard the creature coming up behind him until too late. A cold, sucking pain lodged itself in his back as the demon blade sunk deep. He twisted, lashing out at his attacker. A second dagger buried itself in his chest. He dropped to his knees, shock sapping his strength. He tugged at the second dagger, but he lacked strength, and it wouldn't release its grip.

"Now that was foolish, little demon," the Lady of Battles said. "You have angered my daughter."

"Gregory?" Lillian cried. She called to him again, her voice changing, becoming deeper, more menacing.

CHAPTER FORTY-THREE

Her gargoyle was hurt. Her beloved needed her. No one harmed her gargoyle and lived.

Lillian screamed Gregory's name even as the fraying coil of memories unraveled within her. New strength flooded her body. She burned and itched as her body began shifting into a new form. With a wet sound, the skin of her back parted and wings erupted from her shoulder blades. The new weight altered her balance, and she dropped to all fours. Talons lengthened her fingers even as horns sprouted on her forehead. She shook herself from muzzle to tail tip, stretching and testing new muscles. Then as silent as death on a cold winter night, she stalked her prey.

The demon boy remained hunched over Gregory, one hand braced against the gargoyle's shoulder while the other gripped the hilt of a demon blade, the boy's complete attention focused on killing her mate. Ecstasy radiated off the demon's features as he fed, the look of pleasure made all the worse by the innocence of his softly curved lips, rounded cheeks, and thick lashes dark against his pale skin.

A soft growl escaped her as she lunged at the vile creature. The boy jerked his gaze in her direction, shock clear on his cherub-like face. At the last moment, her opponent twisted with inhuman speed. Her jaws closed on empty air.

With each beat of her heart, her gargoyle instincts sharpened. The breath-stealing stink of demon, a fluttering heartbeat, footfalls crunching through leaves—nothing escaped her heightened senses. Her second lunge landed her half on his back, and she sank her teeth deep into the meat of his shoulder. But this demon was strong, fed additional strength from several of his brethren, and he bucked her off. She crashed to the ground with a grunt of pain. Even before she caught her breath, she rolled to her feet and took up a protective stance next to Gregory.

Anger surged through her veins, pulsing in time to her heartbeat. She charged the demon again, snapping at it in a fit of fury. Another Riven darted into the fight. It slashed at her flank. Its claws dug four shallow grooves across her skin. Snarling, she chased it. It wasn't fast enough to get clear of her leap. She landed on its back and drove it into the ground. One bite to the back of its neck and she severed its spine. With a twist of her powerful neck muscles, she beheaded the creature. The sharp odor of tainted blood and rot overwhelmed her sense of smell. Shaking her head, she sprang away from the demons, then returned to Gregory's side.

At the sight of the demon blades, rage flared to life again. She straddled Gregory, sheltering him from further attack with her own body while she shared magic with him.

"Release him," she ordered the demon blades. Neither was

the one she'd remade, but they sensed darkness greater than themselves and leaped to obey. When the second had fallen to the ground, she nosed Gregory.

Touching him brought her a moment of tranquility, the forgotten key to her innermost self, and the floodgate holding the magic of the Spirit Realm at bay opened.

Power filled her as she stretched her wings toward the sky.

The forest spat out three new demons. They circled her with caution as more of their brethren returned now that the Lady of Battles was gone. Her lips pulled back in a snarl while she waited.

Come closer, she thought, *and meet the Lady's daughter.*

Her wings quivered with the strain of holding back. Blood pounded through her veins. She closed her eyes and waited.

Demon. Dire wolf. Fae-blood slaves. They all returned, drawing nearer.

Just a little more. Almost close enough.

Her ears swung forward. There. The last of them stepped within range.

She snapped her wings down and released the power, directing it as it surged from her body. Like the shockwave from a bomb, the power flew out in an ever-enlarging circle. Wind blasted between the tree branches and howled like a winter's gale. A wild ecstasy filled her.

She fed more and more power into the destroying wave.

It should've been enough to level the forest for a kilometer in all directions, killing every last Riven—but a few of them were escaping her.

Something else fed upon her power.

Fury engulfed her. *How dare it feed upon her?*

She turned toward the great sword at the north end of the

meadow and raised her hand to call defensive magic down upon it. Before she could attack the sword, it tapped into her strength, tearing control of her power from her.

Ropes of fire spiraled up from the ground and covered the blade completely. The sword continued sucking air and magic toward it, until a tornado of fire towered above the trees. With earth-shaking violence, the sword opened the Veil.

The bright flash blinded Lillian.

While she was disoriented, the earth shivered with greater violence. It swayed and pitched under her feet. She rolled and crashed into Gregory.

When the wildly fluctuating powers dissipated, the magic-driven winds calmed. The sword was gone by the time she dragged herself to her feet. It had likely returned to its master to report all it had learned. Lillian flicked her tail in annoyance, but there was nothing she could do now to secure the weapon for the Lady of Battles.

Ash drifted down, and soft flakes coated her and Gregory. The meadow was quiet again. She nuzzled Gregory on the shoulder, and he loosed a pained moan. After sniffing at his wounds, she licked them until they sealed over. He'd have more scars. She narrowed her eyes and growled, angry at herself. In the future, she needed to be more careful of her mate. He had a knack for gathering stab wounds.

The wind picked up again, flowing through the forest from the Northwest. The stench of evil invaded her nose. She sneezed and pawed at her muzzle, but nothing cleared the miasma of darkness that clung to her skin and mane and coated the lining of her throat and lungs. Several of the Riven had escaped, thanks to the Lord of the Underworld's sword.

Had Gregory been stronger, they would have hunted

together and destroyed the last of the Riven. She glanced to the Northwest, uncertain. To let the Riven escape was dangerous. She still had one weakness—her hamadryad. And if the Riven knew about her tree, they would attack her again. But the Riven's territory was far from her tree, and she'd killed enough of the demons to weaken them. With their decreased numbers, the Riven couldn't gather the power required to travel by magical means. It should take them at least two days to cover the distance.

For now, the Riven would survive for a little longer; there was nothing she could do about that.

Clouds gathering on the horizon and the damp smell of rain upon the wind helped her decide. Her mate needed healing and rest. And they both needed a better place to shelter until they were stronger. When Gregory could fly, they would return to her hamadryad and create impenetrable protections. Once that was done, she and her mate would hunt down the remaining Riven. She prodded Gregory again, shoving her head and shoulders under his chest to get him to his feet.

"Get up, we need to find shelter."

Gregory stood on shaking legs, his eyes half-closed and his head hanging. Sweat slicked his sides in a way she didn't like. Seeing him so weak tightened her stomach. She didn't think he was even aware of her new form. Brushing his thoughts, she found he was still in shock and mostly unaware of what was going on around him, but when she started forward, he followed. They made their way clear of what had once been a meadow but now looked more like a burnt-out crater. They walked for a few minutes and came upon a log cabin. It still stood. Only the back of the cabin showed damage like a flash fire had scorched it. She bypassed the cabin, not wanting a shelter so close to the Riven's territory.

After walking for an hour, she found a small pond skirted with trees and a wealth of underbrush. Deer and rabbits moved among the trees, unaware predators walked among the shadows. Here Gregory could rest while she hunted.

He still hadn't snapped out of shock. Her protective instincts roused at the thought of leaving him, even to hunt, but he needed food to grow strong again.

The breeze carried a whiff of a fawn. Her stomach rumbled.

Gregory collapsed among the undergrowth, his eyes closed. He rested, but she knew he hadn't fallen asleep. She waited, hoping sleep would claim him. When it did at last, she rose on silent feet. She'd only taken three steps when he grunted and sat up.

"I'll hunt for us. Stay," she ordered. She returned to his side and rubbed her muzzle alongside his. His scent called to her. It was hard to think when they were so close.

He returned her gesture of affection with a contented sigh. His thoughts were still drowsy, blurred by equal parts magical exhaustion and shock from blood loss. Obedient to her tone, he lay back down to wait.

CHAPTER FORTY-FOUR

The weight of the buck strained the muscles in her neck, but she tightened her jaws and continued to drag the deer along the pond's muddy shore. Two more powerful heaves and the carcass landed next to Gregory.

His nose quivered, but he didn't stir, and she noticed his skin had taken on the seeming of stone. If she didn't get food into him soon, he'd turn to stone to heal. And this location was still too close to where the Riven had established their territory for him to do that safely.

She butted him with her muzzle.

When that tactic failed, she slapped her tail across his flank.

An ear swiveled forward, and he cracked open one eye.

Pushing her kill under his nose, she growled, then slashed her claws along the deer's soft underbelly. Gregory sat up and sniffed at her gift. Then with a vigor which pleased her, he tore into the still-warm beast.

The coppery scent filled the clearing, and her stomach growled a second time.

Licking at his muzzle, she persuaded him to share. When they were both well-fed and drowsy, she lay against him and stretched a wing over him for warmth.

His thoughts were of love, contentment, and mild desire. He thought her lovely. She smiled at his simple thoughts. He still wasn't thinking in complex sentences. It would be easy to get him to give her what the Lady of Battles wanted—a child of their union, a new deity with strength enough to slay the Lady's own twin.

The Lady hadn't specified when, so Lillian waited. Besides, she'd rather have her beloved be in full command of himself when they mated. And she looked forward to the hunt, the slow seduction.

Well, there was nothing to say she couldn't start now.

She intertwined her tail with his and licked at his shoulder while he slept.

When they woke, she'd see how long he could resist temptation. He'd barely maintained his distance when she'd worn the hide of a mere dryad.

CHAPTER FORTY-FIVE

*S*leep slowly fell away. Warmth pressed along his side as the soft, living silk of bare skin brushed his wings. A sweet, musky scent engulfed him. Snorting, Gregory shook his head in confusion. His memories of the last hours were hazy, but thoughts slowly ordered into something he could understand. And he feared to look where Lillian lay next to him. Who had won, his Sorceress or the demon soul?

A gentle brush of his mind against hers told him she still slept.

Thanks be to the Divine Ones for small blessings.

Slowly, he folded his wings against his back and levered himself up. He barely noticed the twinge of stiff muscles. The sight of his lady in gargoyle form held him enthralled. She rested with her head on her forearms, her mane a wild wave of crimson against ebony skin. Black horns spiraled up from her forehead, lightening to a wine color at their tips. Silky black ears twitched in her sleep, and her tail quivered, rubbing against his.

She'd coiled her tail around his in a possessive grip. The strange friction sent his heart pumping. His wings unfurled, trembling as blood rushed to fill them.

Just as quickly as the friction had come, it was gone, her tail relaxing to curl around her flanks. He immediately missed the contact. Though at the same time, he was grateful she still slept. If she'd been awake, she'd probably have made the situation worse, given her purpose was to beget a child with him. He remembered the Lady of Battles saying she could be aggressive.

He needed to get away, clear his thoughts so he could think. There must be a way out of this mess. He just had to find it. Perhaps he could force her back into her dryad form and trap the demon soul by placing new, more powerful wards upon Lillian's mind a second time?

Wings twitching, Lillian whimpered in the grip of a nightmare. A second low moan of terror tugged at his heart. He hesitated, hovering over her, uncertain. It could be a ploy, the demon soul's attempt to manipulate him.

Another helpless sound escaped her. At that moment, he realized he couldn't abandon her—Lillian was in there somewhere, trapped, possibly fighting the demon soul even now. Leaning down, he nuzzled her shoulder. She calmed at his touch. The sap-sweet fragrance of dryad and the warm, fertile scent of gargoyle lost the musky tang of fear.

As he sniffed at her skin, he shifted closer. Bracing his arms on either side of her body, he buried his muzzle in her mane, pushing the strands of hair out of the way until he'd exposed her neck. Unable to help himself, he closed his jaws in the gentlest of love bites. A rumble formed in his chest.

She tasted as good as she smelled. Lillian jerked awake under him, tensed for a fight.

Purring reassurances, he mantled his wings around her so she could catch his scent. She tilted her head to look up at him. Intense, obsidian-colored eyes met his, and after a moment's study, she relaxed and uttered her own deep, rumbling purr.

He growled and took a firmer hold on her neck.

What was he doing? This was wrong, forbidden, a small part of his mind warned. Another part of his soul, far older and more firmly bound to the Sorceress, rejoiced at her response to him. That part scared him more than the newfound heat of desire. He froze, shocked he'd so willingly forsake his duty to the Divine Ones.

This was wrong, he reaffirmed, repeating the words until they were a chant in his head. And still, a part of him didn't agree. This was Lillian, his lady, his Sorceress. Their hearts had always remained loyal. How could their love be a mistake? Did they not deserve a little happiness after all these eons?

Yes, but this was not how he wanted it between them.

Reluctantly, he released her and eased away before his baser instincts won out.

Lillian didn't seem upset by his rejection. On the contrary, she looked completely relaxed as she folded her wings against her back and rolled onto her side, her tail curled along her hips.

The pose gave him tantalizing flashes of her body. One arm rested on the cushion of her plump breasts, paler than the darker skin of her flat belly. Swirls of crimson formed a pattern on the curve of her hips like a tattoo, drawing his eye to her navel and then lower.

A coil of her tail hid where the crimson spirals led. She flicked the spade-like bladed-tip of her tail gently and watched him through thick lashes.

Time to go.

Now.

He turned his back to her and prepared to flee.

"Gregory, wait." Her mellow voice slid up his spine, like fingers caressing his skin.

As easily as that, he was enslaved. The sound of her wings unfurling, the soft rasp of skin on skin, betrayed her movements. Unable to flee or turn and face her, he froze, awaiting her next move. Small, warm hands caressed his sides a moment before her arms encircled his waist, drawing a surprised grunt from his throat.

"Easy. I'm not your enemy. The Lady of Battles doesn't control me to the extent she would like." Her hands slid up to caress the tense muscles of his chest. "I just want to talk, to get to know you better."

"And are you not able to talk without touching me?"

She chuckled. "Yes, of course I can. But it's more fun to watch you twitch."

Her words confirmed his fears. His Lillian wouldn't belittle his feelings. "My emotions are not something to be toyed with for your personal entertainment, demon."

"I'm so much more than that. I'll not harm you, physically or emotionally. The Lady of Battles couldn't change what I feel for you."

Slowly, an image took form and substance in his mind's eye. Lillian as a dryad, her skin pale against his darkness, eyes bright with passion, body coated with the luster of sweat.

"Even when I was a mere dryad, this is what you dreamed of. I can give you what you wish."

A spike of desire shivered down his spine. Worse, he couldn't hide his reaction from her.

"Liked that, didn't you?" She chuckled again, rubbing her cheek against his shoulder. "I haven't even started to court you yet. How long do you think you can resist?"

Her flippant tone dampened his ardor. "Long enough to find a way to get my Sorceress back. Whatever you think you are, you are not her."

"I hear your doubt. You don't believe your own words. Why should I? I know exactly who I was, where I came from, who I am and what I will become." She hugged him, pressing her breasts against his back. Her warm fingers stroked down his chest until she encountered his loincloth.

Rage flared again, and with it, a plan started to form. He would not let a demon soil the love he and his beloved shared.

A shiver of disgust crawled down his spine. Hopefully, she interpreted it as desire. His plan required she believe that lie. He disengaged her clinging hands and twisted around until he held her trapped in his arms. Once he had her in a firm grip, he shifted her until her back was to his front.

Using his tail to trip her, he forced the smaller gargoyle onto all fours. Thrashing and bucking, she tried to shove him off balance. Before she had the chance to dislodge him, he closed his jaws around her neck.

At the soft prick of his teeth, all resistance melted away, and she went limp under him. He loosened his hold on her neck and then licked at her shoulder. She made a small sound of appreciation.

Forcing her to take more of his weight, he leaned over her and licked a trail along her spine, then up onto one shoulder. One quick nip and the heady tang of her blood coated his tongue.

The courtship ritual had begun.

He didn't wait for her to recover from her shock before he bolted into motion. If she wanted to court him, he'd let her do the chasing. But he would decide the direction of the pursuit; a direction that would lead her back to Clan and Coven lands, where he hoped to get aid from Gran, Greenborrow, Whitethorn, and the other fae to help trap Lillian. Once she was imprisoned, he'd have time to worry about what to do with the demon.

Gregory bolted across the clearing and into the tree line. He glanced back once to be certain she followed and caught a glimpse of her black body and burgundy-frosted mane as she raced a hundred paces behind him. Good, she'd fallen for the bait. He slowed his pace to allow her to get closer, then when she was nearly upon him, he lengthened his stride and gained ground.

The sun trekked westward as Gregory continued the game.

His plan was working; they'd traveled a goodly distance. However, he detected a problem with his plan. While his injuries had healed, he still lacked one important thing: Stamina.

CHAPTER FORTY-SIX

Gregory was leaning against a tree for a short rest when she caught up to him.

"I thought you'd let me catch you much sooner than this. Perhaps I was a touch too aggressive with my courtship." Lillian's voice drifted to him from the shadows to his left. "Would you be more comfortable with a familiar face?"

By the time he turned, she was already engulfed in an intense glow of power. When spots no longer flashed before his eyes, he found Lillian standing before him, naked, all pale skin and beautiful dark hair. His lady. But as much as this alluring creature looked like his Sorceress, he knew her allegiance was to the Lady of Battles.

"Gregory, I offer what you've always wanted."

"And what I can never have. I'd be killing Lillian myself if I did. The Lord of the Underworld is nothing like his sister. He has never failed to carry out an edict of the Divine Ones. If I got Lillian with child, he would send every last gargoyle to hunt us down. Demon, think beyond what the Lady of Battles wishes you to be. Can't you see the truth? You won't live long enough to carry any child to term."

Her lips curved into a smile that spoke of assured knowledge. "The Lord of the Underworld isn't infallible. He has weaknesses we can use to our advantage."

"Perhaps you honestly can't grasp what I truly want."

"Your Sorceress." She tilted her head to the side, no longer looking so haughty. "Perhaps the Lady of Battles made a mistake when she created me. A gentler being, one who needed your protection, might have had an easier time seducing you."

He laughed, the sound cold and humorless. "A gentler demon?"

"You'll find I'm very adaptable... and I already know your greatest weakness."

"You don't know me." He turned and loped away from her.

"Gregory, once I have fulfilled my duty, I will return to the battle goddess and this body will revert to the personality you know and fell in love with: your beloved dryad."

After snorting bitterly, he challenged her lie. "Nothing a demon can say will ever change my mind."

He whirled back around to face her, angry enough to confront her in battle.

"Ah, it was a slim hope. But I see you're not interested in the easy path." She smiled as she combed her fingers through her hair. The dark strands fanned out across her shoulders and drifted down over her breasts. She toyed with her hair a moment more, then caressed the upper swell of one breast. The fingers of her other hand trailed leisurely down her abdomen. "That suits me well enough. I like the hunt. And perhaps you will like—"

The creature controlling Lillian's body stiffened. Color drained from her skin. She sucked in a ragged breath—one of pain, not pleasure. When he glanced up to her face, he saw her eyes held the unfocused look of deep concentration.

"Lillian?" he whispered. A small spark of hope kindled in his chest. "My Sorceress, can you hear me?"

Lillian opened her mouth and screamed, a sound of horror and despair. She grasped at her side as a wound opened up under her hands, blood gushing from between her fingers. Moaning in pain, she slowly collapsed to her knees.

CHAPTER FORTY-SEVEN

"*L*illian!" Gregory roared her name as he leaped forward. Catching her in his arms, he gathered her close to his chest. When he touched her, he felt the demon soul within her seeking the spirit link to Lillian's hamadryad. The great tree quaked under another blow as metal bit into her bark.

An axe. Someone was taking an axe to Lillian's tree. The demon soul released control of Lillian's body and focused all its attention upon sending strength to the tree in a frantic attempt to heal it.

But nothing the demon soul did could protect the hamadryad over such a great distance.

"Gregory?" Lillian stiffened in his arms. She shuddered. "What's happening?"

A cold lump of dread, like a frost-chilled stone in winter, weighed heavy in his stomach. He tightened his arms around her. "Lillian, don't give up. Fight. I'll carry you back to your tree. I'll heal you."

He hastily called on his power and wove a ward over her wounds to slow the bleeding.

"My hamadryad... she's dying." She sucked in another short, pain-filled breath. "Let me go. It's better this way. The demon dies with me."

"No."

With that one word, he denied the Divine Ones, the Lord of the Underworld—death itself. He would not serve, not this time. He would not stand by and watch Lillian die.

Cold reason slid over his emotions like a calming blanket. He focused his mind. "What kind of battle are we about to land in the middle of? Can you tell me how many are in your glade?"

"Not sure. Only one, I think." Her answers came in short, pain-filled bursts.

Gregory ached just hearing her soft gasps. But what she said made no sense. It would take at least ten powerful demons working for an hour to break the new stone circle he'd built.

But it didn't matter how many enemies were awaiting him in the glade; he'd fight a thousand Riven for the chance to save Lillian.

"Easy now," he whispered and lifted her into his arms. She weighed so little, as if the loss of her magic were draining her of substance. "I'll keep you safe."

He leaped into motion and spread his wings while he ran. With a thunder of wing beats, he left the ground and flew toward her dying hamadryad.

He circled the hamadryad's canopy, scanning the ground below as he flew lower. The tree shook with each new blow, but he couldn't see who was wielding the axe. The foliage was too thick, the branches too wide near the base. The rest of the clearing looked empty, free of other visible enemies. There was no scent of Riven. And the stone circle still stood, untouched. It didn't make sense.

Four feet from the ground, he folded his wings tight to his body and dropped down onto his hind feet. He deposited Lillian behind him and whirled on his prey.

Partially obscured by the redwood's branches, a slim figure wielded the axe.

As the axe connected with bark in another mighty blow, Lillian cried out. Reason fled before the all-powerful need to protect his lady. He lunged, talons poised for a killing strike. Sable turned to him, the axe lowering, and his blow caught her across the throat.

He blinked in surprise even as blood drenched her pale dress.

The axe slipped from her fingers, and she stumbled back against the redwood's trunk. Instinctively, she reached to cover the deep gash across her throat, trying to stem the flow of lifeblood. She locked gazes with him and attempted to speak. Blood flowed from her mouth instead of words. Panic shone in her eyes, but something else, too: deep sorrow.

"Please," she whispered into his thoughts. *"I have an unborn child. The Riven know the location of my tree. If I don't kill Lillian's hamadryad, they'll kill my daughter. Please. Save my innocent little girl."*

He couldn't lie to the dryad and tell her he'd save her child —he wasn't sure if he had the strength to save Lillian and himself, but he could tell her what he knew about the Rivens' fate at least. "Lillian killed most of the Riven. Those still living are on the run. They'll not have time to hunt down your child before the Clan and the Coven dispatch them." Perhaps she could take comfort in that.

"Thank you, Avatar." Her fear bled away along with the spark of life in her eyes.

Sable slid sideways and collapsed to the ground. Even in death, the dryad Elder retained her grace.

"May peace find you," he whispered.

He returned to Lillian and gathered her up in his arms. She was unconscious. Naked, she looked small and fragile. He didn't like the sickly pallor of her skin. He was running out of time. Fear dug icy talons into his chest. Everywhere their bodies touched, he sent healing magic into her. After a few minutes, she regained consciousness, a look of confusion on her features. She touched his cheek. "What's happening?"

"Don't worry. Everything will be all right."

"I feel strange," she said, her voice groggy and slurred. "Am I drunk? No? Dammit, I'm dying, aren't I?"

He leaned forward and nuzzled her, feeding her more strength as he did so. She returned his caress with shaking fingers, her touch a brand against his shoulder. Her thoughts whispered of her love. He pressed their bodies together and began weaving between the ground-sweeping branches of her tree.

The soft foliage brushed at his arms, and then swept out of the way, making room for him and his burden. They continued to spread until there was a space for him to stand close to the buttressed trunk. Bark pulled back like a seam unraveling, and a fissure opened in the redwood's trunk.

A touch here and a slight push there, and he guided her closer to where he wanted her.

"Relax," he whispered into her hair. "This will come naturally to you. Just give yourself over to your tree. When you are healed, come back to me. Do you understand?"

"Um... I'll come back," she said, sounding like she was on the edge of sleep. "You'll be waiting?"

"Always." *In this life or the next.*

"Goodbye, my gargoyle." She closed her eyes and gave in to a dryad's instincts, her face becoming tranquil. As if a gale blew through the meadow, the redwood shuddered, shaking its branches as the fissure in its trunk widened. Blood-red fibrous vessels, delicate as a spider's web, enveloped his lady's shoulders and crawled across her lower body. Then the cavernous maw swallowed Lillian, pulling her into the tree's embrace. Her arms fell away from him. He held her hand in his for a moment more—a final caress before he let her go completely.

He stared at the tree for a long time after the bark had smoothed over. His heart ached. Dread held him frozen in place. His reassuring words to Lillian did nothing to soothe the chaos of grief and fear in his own soul.

She could still die. Her hamadryad had sustained near-fatal wounds, greater than even what dryad and demon together could heal.

There was one final thing he could do for the tree. Bowing his head, he began reciting a blessing in a deep chant. Drifting into a light trance, he slashed both wrists and allowed his blood and magic to drip down upon the ground. He continued to chant as he walked the tree's perimeter. His powerful heart began to labor after a few moments as more and more of his blood splashed upon the grass and dirt at the redwood's base.

"Drink," he whispered feebly to the hamadryad. "Feed. Grow strong. Then one day, return my beloved to me."

Lightheaded and shivering with cold, he leaned against the trunk to rest. His thoughts blurred as his mind began to shut down.

His heart faltered. The little blood he still possessed retreated from his outer extremities, and his skin grew hard and cold. He stumbled toward his old pedestal and half-collapsed upon the sun-warmed stone. His dying mind noted the random details. Pitted gray stone. A few patches of fuzzy moss. He ran his fingers along the greenery.

As he settled upon the pedestal, his thoughts strayed back to Lillian. He brushed her sleeping mind one more time, sending a wave of love and reassurance to her.

"Live," he whispered into her mind. *"Even if I do not."*

And then, the last of his heat bled from him, hardening his skin to stone. Darkness claimed him.

CHAPTER FORTY-EIGHT

*C*hilled air struck her belly, the fingers of cold invading further into her dreams of warm bedding and soft pillows. Its next strike fell upon her chest and face. The sudden, cold slap shocked Lillian fully awake. She gasped, dragging in a deep breath. The first lungful of air burned down her throat. Spasms tightened her lungs. She gasped and choked with deep, retching coughs. *What? Did I just swallow an entire swimming pool full of water?*

She tried to force open her eyes, but her lids were heavy and stiff. Clumps of damp hair swung across her face, the strands stuck together by some kind of goopy slop. Her coughing subsided. Slowly, her lungs stopped burning. Another gust of cold caressed her thighs, then lower, creeping down her legs a few inches at a time. The rest of her body was as limp and uncooperative as her eyelids. She felt empty. Cored out.

Worse, her sense of balance told her she was upright, but

slumping forward, inch by inch. She couldn't move her limbs to fight the slow workings of gravity. Whatever was holding her up seemed to be letting go.

With nothing else to do, she waited, barely daring to breathe. A slight tingling encroached upon her silent, unfeeling world. It started in her shoulders and worked its way up her neck. Feeble energy stirred.

She ran her tongue along her lips. They tasted sweet. It was a strangely familiar flavor. A moment later, she had it. The watery sweetness of tree sap.

Feeling slowly returned in the wake of the tingling. Her eyelids opened. After blinking several times, the gray world sharpened into strands of her dark hair coated with tree goop. She gave her head a shake. The motion lacked the strength to toss the lank strands over her shoulder, but it swung enough that she could see the ground. Knee-high grass waved in a breeze. Now that her wet skin was adjusting, the air felt warmer.

Lillian sighed and rested her chin on her chest. Thinking required too much energy. It was easier to relax and be lulled by the sounds of the breeze blowing through tree leaves. She supposed she was in her glade. It smelled like it. And she'd always felt safe in her glade until... until when? No, she didn't want to think about it.

Sleep was encroaching upon her consciousness again when Lillian's world shivered. An earthquake? Here? The strange sensation subsided after a few heartbeats. The silence and stillness lasted for a minute more. Then a deep groaning like the wind in an old tree, its branches creaking in winter, echoed all around her. The world tilted on its head. Whatever was holding her upright loosened. One arm came free. Her upper body lurched forward. She was pulled up short by her other arm, still trapped within the same warm, wet blanket that held her thighs and lower legs. A pained gasp escaped her. By the radiating pain in her shoulder, she'd damn near dislocated it.

She was hanging upside down, bent almost double at the waist, hair pooling on the ground. Her new position showed her something she'd missed before. It was impossible to miss now because her nose was almost touching it.

And the "it" was the exfoliating bark of her redwood. The rough bark grew up and over her legs, midway up her thighs. Her upper body had emerged faster than the rest of her. One arm was still trapped within the trunk, but she could feel the arm slipping.

"This can't end well."

The prickling bite of returning sensation crawled down her body in a hot wave. A few more minutes and she might be able to move, maybe even extract herself from the tree without harm.

The tree gave another series of contractions.

"Ah, my usual luck, I see."

Her arm came free from the tree's hold. At the same time, the fissure in the trunk widened, releasing her legs. Lillian started to fall head-first toward dew-covered grass. Desperate to protect her head, she tucked and rolled. Or at least tried. She hit the ground with an expulsion of breath, then grunted in pain when she rolled onto her strained shoulder.

Judging by the throb, her shoulder would be colorful come tomorrow morning, but she didn't think it was dislocated. Her midair twist and roll hadn't been pretty. Actually, it probably resembled something a sea lion on land might do, but the maneuver worked for the most part.

"Nastiest wake-up ever," she mumbled as she stared up at her tree. The fissure she'd just fallen from was closing, the bark healing over the mass of red tissue and wood fiber. When it was healed, it looked like any other redwood trunk, nothing like a tree that had just given birth to her.

"Yep, a tree just gave birth to you," she muttered.

With a small part of her brain that decided to work, she realized, with a hint of amusement, she was probably in shock.

The grass was cold and wet from recent rain. She was buck-naked. Tree sap and blood covered her from head to toe. Her mind flailed for a moment, and then she remembered everything. The Riven. The demons trying to sacrifice her so they could corrupt the Lord of the Underworld's sword. The demon within her awakening and saving her and Gregory from the Riven.

Events were blurry after that point, but she remembered the demon using her body to seduce Gregory, or at least trying damn hard and failing. Then the agony of an axe biting into her hamadryad. Sable with an axe, tears running down her cheeks.

The last lucid thought was of her gargoyle placing her in her damaged hamadryad in a desperate bid for them both to heal. Then Gregory whispered his love and told her to "live." She remembered the loving touch of his mind. But there was something else, too: "Live, even if I do not."

That horrible emptiness. The sensation of being cored out. God, no. No, no, no, no!

"Gregory!"

Lying on her side, propped up on one shoulder, she was facing the wrong direction. She struggled to get her muscles working. The pins-and-needles sensation intensified. After a few moments, feeling returned to her legs and she rolled over.

He was there on his pedestal.

Head bowed, unmoving stone.

She tried to touch his thoughts, but no magic stirred within the emptiness inside her. His last words to her echoed in her mind once more.

Live, even if I do not.

She crawled toward him. The sweet fragrance of sun-warmed grass coiled around her. Bees and insects buzzed close to her head, sounding loud to her ears. Everything was as it had been all her life. The maze. Her glade. Her redwood rustling in the breeze. Her silent stone guardian.

But it was all wrong.

"Gregory, please," she whispered as she continued to crawl closer.

Horrible emptiness crushed all hope. She'd felt his willingness to sacrifice himself if it would save her. Gargoyle blood could heal a hamadryad. Her hamadryad had been grievously wounded. It would have taken a lot of Gregory's magic-laced blood to heal those kinds of injuries.

Gregory's pedestal loomed in front of her. Her fingertips brushed the rough stone. Then she reached up and grabbed a handhold to haul herself to her feet. She swayed but held on to her gargoyle's leg. After struggling up onto his pedestal, she looked up and stared into his beloved face. It didn't matter what form he wore, she loved him regardless. Fingers shaking, she caressed his muzzle.

Words she'd spoken once before whispered across her memory.

"I trust to the Father's choice."

She leaned against her beloved, breathing across his stone skin, trying to pick up even a hint of his scent.

"Dark Watcher, immortal servant of the Light, with my power, I summon you to wake."

No power stirred at her command. She fought back against a sob and continued in a shaking voice. He couldn't be dead. Not after they'd defeated the enemy.

She couldn't be alive, and he be dead.

"With my will, I do claim you."

She focused all her shock-benumbed thoughts, her sense of purpose, her love—everything she was—and willed it into the stone under her hands and prayed some part of her beseeching litany reached Gregory.

"Hear me and awake. My friend. My soul." She pressed her lips against his forehead. The stone was as rough and cold as the rest of him.

"Evil walks the land."

She paused and then continued weakly. "I have need." *Of you. Forever. Beloved.*

Nothing happened. At that moment, hope died within her. As she had since childhood, she dropped down onto his stone knee, then she wrapped her arms around his neck and sobbed. The echoing hollowness within her opened wider, threatening to devour her soul. Agony built within her until she couldn't hold it back. She screamed great gasping howls that hurt her throat. Tears flowed onto her lips, their taste salty.

When her voice failed, she continued to sob in silence. But no tears could fill the void within her.

"Listen. Hear me, my lady."

She jerked in surprise and looked into his face. Still cold, unmoving stone. Her grief must have been playing tricks on her mind.

"We are one entity, one soul. We are the two halves of the Avatar. Nothing can part us. Not even death." Gregory's words echoed back to her from her memories. Either that or grief had broken her mind.

"My love, you are sane. At least as much as anyone on this cursed, magic-less world."

Lillian couldn't prevent her arms from tightening around his neck. Could it be?

"I live. And for you, my lady, I will try to wake. I think I'm healed enough to resume warm flesh."

Worry made her stomach tense.

"Gregory, don't endanger yourself for me." She hugged his stone neck harder. At that moment, she didn't care if she had to wait another twelve years for him to heal enough to be with her again. He was alive. She'd give daily thanks to the Divine Ones while she waited. "Rest. Finish healing and then come back to me."

"I'll not make you wait another twelve years." There was a smile in his mental tone.

The stone warmed under her hands, then all along her body. She didn't care if he gave her a scorching sunburn; she wasn't moving. The shadow of his wings moved up and away as his arms encircled her shoulders. A warm tongue slathered across her cheek and Gregory's rumbling purr broke across her hearing.

"Tickles!" she gasped as tears streaked down her cheeks. She squirmed to get away. Helpless to stop, she continued crying, laughing, and shaking.

Gregory licked up her tears. To her utter surprise, his shoulders began quivering, shaking Lillian's entire body with the force of his silent sobs. The need to protect and comfort, as compelling as anything she'd ever experienced, had her rocking him back and forth, murmuring meaningless words into his neck. "Hush now."

"I didn't know if your tree could heal you. The thought of losing you again..."

"We survived."

"Yes, you're a tough little dryad."

She gently pushed away from him just enough to look up into his face. His dark eyes tracked the motion of her hands as she reached up to caress his cheeks. "I love you, too, gargoyle."

Stretching up on her toes, she tried to plant a kiss on his cheek. Her foot slipped, and she lost her balance. He caught her but was far from steady himself, and they both pitched sideways. She yelped in surprise as they toppled off the pedestal. Gregory reacted faster and turned them in midair. He landed first, taking the brunt of the impact on his back. She still slammed painfully into his chest, knocking the breath from them both.

"Thanks," she managed between bouts of laughter. "Having an eight-foot-tall gargoyle land on top of me isn't on today's to-do list."

"I think I'll just stay here for a few minutes until I figure out which way is up." He lay underneath her, panting, his wings spread to their fullest on either side. After a moment, he started to chuckle. "You're welcome to use me as a pillow for however long you like."

"And would your willingness have anything to do with the fact I'm as naked as the day I was born?" She decided modesty required too much energy and simply snuggled closer.

His eyes remained closed, and he replied in a slow, lazy drawl. "Entirely possible."

"You're incorrigible. You know that, right?" Her words were playful, but a sense of seriousness was settling over her heart, eroding her earlier joy. She remembered the demon all too clearly. And she didn't believe for a minute the demon was gone, even if she couldn't feel it slithering around in her soul. It would only be a matter of time before the demon grew strong enough and made its reappearance.

"My little dryad, you do feel different," Gregory said.

She frowned as she mused over his words. She did feel different and wasn't sure if that was good or bad. "My magic is gone. I've been cored like an apple."

"Hmm... that explains it," Gregory rumbled by way of answer, sounding more relaxed than she ever remembered hearing. He nuzzled her hair, making sounds of contentment deep in his throat. A large, warm hand settled on her shoulder, then moved down leisurely to stroke her back.

"Explains what, exactly?" she asked, though she wasn't certain she wanted to know. His answer might destroy the pleasure she took in his petting. He switched to running his hands along her hair before trailing his fingers down her back.

Resisting the urge to arch her back in cat-like fashion, she instead lifted her head to meet his eyes. He wasn't looking at her. His focus was on her hamadryad. By the curve of his smile, which showed a generous amount of fang, he was pleased with what he saw.

"Gregory?"

"It's easier if I show you." He rolled her off to the side, then sat up. When he'd gained his feet, he reached down and pulled her up after.

Now that she was standing, looking down at herself, she no longer felt sexy—not covered in tree sap and bits of grass, dirt, and other plant materials. "A bath and some clothing would be nice," she mumbled to herself.

With a slight motion, Gregory stirred the air with one hand. Shadows, flecks of sunlight, and bits of soft moss came to his hand. While she watched in silence, he wove a skirt and vest from the materials. It wasn't as sophisticated as what the other dryads had made for her, but she was twice as happy. "Thank you."

After she donned her new clothing, Lillian let herself be led back to her hamadryad. She even managed to swallow back the numerous questions floating through her thoughts.

"You said you felt empty?" he asked.

"Yes, nothing happened when I tried to call my magic. I thought you were dead and a part of me had died as well... but you weren't... and you heard me, even though I had no magic left."

"I'll always feel your joy and your pain; any powerful emotion will touch me. You don't need magic for that."

"I'm glad." Her words couldn't convey the slightest drop of what she felt for him, but her throat tightened and blocked any more words from escaping.

He reached for her hand. "Do you trust me?"

"Of course," she agreed but didn't know what he was

getting at. Now she could add feeling perplexed to the riot of emotions bubbling up inside.

"The demon is gone from you. In part, that is why you feel empty."

"How? I thought you couldn't remove it without killing me."

"I couldn't. Your hamadryad did what I couldn't—feel." He took her hand and pressed it against the rough bark of the trunk. "I didn't expect this."

At first, she felt nothing except the tree, then Gregory put his hand over hers and called power. It washed into her.

"There is no danger," he whispered above her, "not while I'm here with you."

His mind touched hers, then his thoughts flowed away into the hamadryad. He tugged Lillian along after him.

"Do you feel it?"

Just as she was going to say no, she heard the distant echo of another mind, its enraged thoughts broadcasting its loathing. She sent her consciousness in the direction of the disturbance. Her hamadryad's mind surrounded hers. It was strangely comforting, and Lillian forgot what she'd been doing until Gregory mentally nudged her.

"Come. You need to see this, so you'll no longer doubt yourself."

Another tortured, infuriated scream reverberated throughout the internal world of the hamadryad. It was so full of hatred Lillian shivered at the sound.

"That's my demon, isn't it?"

"Yes. Your hamadryad has trapped it."

The demon howled again.

Lillian continued to follow Gregory's spirit until she sensed they were deep in the hamadryad's wooden heart.

Ahead of them, golden power coiled and twisted around something of darkness. The two forces were joined in a fierce battle beyond Lillian's understanding. What she saw wasn't fought in the physical world; this was a battle between two spirits. Somehow Gregory was using his power to show her what was going on inside the hamadryad.

Gregory drew back from the fight and urged her along with him. Lillian swayed and found herself again in her body, staring at the trunk of her redwood.

"I don't understand. How can my hamadryad trap the demon soul? Wasn't the demon... part of me?"

"The demon was grafted onto your soul—the ancient essence of the Sorceress. You feel empty because you are no longer the Mother's Avatar. That power now belongs to your hamadryad. In essence, she is now the Sorceress."

"Gregory—" she held up her hand, "—you're giving me facts, not an explanation."

"Sorry." He had the grace to look embarrassed. "I've been telling you half-truths for so long..." He sighed and bowed his head. "While the hamadryad was healing you, she saw a way to strike at the demon. One I hadn't thought of. Apparently, the demon hadn't, either. To heal you, your tree needed to call power from the Spirit Realm. Something both you and the demon were too weak to do, so the hamadryad called your shared soul to her. The tree became the Sorceress. Seeing no other way for its host to be healed, the demon allowed this, but it had to go with the soul, into the hamadryad."

"The hamadryad took my soul?"

Gregory curled a wing around her shoulders and guided her away from the tree. The warmth of his body pressing against hers triggered an answering heat in her belly. As if he read her thoughts, he bowed his head and nuzzled her shoulder.

"Stop that." She slapped his nose away. "You're trying to distract me. Did you just say I'm soulless?"

"Of course not. Your hamadryad is a part of you. It doesn't matter to me which vessel the other half of my soul inhabits. In my eyes, you are one being."

Easy for you to say, she thought to herself. *First my memories and now my soul.*

But it wasn't Gregory's fault, either.

Focus, Lil. You're just scared shitless. Suck it up.

She glanced in the direction of the hamadryad. "So, my tree has trapped the demon?"

"Yes. The demon is tied to the Sorceress's soul and can't escape. A hamadryad is different than her dryad. A demon must prey on emotions of jealousy, greed, rage, and fear to overwhelm its host's mind and take command of the body. Unlike a normal host, a hamadryad lacks the type of emotions a demon can manipulate. The demon has been rendered impotent."

"I don't trust the demon. She's a cunning bitch. She'll find a way to hurt or corrupt my hamadryad."

"The demon can't hurt your tree. And your hamadryad is doing more than passively trapping the demon." Gregory pointed at the redwood, then made a sweeping motion to indicate the far distant forest. "What do all trees do?"

Lillian didn't think Gregory wanted a scientific answer, so she arched a brow and waited for him to answer his own question.

When he realized she wasn't going to answer him, he

continued with his explanation. "A normal tree can purify the soil and water. A hamadryad does much more."

Lillian looked back to her hamadryad with renewed interest. "My redwood is purifying the demon?"

"Yes. Killing its evil. Unmaking it. Eventually, she'll release that second, damaged soul back to the Spirit Realm. But hamadryads work slowly."

A new concern wormed its way into Lillian's mind. "How long will this process take?"

"Perhaps a season. Maybe two," Gregory answered.

"If I can't reclaim the powers of the Sorceress until then, that's going to be a problem."

Gregory nodded. "There is that concern. The Lady of Battles will likely send her minions before the hamadryad has killed the demon. You can't merge with your tree at all until the demon is dead, or it will migrate back to you with your soul. And it isn't stupid enough to be tricked a second time."

"What can I do?"

"We'll unite all the Clan and the Coven and create a force to fight the Lady of Battles herself. And I still am the Father's Avatar; I'm far from helpless. As long as the hamadryad holds the demon trapped, it can't reach me through you."

"I'm glad you're safe from the demon, but we've just traded one problem for another. Without magic, I'm useless. I'll be a liability when the Lady of Battles comes calling."

"The Battle Goddess can't actually come to this Realm. We'll just have to deal with her underlings." A glint of humor sparked in Gregory's eyes. "I don't think you're half as helpless as you think. The demon is gone, and your hamadryad has blocked you from touching your dryad magic, and that of the Sorceress. But if I am not mistaken, you still have one formidable talent."

"What? Polishing swords?"

He looked baffled for a moment and then chuckled in understanding. "It does have to do with weapons. Natural weapons." Gregory flared his wings and gave them a little shake.

Lillian's mouth dropped open. He didn't mean...? Surely not.

"The power to shapeshift into a female gargoyle is a power that has nothing to do with your power as the Avatar. Up until now, there were no female gargoyles but because of the Lady of Battles—" Gregory paused, seeming to search for the correct words. "Because of her breeding program, you are now the first female gargoyle. You are equal parts dryad and gargoyle. Where the other female dryad children sired by gargoyles carried the potential, none of them could take that next step and become gargoyles themselves."

"You're talking about the genetic code—recessive and dominant genes."

Gregory looked uncertain.

"Never mind." She grinned from ear to ear. "I can be a gargoyle if I choose?"

"You'll need rest and then training first, but yes, my lady, you are still a gargoyle." He reached for her hand, his engulfing hers.

She squeezed his fingers. After what the demon had forced her to do, Lillian wasn't sure what Gregory wanted. Yes, he loved her. He'd always loved his Sorceress. But she was no longer the Sorceress. She didn't even have a soul.

"You are my beloved companion regardless if you're a

dryad, a gargoyle, or demon possessed." He tapped his fingers on the back of her hand.

Of course he knew her thoughts, they were touching. He could read her every thought and emotion. Heat mounted her cheeks, and she stared at the ground.

A finger under her jaw tilted her head up. She was just wrapping her arms around his neck when the sound of hooves on gravel intruded.

Gregory sighed, then rested his chin on the top of her head. "It's probably that one-horned fool."

She chuckled as she curled her arm around his waist instead. "If he's here, Gran can't be far behind. She always knows what I'm thinking before I do—she probably knew down to the hour when my hamadryad was going to go into labor."

As Gregory had predicted, it was a white blur that bolted from the nearest maze entrance. The unicorn galloped toward them, grass and clumps of dirt flying in his wake.

"Bet Gran has a feast laid out for us."

"I hope so."

Lillian took note of her gargoyle's eagerness at the mention of food. "Come on, let's go greet the unicorn and then eat."

"Mmm, roasted unicorn meat."

She swatted Gregory in the arm, then took his hand as they walked out from under the canopy of her redwood. Once again, her maze felt like home, her life complete, the void of missing memories no longer important. Some things she could live without. Gregory wasn't one of them.

For the first time in days, she felt hopeful that there might be a future where both she and her gargoyle protector survived all the trials ahead of them and got a chance to—if not actually grow old—than live a full life before returning to the spirit realm.

Surely that wouldn't be too much to ask, she mused as she headed back toward the house to learn all that had happened while she'd slept in a tree.

*L*ord Draydrak galloped down the sandy beach of his island home. The ocean breeze blew warm and strong, driving the waves high up the sands to wash around his hooves. As soon as he'd felt the sword's return, he'd bolted from his temple, through the terraced gardens, down hundreds of stone stairs, and finally onto the warm sands.

As pleasant as his surroundings were, he wasn't out for a pleasure jaunt. He slowed when he approached the sword lying half in the ocean and half on the shore.

He hadn't expected the sword to return so soon, but then again, he hadn't planned for the misbegotten Riven to find it either. His original plan was for the sword to provide the Avatars with enough power to allow them to heal swiftly and return to the Magic Realm where he could free the female half of the Avatars' soul to be cleansed and reborn.

But his twin and her Riven beasts had disrupted his plans.

Now, even with the male half of the Avatar having

survived, a great divergence was still forming in the flows of creation's possible futures, and none—not even Draydrak with all the gifts bestowed on him as the Lord of the Underworld—could foresee which of the many possible futures would hold dominance over all the others.

Though the death of the male half of the Avatar soul would have made Draydrak's task easier, that wasn't what had happened. Which wasn't really a surprise. He knew the Avatar well. That being was too old and stubborn to allow death to claim it easily. And Draydrak secretly thought the male half of the Avatar soul got a larger portion of that stubbornness.

But none of the possible futures Draydrak foresaw showed a hint as to which one would come into fruition.

Never one to leave an outcome up to chance, he knew he must come up with another strategy to force the Avatars' return.

He couldn't allow his sister to sink her claws into them more than she already had.

The Divine Ones were clear on that. All of creation would suffer if his twin succeeded with her plan.

If he couldn't orchestrate the Avatars' return on his own, then he would need help from a powerful ally to capture them both and bring them to his island home where he would do what was necessary to free their souls.

The Avatars' current location presented a problem. While that pretty blue planet teemed with life, it was also poor in magic. Long term, it simply could not support a member of the Magic or Spirit Realms' upper echelon of magic wielders, like a djinn or a celestial warrior, without harm befalling that world. And only an upper echelon being had any hope of defeating the Avatars in battle.

Hmm.

But what if raw power and brute force were not needed at all?

Sometimes persuasion could be far more powerful than any weapon.

He knew of several beings possessing great enough skills that it had allowed them to master persuasion and take it to the next level. One such being, an ancient siren known as Tethys, had made the journey to the blue planet many eons ago. She was very nearly a deity in her own right.

Yes, he decided. She would do nicely for his plan.

And his ability to track souls allowed him to know she hadn't yet taken the journey home to the Spirit Realm. She was still somewhere on that magicless blue planet.

Turning his muzzle toward the ocean, he closed his eyes and drew on his power. Once sufficient magic danced in the air around him, he sent it racing toward the Veil Between the Realms. In less time than the moments between two thoughts, his power sped through the veil and into the Mortal Realm. It didn't take him long to find the planet he sought and soon his magic was spreading out to blanket that world, hunting for ones of power.

Ah.

There.

He found her deep in a ravine in the ocean floor, sleeping away the eons as she gathered power to her.

Reaching out with more magic, he sought a weakness in the ocean floor, one already under great strain and soon to give way even without his aid.

He stilled, his power at the ready to unleash an ocean's destructive force, time meaning nothing to him as he waited for a confirmation. Then as he expected, his gift of sensing possible futures shifted suddenly as one formed more strongly than the others, snapping into place. It was always so when the Divine Ones deemed it was time for an alteration in their design.

Their Blessing having been bestowed upon his plan of action, he carried it out by nudging the faultline, starting up a great shaking deep in the rock. Destruction would arise to sweep across a distant land, freeing many souls to start their journey home. His actions had changed little, merely hurrying events.

Still, he never liked when a soul's chance to learn and grow was cut short, even if only by a few planetary rotations.

And he knew setting loose Tethys upon that unsuspecting world would lead to many deaths. But the collateral damage caused by the siren would be small compared to what the Lady of Battles would do if she ever enslaved the Avatars to her will.

At least the deaths brought about by the siren would help maintain the balance and protect the rest of the Universe.

Satisfied the tremor he'd unleashed would serve its purpose and wake the siren, he opened his eyes.

Gazing out at the white capped waves of the ocean for long moments, he basked in the beauty of the scene before silently musing that this one act felt like a great betrayal, but then he reminded himself that the Divine Ones would not have set him on this path if they hadn't seen an outcome that would serve the greatest good.

If the siren was successful, she would bring him the flesh

and blood Avatars in the coming weeks, and he would free their souls to be reunited and healed in the Spirit Realm.

It would only require him to kill two halves of a being he considered his friend.

With a sigh, he at last turned his magic back to its primary task of guiding all the souls of the newly dead to the safety of the Spirit Realm.

Slowly the sound of the ocean loosened its hold on his senses, if not his heart.

THE END

Lillian and Gregory's adventures continue in Sorceress Rising.

Hey before you go, can I interest you in signing up for my author newsletter?
You get my free starter library as a gift for joining.

http://lisablackwood.com/join-the-newsletter-here/

Did you enjoy Sorceress Awakening?

If you have a moment and wouldn't mind leaving a review, that would be greatly appreciated.
Reviews help other readers to decide if a book is something they would like.
It doesn't need to be long. Even a few words is tremendously helpful.

None of this would have been possible without, you, my readers. You're awesome!
Thank You!

Bye for now,
Lisa Blackwood

ABOUT THE AUTHOR

Lisa Blackwood is the author of the bestselling Gargoyle and Sorceress urban fantasy series. Her work has also landed on the Wall Street Journal and the USA Today Bestseller lists as part of the Dominion Rising Anthology. When she's not reading and writing, she also enjoys gardening and spending time with her horse and her dogs.

At present, she grudgingly lives in a small town in Southern Ontario, though she would much rather live deep in a dark forest, surrounded by majestic old-growth trees. Since she cannot live her fantasy, she decided to write fantasy instead

BOOKS BY LISA BLACKWOOD

Gargoyle & Sorceress

Dawn of the Sorceress

Sorceress Awakening

Sorceress Rising

Sorceress Hunting

Sorceress at War

Sorceress Enraged

Legacy of the Sorceress

Sorcery & Firedrakes

Scion of the Sorceress

Sorceress Eternal

In Deception's Shadow Series (Epic Fantasy Romance)

Betrayal's Price

Herd Mistress

Maiden's Wolf

Death's Queen

The Prince's Gryphon (forthcoming)

Ishtar's Legacy Series (Epic Fantasy Romance)

Ishtar's Blade

The Blade's Beginning (short story)

Blade's Honor

Blade's Destiny

The Blade's Shadow

First Queen of the Gryphons

The King of the Anunnaki (forthcoming)

The Anunnaki's Blade (forthcoming)

Huntress vs Huntsman (Epic Fantasy Romance)

Master of the Hunt

Night Huntress

Dragon Archer

Soul Mage (forthcoming)

Lightning Source UK Ltd.
Milton Keynes UK
UKHW010750060223
416537UK00003B/736